RENNO—Young, impetuous, and brave, he must prove himself worthy to be Sachem by carrying out one final mission—to track down and destroy his father's killer. But the strange power that guides his destiny will make his odyssey of vengeance a deadly test of courage . . . a heart-stopping adventure in the land of the people called Seminole.

EMILY—The golden-haired beauty who won Renno's heart now excite the passions of a dangerous man . . . and instead of the glorious wedding she dreamed about, a nightmare of abduction and terror become her fate.

CAPTAIN BEN WHIPPLE—A soldier turned renegade and murderer, he gives full rein to his basest desires, robbing with impunity, killing with joy, and stealing the one woman he both desires and despises.

DURATI—Mighty Chief of the Seminole, no man is his equal in battle, no woman dares to refuse his commands . . . not even a fair-haired captive beauty who belongs to another, but is chosen to become a Seminole bride.

ADMIRAL RILEY—Mad corsair whose pirate band plundered the rich sea trade to America, a curved sword which has replaced his missing hand spills the blood of the evil and the innocent alike . . . and is aimed at the heart of Renno.

RUSOG—Noble leader of the Cherokee, a white man's treachery puts him on trial for his life . . . and the verdict could be the spark which would light the fire of battle between Indian and pioneer.

P9-EMH-606

The White Indian Series
Ask your bookseller for the books you have missed

The White Indian Series
Book XII

SEMINOLE

Donald Clayton Porter

Created by the producers of
The Holts: An American Dynasty,
The First Americans, and **The Australians.**

Book Creations Inc., Canaan, NY • *Lyle Kenyon Engel, Founder*

BANTAM BOOKS
NEW YORK • TORONTO • LONDON • SYDNEY • AUCKLAND

WINTER PARK PUBLIC LIBRARY
460 E. NEW ENGLAND AVENUE
WINTER PARK, FL 32789

SEMINOLE
*A Bantam Domain Book / published by arrangement with
Book Creations, Inc.*

Bantam edition / February 1986

DOMAIN *and the portrayal of a boxed "d" are trademarks of Bantam Books,
a division of Bantam Doubleday Dell Publishing Group, Inc.*

*Produced by Book Creations, Inc.
Chairman of the Board: Lyle Kenyon Engel*

*All rights reserved.
Copyright © 1986 by Book Creations, Inc.
No part of this book may be reproduced or transmitted in any
form or by any means, electronic or mechanical, including
photocopying, recording, or by any information storage and
retrieval system, without permission in writing from the publisher.
For information address: Bantam Books.*

*If you purchased this book without a cover you should be aware that this book is
stolen property. It was reported as "unsold and destroyed" to the publisher and
neither the author nor the publisher has received any payment for this
"stripped book."*

ISBN 0-553-25353-0

Published simultaneously in the United States and Canada

*Bantam Books are published by Bantam Books, a division of Bantam Doubleday Dell
Publishing Group, Inc. Its trademark, consisting of the words "Bantam Books" and the
portrayal of a rooster, is Registered in U.S. Patent and Trademark Office and in other
countries. Marca Registrada. Bantam Books, 666 Fifth Avenue, New York, New York
10103.*

PRINTED IN THE UNITED STATES OF AMERICA

OPM   15 14 13 12 11 10 9 8 7 6 5

499

To the Seminole, the only Indian nation within our boundaries that has never surrendered to the United States or signed a peace treaty.

murrah fund
B+T

5/92

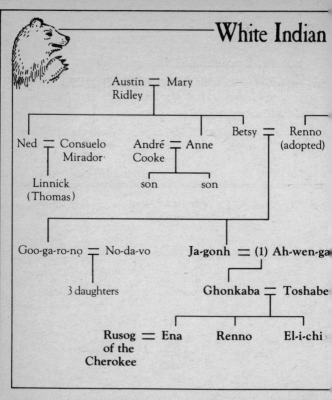

White Indian

Austin Ridley ═ Mary

Ned ═ Consuelo Mirador   André Cooke ═ Anne   Betsy ═   Renno (adopted)

Linnick (Thomas)

son   son

Goo-ga-ro-no ═ No-da-vo   **Ja-gonh** ═ (1) **Ah-wen-ga**

3 daughters

Ghonkaba ═ **Toshabe**

Rusog ═ **Ena**   **Renno**   **El-i-chi**
of the
Cherokee

A Seminole Village

© 1985 BOOK CREATIONS INC.

Family Tree

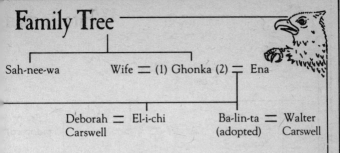

Sah-nee-wa   Wife = (1) Ghonka (2) = Ena

Deborah = El-i-chi   Ba-lin-ta = Walter
Carswell   (adopted)   Carswell

**People of
the Cherokee**

(2) = (2) **Loramas** (1) = Mirala

= **Wegowa**

Rusog = Ena
of the
Seneca

Chapter I

Late in the autumn of 1783, as white men measure the passage of time, peace came at last to the New World. The long War of Independence had reached an end when Great Britain finally recognized her former colonies as a free and separate nation, the United States of America.

As citizens of the new nation rejoiced, nowhere was the joy more unconfined than in the region west of the Appalachian Mountains. There, in the territory that would later comprise eastern Tennessee, lay the boundaries of a new state; its founders were calling it Franklin, in honor of America's revered elder statesman.

Beyond the limits of Franklin to the south and west was the vast forest home of the Cherokee, a nation that had cast its lot with the colonial patriots and now with the United States. New blood and spirit brought by several hundred warriors of the Seneca, the famed tribe of fighting men, were reviving the ability and will of the Cherokee, who—abandoning their peaceful ways—had resolutely pushed across their borders to battle, defeat, and conquer the Choctaw, the Creek, and other lesser nations.

"We bow our heads to no tribe!" proclaimed Wegowa, principal warrior of the Cherokee and heir to the leadership of his nation.

No one agreed more heartily than did Renno, the young warrior who ultimately would succeed to leadership of the Seneca band that had traveled southwest after fighting valiantly in George Washington's army. Possessing the most renowned name of any Indian in the country, he could boast a distinguished lineage. Ghonka, the first of his family who became Great Sachem of all the Iroquois nations, had established the line, and his foster son, the first Renno, was the original white Indian whose feats of bravery and daring were legendary. In the next generation, Renno's son, Ja-gonh, had led his people in support of the English loyalists, but Ja-gonh's own son, Ghonkaba, had fought with distinction for the separatists in the War of Independence. Since Ghonkaba's death at the hands of a vicious murderer, young Renno had been marked as the future leader of the Seneca. Because he was judged too inexperienced to take active command as yet, the Seneca remained in the charge of a regent, Casno, who had been Ghonkaba's lieutenant. Renno's day would come.

Shortly after Ghonkaba's death, he appeared to Renno in a dream, his wounds caked with his life's blood. His murderer, Captain Ben Whipple, a ruthless militia officer, had fled. As Ghonkaba related to his son, it was essential that Renno find Whipple and avenge his father. Until then, Ghonkaba could know no peace, for he had been denied admission by the gods to the land of his ancestors, where his forebears awaited him. He would not be permitted to cross the Great River until Renno had slain Whipple with his own hands. The gods must be satisfied so that they no longer would punish Ghonkaba.

Striving toward that goal, Renno had searched the forests west, south, and north of the fortified town of Knoxville, without finding a sign of his quarry. Whipple had vanished with the elusive ease of a Seneca warrior.

The day was warm, with a gentle breeze blowing northward, but Renno, sitting motionless on a boulder overlooking the Tennessee River, felt as cold as death itself. In his mind, he lived again the vision that had so shocked him and disturbed his soul.

In his strong, capable hands, Renno was gripping a curiously tapered spike of hardwood. He had taken it from his father's funeral pyre. According to the vision, he would use this tool to kill Whipple.

Though he seemed outwardly passive, a terrible inner restlessness gripped Renno. Even if time in the land of the ancestors was not measured as living people count its passage, he was anxious to end his father's ordeal as quickly as possible.

Straining as he gazed toward the horizon, Renno prayed with all his heart to the manitous, the intermediaries who interceded with the gods on behalf of man. He pleaded for the opportunity to end his father's banishment.

Despite Renno's preoccupation, he could hear the approach of soft, stealthy footsteps through the forest. Instinctively, he grasped the hilt of his tomahawk, a ferocious instrument when he chose to wield it.

Within a minute, he saw through the trees a tall figure and promptly relaxed his grip on the tomahawk when he recognized Wegowa. To Renno, Wegowa was like a father. His respect and admiration for the older man was great. Raising his left hand in amicable greeting, he called out, "What brings you so far into the forest from the homes of the Cherokee and the Seneca?"

"You do, Renno," came the blunt reply. "I have been searching for you because of concern for your prolonged absence. I had not realized you had gone so far. Your spirit must be troubled indeed when you roam this great a distance from your dwelling."

"My soul is exceedingly troubled," Renno admitted.

"I would have expected," Wegowa replied, "that despite your burden of grief for your father, you could also find time to be light of heart, rejoicing at the prospect of your forthcoming marriage."

"I truly do rejoice, because Emily will soon become my wife," Renno acknowledged, "and because— even at this very moment—she is learning the ways of our people from my mother and my grandmother."

Emily Johnson, the daughter of the colonel who commanded the Franklin militia and also was its highest-ranking judge, had fallen in love with Renno several months earlier, and despite initial misgivings about whether she could live successfully and happily as a member of an Indian family, she had finally agreed wholeheartedly to marry him. Their wedding would take place in her hometown within the next several weeks.

"All the same," Renno continued, "my heart shrivels within me, and I am overcome by sadness, because of the loss of my father."

"Ghonkaba was my great friend and my valued comrade in arms," Wegowa said. "I mourn him almost as you do. But if he came to life and stood beside me here, he would remind you that life must be lived for the sake of the living."

Reluctant to reveal that his father's spirit had sought his help, Renno remained silent.

"I also bring you word," Wegowa went on, "from my father, Loramas, who leads all the Cherokee and the Seneca who live on this side of the mountains that separate our people from the great sea."

Renno folded his arms across his chest, bowed his head, and waited to hear of the commands of Loramas.

"My father has selected you to receive this message," Wegowa explained, "because of your special association with the settlers who make their headquarters at the fort they call Knoxville. They have elected John Sevier, whom we know and respect, as governor of the territory they have chosen to name Franklin, and they have made Roy Johnson the chief of their warriors. You speak and write the language of these people who proudly describe themselves as Americans. And you enjoy a relationship with Colonel Johnson as the father of your future wife. Therefore, Loramas deems you to be the appropriate delegate to go to them and sign a treaty of perpetual friendship on behalf of the Cherokee and of the Seneca."

"It will give me great joy to accept this mission," Renno assured him, thinking that on a journey to Knoxville he could have the opportunity to explore more territory in his search for Ben Whipple. "Perhaps," he added, "it will also prove possible for me to escort Emily when she returns to her home prior to our wedding."

Shocked by Renno's apparent disregard for certain ancient customs, Wegowa spoke severely. "That is something," he said, "that I know your mother will never permit. You are not allowed to act as Emily's escort until you and she are married."

Renno saw the futility of trying to argue the matter, so he merely inclined his head. In fact, he thought, it was perhaps just as well that he not accompany Emily. He would instead be able to concentrate his full attention on finding Whipple in the vast reaches of the wilderness.

Reflected by the pale, blue-green waters of the Atlantic and by the yellow sand of the beach, the sun was dazzling and its humid heat intense. A slight breeze barely rustled the tops of the palmetto trees that rimmed the beach. Here, on the Florida seacoast, far south of St. Augustine, the climate was considered unfit for human habitation.

But one man, living by his own rules, chose to ignore the judgment of the Spaniards, in whose territory he owned a cabin hidden amid palmettos and scrub pines. The master of a sleek ship that sailed the waters off Florida, preying on legitimate commerce of America, France, and Great Britain, Emil Whipple was wanted for piracy by all three nations.

At peace with the world, Emil sat now on the cabin's crude porch, his feet propped on the railing. The large *segaro* riding at a jaunty angle in his mouth was a token of the prizes taken when he captured a merchantman out of Havana.

His tranquility contrasted strongly with the restlessness of his companion. Ben Whipple, his cousin, had made his way from the Tennessee frontier where he was wanted as a traitor to the United States.

"I have spent a month with you, Emil, and have done nothing but fish in the shallows and relieve the monotony by swimming in the surf. This is a fine hideout, but I need more than that."

Emil Whipple reached down and picked up a mug of rum and water from the porch floor. After taking a long swallow, he belched and wiped his mouth with a frayed sleeve.

"If it's action you want, lad," he said, "come to sea with me. You will get your fill of action when we attack a merchantman that looks helpless but carries some concealed cannon as protection. Then you will wish you were back here on this porch."

Ben's mind had been busy during the weeks at his cousin's hideaway, and he had another plan, which he presented cautiously. "Instead of my going to sea with you," he said, "would you consider an overland raid into the Tennessee country?"

Emil was amused. Grinning broadly, he asked, "What is up there that could possibly lead me to endure the discomforts of a long, uncomfortable trek through the wilderness of this godforsaken land?"

"Perhaps this would persuade you," Ben answered. "Money—a small fortune—has been provided for the state militia, and I know exactly where to get my hands on it. There's enough to keep us living in comfort for many years."

Secretly, his goal also included abducting Emily Johnson and forcibly carrying her back to Florida. She had rejected him as a suitor, but he intended to have her nonetheless. This had become an obsession in his twisted mind, greater than his desire for money or even concern for his own safety.

"I thank you for the very kind offer, cousin," Emil said with a chuckle, "but I'll take my risks at sea."

Ben was not surprised. "I reckon we're not destined to join forces, Emil," he said. "I would feel as uncomfortable at sea as you apparently do in the wilderness. You go on capturing merchantmen if that's what you want. But as for me, I've decided to head north as fast as I can get organized. I thank you for the hospitality that served my purposes so well. And now I must move on. I have my own fish to fry, and they'll taste better than any I've caught on this beach!"

Friends in Knoxville who had known Emily Johnson all her life would not have recognized her as she sat cross-legged before a fire burning in the stone-lined pit. The scene was an open courtyard adjoining a large dwelling in the town of the Cherokee, deep in the Tennessee wilderness. Clad in a shift of butternut-hued leather, she had matching moccasins laced around her bare ankles. Her wheat-colored hair tumbled down her back, restrained only by a leather headband. Two feathers affixed to it signified that she was an unmarried maiden. She had fashioned earrings of smaller feathers, and on a bare upper arm she wore a thick bracelet of hammered copper. It was a remembrance from Renno, who had made it for her.

With a ladle-shaped gourd attached to a pole, Emily stirred the contents of a large pot, which rested on the edges of four stones surrounding a small fire. Her eyes watchful, she concentrated on her task. Two women of the Seneca stood near, intently observing her. One was Toshabe, widow of Ghonkaba and mother of Renno, and the other was Renno's grandmother, Ah-wen-ga, widow of Ja-gonh, who was the son of the earlier Renno and in turn, Ghonkaba's father.

Toshabe broke the silence. "Relax, my child," she advised. "The muscles in your neck and in your arms reveal too much tension. Relax them, so that no one may gather that you might be worried or afraid."

"She speaks wisely, my granddaughter-to-be," Ah-wen-ga said. "A woman of the Seneca is the mistress of her own domain. When she is cooking a meal, she alone is in charge. None may interfere with what she does."

"I am concerned," Emily admitted, "because this is the first time I have ever prepared a stew of buffalo meat. I want to be sure that the dish is done to everyone's taste."

Ah-wen-ga chuckled. "When you prepare the meat of buffalo for eating," she said, "you first boil it with herbs and roots until you believe it is done. But then you continue to cook it on a smaller fire until you have been forced to rebuild your fire, and not once but twice."

Emily smiled broadly. "I shall remember your instructions, my grandmother-to-be," she said in the Seneca tongue. She was discovering, to her own pleased surprise, that it was becoming easier to speak and think in the Indians' language.

"That's better!" Toshabe commented. "Now you look as though you are enjoying yourself, and fully in charge of your own destiny."

Composing herself under their watchful eyes, Emily realized that the supreme calm demonstrated by women of the Seneca in almost any circumstances was by no means merely for appearance's sake. A Seneca woman could look serene because she actually was at peace with herself.

Over the years, Emily had heard settlers, including her own parents, refer to Indians as "woodenfaced." But now she was learning that this was far from the truth. Though susceptible to the same emotions as those of the settlers, they cultivated an enduring inner tranquility.

At last the stew, the main dish for the evening's meal, was ready. Emily removed the pot from the fire, intending to return it later to the coals for a short time to heat before serving it.

"Now," she said with a smile, "I'll have time to mend that tear in Renno's cloak."

"No!" Ah-wen-ga commanded, and then she softened slightly. "Do as I do," she said, folding her arms across her breasts. "There comes a time in the daily life of every squaw," she continued, as Emily obediently crossed her own arms, "when she must take stock of herself and of the life she is leading. She must contemplate the good that she is doing, considering honestly what she has accomplished that day. She must determine what tasks remain and decide which are important enough to require her immediate attention."

"It is not seemly," Toshabe interrupted, "for a squaw of the Seneca to feel harried, and so to race from one task to another. At all times, she must remain calm and dignified, setting an example for her husband and her children."

Emily lowered her head as she had been taught, to show that she understood and would obey.

"Now," Ah-wen-ga said, seating herself beside Emily and motioning to Toshabe to sit on the other side, "I have a matter of mutual interest to tell you about."

As they settled themselves on the stone flooring, Emily felt flattered that she should be included in what apparently was to be a full-scale family conference.

"Loramas," Ah-wen-ga began, "has spoken to me on a matter that concerns all of us."

Looking into the expressionless face of Toshabe, Emily believed she knew what her future mother-in-law was thinking. It was no secret that Ah-wen-ga and Loramas of the Cherokee were enjoying a touching romance. In fact, Toshabe had told Emily that she was confident Ah-wen-ga would have been married to Loramas already except for the untimely death of Ghonkaba, her only son.

"It has become advisable," Ah-wen-ga explained, "for Loramas to send an emissary to sign a treaty of peace with the new governor of the State of Franklin and the commander in chief of the Franklin militia. After consulting with me, he has decided to dispatch Renno for this purpose."

Emily beamed. "How very nice!" she exclaimed. "That probably means that Renno would be going to Knoxville at about the same time that I have been planning to return home after my visit here. Perhaps we will be able to travel together, with him acting as my escort."

"This you may not do," Ah-wen-ga replied quickly and severely. "It is not seemly for a maiden to spend nights in the wilderness alone with a man. Even with the man she intends to marry."

Emily sighed and bowed her head. Ah-wen-ga sounded much like her own mother, for the settlers' standards and those of the Indians were virtually identical in such matters. Reared as she was in accordance with those standards, she could not dissent from them, no matter how much she yearned to be with Renno. She realized that the time would come soon enough when they would be able to go off alone, wherever they decided to travel.

"When will Renno depart for Knoxville?" Toshabe inquired.

"He must appear before the Grand Council of the Cherokee and the Seneca at this hour tomorrow to receive his instructions," Ah-wen-ga replied. "And he will go forth into the wilderness the following morning."

Toshabe smiled at her future daughter-in-law. "Your lot will not be too hard to bear," she said. "Within a few days' time you, too, will leave, escorted by my son-in-law, Rusog, the son of Wegowa. You will arrive soon after Renno, and you will have an opportunity to see him there for a few days before he returns home as a bachelor for the last time. I fully realize you do not find it easy to wait to become his bride, but look at the bright side of what is about to happen. When the moon is full and then once again goes through its cycle, you and Renno will become man and wife. In your memory, this necessary time of delay will become as nothing."

*   *   *

The informal conduct of the highest officials in Franklin would have shocked their counterparts in the older states such as Massachusetts and Virginia. In a log cabin that served as the governor's office and personal parlor, Governor John Sevier, having pulled off his boots, sat with his stockinged feet propped on his desk as he waded through a stack of documents. He chewed absently on a wad of tobacco, and from time to time he unleashed with unerring accuracy a stream at a cuspidor several feet away. He never missed, as his aides who had served him throughout his distinguished career as a frontier Indian fighter readily testified.

Roy Johnson, tall, spare, and gray-haired, chief judge of the new court of the State of Franklin, opened the door and peered in. "Can you give me a couple of minutes, Jack?" he asked.

"Come in, Roy!" Sevier boomed cordially. "It will be a sad day for the people of Franklin when I lack the time to see you. How be you?"

Johnson chuckled. "Folks hereabout are so unaccustomed to having their own judiciary system that I've had no business yet," he said. "Not one case is on the docket for us, so I've been spending the past few days as militia chief of staff, reviewing our overall situation. I'm here to report to you, as commander in chief."

John Sevier opened a drawer in his desk, removed a whiskey bottle and two small tumblers, and proceeded to fill them. "I'm all ears, Roy." He raised his glass in salute.

They both finished their drinks in quick gulps, and

belching politely, Johnson resumed. "The militia is in good shape, Jack, the best of good shape. We have two hundred and sixteen officers and men on our muster rolls. In an emergency, I reckon we could raise an additional fifty. But I fail to see any real emergency threatening. Off to the west are the Cherokee and the Seneca as allies. Personally, I expect that Emily's marriage to Renno next month should help to cement that relationship for a long time to come. As you requested, they are sending an emissary to sign a long-term peace treaty."

"I, too, have no doubt in my mind about the loyalties of the leaders of the Cherokee and Seneca," Sevier said. "I wish I could feel as certain about the motives and character of all Indians. I particularly respected Ghonkaba of the Seneca, and we will miss him sorely. I could deal with him man to man, honestly and honorably on both sides, and successfully too. That's the way I wish it could be with all of them, in all tribes. But I've had a lot of grief from Indians, and to say the least it has made me more than a mite wary. Suspicious, some people may call it. But go on, Roy—I interrupted you."

"Off to the southeast are the Creek. We defeated them last year with sufficient decisiveness that they no longer threaten us in any way. But directly south of us are the Choctaw. They're a different story—"

"Hellfire!" Governor Sevier interrupted again. "We, with some help from our Indian allies, whipped the daylights out of the Choctaw earlier this year. They and the Creek are fine examples of the Indians I can never trust. What more can we do to guarantee our safety from them?"

"Unfortunately," Roy Johnson replied, "the Choctaw are like counterfeit money. They keep showing up when you least expect them to appear. Sure, we beat them to a standstill in battle. But they know their nuisance value. Most likely they will launch a fresh campaign, even though they know they would lose again. I regret to say this, Jack, but my own estimate, and that of my lieutenant colonels, is that we must control the Choctaw. Unless we can, they are likely to counter our hopes to expand the border of Franklin southward as more people cross the mountains to join us."

"I suspect you're right, Roy," the governor answered. "What's more, I would hate like the very devil to fight the Choctaw. I find it too damned hard to have to explain to the widows and parents of men who are killed in such a war."

"The last thing on earth that I would want to do," Colonel Johnson said, "is to dump the burden back on you, Jack."

"We're in the same boat, Roy," Sevier replied gruffly. "We will either sink or float together. I have to consider the Choctaw as untrustworthy bastards—how about you?"

"I call them the greediest damn good-for-nothing tribe of Indians I ever encountered," Johnson declared emphatically. "I'm convinced they would sell their very souls to the devil! They became allies of the British just because they hoped for more land, and they also wanted to receive guns and other goods."

"We might find it worth feeding their greed," Sevier said thoughtfully. "In fact, in the long run we could save the lives of a lot of our people who might die fighting the Choctaw."

"I don't understand," Johnson said in some confusion.

The governor rose from his desk and crossed the office to a wooden cabinet. He unlocked it with a key attached to a heavy chain that he took from a pocket. Opening a cardboard box, he removed several coins of shining gold, each about three quarters of an inch in diameter. "Take a look at these, Roy," he said. "They are the first coins made for the State of Franklin."

Judge Johnson picked up one of the coins, held it in his palm, turned it over, and examined it at length. "Real beauties," he said. "They're a sign of the progress we are making in bringing civilization to the wilderness."

Sevier nodded and counted out a portion of the box's contents. "Take these coins, Roy. They are worth around two hundred dollars. Go quickly to the Choctaw. Make a deal with their chief. Offer the money in return for an ironclad promise to keep the peace."

"The Choctaw are two-faced and unreliable," Johnson replied, "but if they do accept gold from us—as I predict they will—they could be expected to keep their word and not break the peace."

"Now that America is independent," the governor said, "I anticipate that migration from the British Isles will become much greater. We have many peo-

ple here from Scotland and Ireland who have been
corresponding with relatives in the Old World. We
can expect immigrants by the thousands, coming to
join their families and friends. Settlers will be filling
the whole Tennessee country, not just Franklin.
To have real peace in the area would be a great
advantage."

"You're right, Jack, no question about it." Johnson
picked up the coins, one by one, and dropped them
into a long, thin wooden box. "Two hundred dollars,
more or less, would be a small price to pay for real
peace on the frontier. Never fear, I will work out a
binding deal with the Choctaw!"

The band of Indian braves, twenty strong, strode
in single file out of the Everglades, the vast swampland in the southern part of Spanish Florida. Their
red and yellow war paint identified them as Seminole, unique among all tribes on the continent.

The Seminole were proud that they were a self-
created nation. Their numbers had been made up
originally by outcasts from several other nations, the
Cherokee, Choctaw, and Creek among them. When
a criminal was condemned by any of such tribes and
was expelled, forbidden to live any longer in their
territories, he almost invariably fled south to seek
refuge among the Seminole. So did runaway slaves,
who could find a safe home there. Over the decades,
as the fugitives intermarried, their offspring had become darker than the members of most Indian nations, a mixture of Indians and blacks.

The Seminole lived beyond the reach of the authorities who ruled Florida or of any Indian nations that might seek vengeance against them. Deep in the Everglade swamps, they were surrounded by alligators, poisonous snakes, and other intimidating creatures, so would-be intruders gave the area a wide berth.

With few exceptions, the Seminole warriors were quite tall and husky and possessed unusual skill with tomahawks and bows. In an environment alien and dangerous to all other humans they were at home.

They were on one of their rare expeditions out of their area, to determine what conditions now prevailed in the area to the north from where their ancestors had fled. In carrying out their surveillance, they would be scrupulous to observe from a discreet distance, never coming into contact with other tribes, who would outnumber them. They were confident that they could skillfully avoid being seen by scouts from other Indian tribes.

At the head of the column marching northward through the forests of palmetto and scrub pine was a strapping young man, striking in appearance. No more than thirty years old, he showed a self-assurance that, with the many feathers in his headdress, marked him as a chief.

Chief Durati was recognized as the bravest of the brave, the most skillful of the skilled. Seminole were evasive and tricky if forced to deal with outsiders, but Durati was noted as a man of integrity who always kept his word.

As he marched, he occasionally slowed his pace and looked back at his followers. He paid special attention to four stalwarts who carried long poles from which were hung the carcasses of two deer that had been shot on the outskirts of the Everglades. The men marched vigorously, in spite of their burden. In this, the Seminole were much like the Seneca; despite any difficulties, nothing would prevent them from carrying out their duties.

Suddenly, Durati heard a faint rustling in the underbrush ahead and to his right. Without missing a single stride, he scanned the area with care and finally found what he was seeking. Turning to a warrior directly behind him, he mouthed a single word: "Jeana."

The word was passed down the line swiftly and almost silently. Within seconds, the entire force had been alerted. They were being observed and shadowed by braves of the Jeana, a small but ferocious nation that lived along the Atlantic coastline northeast of the Everglades.

Durati put one hand behind his back and signaled with his fingers. The warrior behind him interpreted his wigwagging to mean six braves were in the enemy party. He passed along the information to the rest of the contingent.

The party continued marching for three hours, never pausing or slowing its pace. Finally, Durati gave an open signal and the entire line veered to the right, reaching several dead trees, where they broke off limbs to provide many armloads of firewood. As they again proceeded forward, they arrived at the inner rim of a crescent-shaped beach, fringed with palm trees and tall bushes. Halting here for the night, the warriors sprawled indolently near the crest of a dune. A few men busied themselves butchering the deer carcasses.

Sitting with his back propped against the side of the dune, Durati appeared to be asleep. Actually, he was listening to every sound, analyzing it, and preparing for the moment when he would issue the call to action.

Suddenly he sounded the Seminole war cry.

The bloodcurdling call was picked up by his men, who seized bows and arrows and began firing into the semitropical forest that surrounded them on three sides. Their fire was accurate, as befitted Seminole marksmen, and three of the six Jeana were killed. Within minutes, the surviving Jeana warriors were captured. Their hands were securely bound behind their backs.

Realizing that the venison would soon be ready to eat, Durati cut short the long ceremony. Instead of lecturing his unfortunate captives for hours, he limited himself to a few remarks.

"The warriors of the Jeana," he told them, "are not men. They are fools. They expected to attack the Seminole and to steal the deer that we shot and that rightfully belong to us. Since the braves of the Jeana are less than men, I order that they be reduced to their rightful state and sent back to their own people with a warning never again to trespass on the Seminole or to attack us under any circumstances. Let them learn from this that the Seminole are to be treated with the utmost respect at all times."

Drawing his tomahawk, he wielded it with ruthless efficiency and removed the testicles of one of the captives.

The unfortunate man was still bleeding profusely, his screams of pain and terror filling the soft night air, when his two companions received the same punishment. Then all three were cut loose from their bonds and pushed out into the wilderness, free to make their way home as best they could.

It would be a very long time, Durati reflected wryly, before the Jeana were again foolhardy enough to attack Seminole warriors. They would understand that like a nest of rattlesnakes, the Seminole were to be avoided.

Sniffing, Durati smelled the delicious scent of roasting venison and smiled gently. "The time is at hand for us to eat our supper," he called. "The gods favor those who are strong in their own protection and in the guarding of their rights. Put aside your cares and eat heartily. Rejoice that you are men of the Seminole, because the whole world trembles before you!"

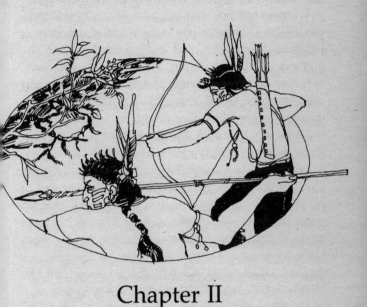

Chapter II

Ben Whipple suffered no illusions about the character of his companions as he sneaked cautiously through the wilderness toward Tennessee. Without exception, his five comrades, members of the crew of his cousin Emil's pirate ship, were hard-bitten desperadoes. They had joined him because he had promised even more loot than they could capture at sea. He knew that he could not depend on them in a crisis and that they would undoubtedly turn on him if he could not provide the booty he had promised.

Whipple was not worried, however. A former military officer, he knew where the funds of the State of Franklin were kept, and he intended to use the pirates to raid the building. With any luck, he should come away with thousands of dollars, enough to satisfy the greed of his comrades and take care of his own needs.

Game was plentiful, and the journey without incident. Whipple took few risks. Drawing on his experiences as a woodsman and militia officer, he often climbed the tallest trees or stood on high ground to survey the countryside and assure himself that no other travelers were in the vicinity. He was not even aware that his little band was under constant surveillance by scouts of the major tribes of the territory through which they passed. The Choctaw and the Creek, who could have set upon them at any moment, disdainfully refrained from attacking white men, although they would have tried to ambush any unwary Indians who might venture through their lands.

One afternoon, as Whipple scoured the surrounding area from a towering oak, his vigilance was rewarded. He glimpsed three white men heading directly toward the tree.

Studying them, Whipple was elated when he recognized the leader of the little group as Roy Johnson. He was accompanied by two younger members of the militia. What Whipple found most intriguing was the fact that under one arm Johnson carried a long, thin wooden box. It bore a striking resemblance to a strongbox, and he promptly convinced himself that for some reason Johnson was traveling with a state treasure.

Whipple climbed down and described for his companions what he had seen. They listened avidly, their eyes shining with greed, and were immediately eager to attack the group and snatch the strongbox.

Whipple ordered them to hide in dense foliage on either side of the trail. Satisfied with his scheme, Whipple waited for the unsuspecting trio to walk into his trap.

At last, Johnson and the two militiamen appeared, moving slowly but steadily. Unaware of impending danger, they carried their rifles in slings on their backs.

When all three were in the clear and ideal targets, Whipple shouted a command. His companions joined him in opening fire with their old-fashioned muskets. They were all expert shots and the militiamen were killed immediately.

Only Roy Johnson had survived, and he was unhurt. Reaching over his shoulder, he plucked his rifle from his back and swung it into position, pausing to find a target in the dense brush.

Whipple, concealed directly behind him, had no time to reload. He grasped his musket like a club, stepped into the open, and swinging viciously, brought the butt around against the right side of Johnson's head.

The officer was knocked unconscious, dropping to the ground like a stone.

Whipple assumed he had killed the colonel, his former commanding officer. He snatched up the wooden box from the ground and then took from Johnson's belt a small bag, which he thought might contain additional valuables. Then, picking up the colonel's rifle, he followed his companions, who had seized the rifles of the other militiamen.

They jogged rapidly along the trail to the north, putting distance between themselves and the bloody scene.

But curiosity soon overcame Whipple. He halted, and the desperadoes crowded around as he pried open the lid of the wooden box. In it were the newly minted gold pieces bearing the name and seal of the State of Franklin. Counting them quickly, Whipple realized that he had made a haul of only about two hundred dollars. In the colonel's bag, he found only a pipe with the initials "R.J." etched in silver and a pocketknife with the same letters carved into the ivory handle.

Whipple quickly distributed the money, giving a few gold pieces to each of the men, while he kept the remainder, together with the pipe and the knife.

He realized that the coins, pipe, and knife were proof that he had robbed and killed Roy Johnson. If he were caught with the loot in his possession he would be hanged.

The possibility made him extremely uncomfortable, more nervous than he had been after murdering Ghonkaba. A civilized community would take

much more seriously the death of one of its leading
citizens.

Renno sat opposite Nora Johnson, the woman who
was to be his mother-in-law, in the dining room of
her Knoxville home, happily demolishing a platter of
roast beef with baked potatoes, corn, and squash.

"I'm sorry that you missed the colonel," she told
him. "He was sent unexpectedly by Governor Sevier
on a mission, and I don't know when he will be back.
I really can't expect him to return home until next
week at the earliest."

She noticed, as she often had before, that Renno
handled the knife and fork of civilization with practiced ease. It was traditional particularly for the first-
born of each generation descended from the first
Renno to become familiar with the ways of civilization and to conduct himself accordingly.

"I am sorry, too, but I understand," he said. "I do
not know that I will still be here by next week. I was
sent only to sign a treaty on behalf of the Cherokee
and my own Seneca. With that accomplished, I am
expected to go home. But if I do not see the colonel,
we will meet when I come back for the wedding. I
have signed the treaty, and so has the governor.
Therefore, I will be leaving soon for the land of the
Cherokee."

Mrs. Johnson smiled. "Won't your path and Emily's cross in the wilderness during your journey?"

"No, ma'am," Renno said with a chuckle. "You do
not know my grandmother or the sachem of the
Cherokee. They are both old-fashioned and very rig-

orous in applying their standards to my generation. Since Emily and I are not yet married, it would not be regarded as proper for us to be together in the wilderness, so you can be sure that no accidental meeting will occur. Whether she will arrive here before I leave or after I reach the land of the Cherokee, I can't predict."

Mrs. Johnson shook her head. "I had no idea," she said, "that the Indians of any nation were so strict in such matters."

"I think you will find," Renno told her, "that the standards of most Indian nations are similar to those of the Americans, or the British, and certainly better than the French. From the little I have seen, the Spanish are more severe in their treatment of their young. For all I know, people of some other nations may be more lenient, but most probably are generally alike."

"I think it's admirable," she said, "that you know so much about the customs of so many different peoples."

"My familiarity with the ways of many is not accidental," Renno said. "My ancestor, the first Renno, discovered at an early age that he had been adopted by Ghonka, and realized that because of his white skin, he was different from all other Indians. Later, he made it his business to learn all he could about the colonists in Massachusetts, because he knew he was descended from some of them. Renno married a white-skinned girl from Virginia, and he and Betsy raised their son, Ja-gonh—my grandfather—to be as much at home in her civilization as in his. Since that

time, we have had a family tradition, and each generation learns to adapt to the ways of both the Indian
society in which he was born and white society. Now
you may see why I am not worried over the ability of
Emily to grow accustomed to the ways of the Seneca,
and to a lesser extent, of the Cherokee. My family
and I are already very close to the Americans in the
way that we live and think and act."

"I'm pleased we are having this talk," Mrs. Johnson said. "You've answered some of the questions in
my mind that I have not yet asked. I feel much
easier now, greatly relieved, to be reassured again
that you and Emily don't come from worlds as different as they may seem on the surface."

"Just as my sister, my brother, and I learned from
the best of American civilization, as well as the civilization the Seneca could offer us, so my children also
will learn," Renno said. "The face of this land is
changing swiftly, and the pace will be even more
rapid now that the war has come to an end. The
Indian nations are becoming more accustomed to
seeing white men within their lands, and they are
adjusting to the need to change their ways. No one
can predict what this land will be like when our
grandchildren and their children inherit it. But I
predict that none will be better prepared for that
world than those who are descended from Emily and
from me. They will enjoy the best of both our worlds,
which will become one world in the America of
tomorrow!"

*   *   *

Emily Johnson was designated to prepare the evening meal on her last night in the land of the Cherokee. Toshabe pronounced her efforts good, as did Ah-wen-ga.

Early the following morning, she was awake in time to drink a gourd filled with the cool liquor of several herbs before she began her journey under the escort of Rusog, the large, muscular Cherokee war chief who was married to Ena, Renno's sister. As the grandson of Loramas, he belonged to the most distinguished family in the land. The fact that he was assigned to escort Emily was a sign of his high regard among the Indians with whom she would be making her home.

Rusog showed great consideration for her, never traveling at a pace too difficult for her to keep up, and always pausing long enough to allow her to rest. She surprised him, however, by the help that she gave him. Whenever he brought down small game or caught fish for their meals, she skinned, cleaned, and cooked the meat and prepared the fish unaided. She even collected firewood and built the fires, having learned well from the Seneca women. She made no complaints, and Rusog was much impressed. One night, as they sat at their small fire eating the meal Emily had prepared, Rusog spoke more confidentially than usual. "Ena and I were sad," he said, "when we first learned that our brother Renno would marry a woman from another world. It was our belief that great unhappiness was in store for Renno, as well as for her. But we were wrong."

Emily realized he was complimenting her and was pleased. "You are sad no longer, then?"

"I am not," he said, "and when I see Ena again, she will share with me my newfound happiness. I will have pleasure in telling her that the woman Renno will marry is as adept in the ways of the wilderness as is any squaw. I did not know that in your world you gather wood and make fires, or that you could cook meat and fish and make them good to eat."

"I must admit," Emily said with a light laugh, "that I learned how to accomplish those things in the weeks that I spent in the land of the Cherokee. There I was taught by Toshabe how a woman must act."

"That is good," Rusog said earnestly, "but many things you have not been taught, but have yourself known. You have not cried out in distress even one time when I have kept you traveling longer than you might have wished and have become weary."

They smiled, then lapsed into silence and did not speak again. Emily had also learned the art of refraining from conversation when talk was unnecessary, and she demonstrated now that she understood the moods of Indian men, sometimes even before they themselves were aware of their state of mind.

After they finished eating and washed in a nearby stream, Emily helped Rusog tamp down the fire. Then she curled up in her blanket for the night.

Rusog chose a spot beyond her, closer to the wilderness and farther from the fire in the little clearing. He, too, wrapped himself in his blanket and did not even bother to say good night.

It was true, Emily thought, that she was returning far better prepared for marriage than she had been before visiting Renno's mother and grandmother. She had acquired a familiarity with the customs of the people whose world would become hers, but even more important, she had become more familiar with the wilderness itself. During her years of living in a frontier fortress town she had come to regard the omnipresent wilderness as a friendly place. When treated as a friend, it could be helpful and kind. She had learned to obey the laws of self-preservation that the wilderness imposed and was prepared to accept the best that the forest had to offer.

Consequently, she had no difficulty in drifting off to sleep. She was confident that the combination of the nearby fire on one side of her and Rusog's presence on the other would protect her from any wild beasts that tried to come close. Otherwise, she felt no cause for fear.

In her reckoning, however, Emily somehow overlooked one element—man. Some savages and even some men who came from her own world, men with pale skins who considered themselves civilized, were to be feared and avoided.

She had no idea that men who embodied the very worst of every aspect of so-called civilized human beings were only a few miles away from where she and Rusog had made their camp for the night.

Even though his loot from the robbery of Colonel Johnson had fallen short of the larger treasure he had dreamed of capturing from the treasury at Knoxville, Ben Whipple soon decided to amend his plan and head back south. He had chosen the wrong kind of associates for his expedition.

He had made a mistake in giving them the gold coins; they got out of hand and were proving too much for him to control. In Knoxville this uncouth greed could only result in big trouble.

He changed the route as the freebooters became increasingly troublesome and all but unmanageable, resenting and resisting his efforts at discipline.

Feeling the weight of their gold pieces, they were happy enough to turn around and start the long walk back to the port in Florida where Emil Whipple held forth.

Each man carried his own supply of liquor, and some men drank too much. Quarrels and fights broke out. Whipple's attempts to stop them failed miserably, and he could no longer persuade them to work together.

The situation worsened. Three violent quarrels erupted in one day; it was impossible to continue the journey, and Whipple's patience gave way.

Never the most even-tempered of men, now he exploded. "Sit down, you bastards, and listen to me! You've been unmanageable for too damn long. You've done nothing but fight and carry on ever since I gave you the gold."

One of the men muttered under his breath.

Whipple pointed an accusing finger. "I'm not trying to reform you!" he shouted. "I don't give a damn if you kill each other. I brought you with me and I've taken responsibility for you so far. You forget that we're not just a few miles from Emil's ship. We're hundreds of miles away, and we have a long trek through a wilderness filled with hostile Indians and worse dangers. I will guide you back home on one condition: that you behave yourselves. We'll have no more drinking along the trail and no more of your senseless quarrels. If you want to fight, go ahead. I'll leave and go my own way to Knoxville, and you can find your way back to the coast as best you can. You'll see just how far you can go on your own."

His words had a sobering effect. Self-satisfied smirks vanished from the desperadoes' faces, and they listened quietly, aware that they needed him if they hoped to survive in the wilderness and reach the Florida shoreline in safety. Realizing that Whipple was capable of carrying out his threats, they quieted down and began to march along in some semblance of disciplined order.

Shortly after noon, Whipple once more climbed into a tree to check the area for Indians. He was astonished to see, in a clearing less than two hundred yards ahead, a man and a woman eating their midday meal. His surprise mounted when he recognized the woman as someone very greatly resembling Emily Johnson.

At first he thought his eyes were deceiving him. Long attracted to Emily, Whipple had become embittered when she rejected him to marry Renno. Now, staring at her, he finally realized he was not looking at a mirage. It was indeed Emily, and she was accompanied only by one Indian brave, who was wearing the war paint of the Cherokee.

Even as he exulted, Whipple's mind worked rapidly. How could he turn this unexpected encounter to his advantage? The answer was very simple, and he knew precisely what he needed to do.

"Gather around me, lads, and listen," he excitedly told his companions when he rejoined them on the ground. "I'm about to have a wonderfully lucky break. My woman, with whom I had a falling out, is only a short distance away on the trail, coming from the opposite direction. With her is a big Cherokee brave. We'll put him out of the way and then take the woman captive. Just remember—she's mine. I'll kill any man who lays a hand on her!"

He and his men hurried forward, making a wide detour around Emily and Rusog, who were still engrossed in their meal. As soon as the couple was surrounded, Whipple gave a signal and the men closed in.

It was impossible for men unaccustomed to the forest to move silently, and Rusog heard them coming. Leaping to his feet, he grasped his bow and reached over his shoulder to take an arrow from his quiver.

Before he had a chance to nock it, however, a rattle of gunfire erupted, and suddenly four of the desperadoes broke into the clearing.

"Hide in the brush!" Rusog called to Emily in the tongue of the Cherokee. "Hide, and let me take care of this!"

Emily obediently began to back away out of the clearing. She inadvertently backed into Ben Whipple, who was approaching from the rear.

Giving her no opportunity to protect herself, Whipple grasped her by both arms, and taking a bandanna handkerchief from his pocket with his free hand, he stuffed it into her mouth. Then he tore a supple vine that was within reach and with it bound her wrists behind her back. As he threw her to the ground, she caught her first glimpse of her tormentor, and the shock and contempt he read in her eyes infuriated him. With far more force than was necessary, he tied her ankles with another length of vine. Then, chuckling, he told her softly, "You're not going anyplace. I will attend to you shortly." He snatched up the rifle that had been her father's and advanced into the clearing.

Rusog was demonstrating that he fully deserved his promotion to the rank of war chief. Wielding his tomahawk with great ferocity and determination, he had struck one of the desperadoes a glancing blow and was holding him and three others at bay. His long brawny arm swept back and forth in a wide arc, and the corsairs were intent on staying beyond his reach.

Whipple approached Rusog from the rear, unseen. Whipple was reluctant to fire his rifle; his own men were too close. Much as he had done when surprising Colonel Johnson, he grasped his rifle barrel like a club. With all his strength, he slapped the stock hard against the warrior's face.

Though endowed with far more than average strength, Rusog was only human, and he toppled, unconscious, like a majestic oak felled by a sharp ax. His face was covered with blood; he looked dead.

As he looked down on the bloody body, a diabolical plan was taking form in Whipple's fertile mind. He dropped to one knee beside Rusog; it did not matter whether the Cherokee was alive or dead. What mattered was that he had found a convenient scapegoat for the attack on Colonel Johnson. The unprovoked assault on the colonel and the theft of the gold were criminal offenses. Now Whipple had unexpectedly found a way to shift the blame to this Indian, a savage who would be a natural suspect and hardly in a position to defend himself.

Removing the colonel's initialed pipe and knife from the pouch he carried in his own waistband, Whipple took a small bag from beneath Rusog's belt and dropped the objects into it. Then, after a moment's hesitation, he added two gold coins, sacrificing them to make certain that the Indian would be blamed for the attack on the colonel. They were sufficiently close to the fort, he knew, that the body of the Indian would be certain to be discovered. As soon as that occurred, the Indian's guilt would be established and he, Ben, would never pay the penalty for his crime.

Chuckling quietly, he aimed a kick at Rusog's bloodstained head before heading south again.

He found Emily Johnson stretched out on the ground, facing away from the clearing.

"On your feet, woman!" he ordered as he slashed the vines that bound her feet together. He did not untie her hands or remove the gag from her mouth.

Emily slowly struggled to her feet. There was an icy hatred in her eyes when she looked at Whipple.

He laughed openly at her. "You're my woman now, and don't forget it, not for a single second," he told her with a sneer. "You'll do whatever I tell you, whenever I tell you to do it. Disobey me just once and I'll turn you over to the lads with whom we'll be traveling. There's not a single gentleman in the company, and I don't mind telling you they're all freebooters of the sea who would treat you in a manner you'd hardly like once they got their hands on you. Just remember, you depend completely on my generosity for your own welfare and protection." He snapped his fingers imperiously. "Come along," he ordered.

Emily hesitated for a long moment and then obediently followed him. She knew he was not exaggerating about what could happen. Whipple was sufficiently vindictive to keep his word and hand her over for their amusement any time she failed to do his bidding. She was trapped, at least for the immediate future. She would gain her bearings as soon as she possibly could and then concentrate on escaping from Whipple. Until then she would be well advised to pander to him, no matter how distasteful that was.

The trek southward seemed endless, and Emily felt that she had spent months rather than mere days walking through the limitless wilderness. Every morning, her wrists were bound behind her back before the day's journey began, and her bonds were not removed until the party halted at nightfall. Though she no longer had a gag in her mouth, she rarely spoke, replying in curt monosyllables when Whipple addressed her.

She held herself apart as best she could, hoping
the men would begin to take her for granted and pay
no attention to her. So far, her scheme appeared
effective, and she was grateful for the way they ignored her.

The attitude that Whipple displayed toward her
was very different, however. She was forced to walk
behind him all day and to sit beside him at meals.
He seemed conscious of her whereabouts at all times,
so she could not understand why he had made no
advances toward her.

At last it dawned on her that he was not being
considerate but was thinking only of himself. He was
holding back from making love to her until they were
sufficiently far from Knoxville that she could have no
hope of returning there without his help. He began
to make his bolder attitude plain by placing a hand
on her shoulder or arm in a proprietary way, and
even when she moved away or tried to shrug him off,
he became increasingly difficult to dislodge. Something would happen soon, but she had no idea when.

The weather became warmer and more humid as
the party traveled south beyond the land of the
Choctaw, and although nothing was said directly to
Emily, she gathered that if they continued their
journey south without changing direction, they would
walk the length of the Florida peninsula. She knew
little about that area except that Spain had recovered
it from Britain only earlier that same year, as one of
the conditions of the treaty ending the American
Revolutionary War.

Her sense of isolation and helplessness grew until

it encompassed her completely. She was far from home, from her family and friends, from her beloved Renno. No one could help her, and she was totally under the power of Ben Whipple, who did not hesitate to demonstrate each day how completely she was within his control.

Every day she was more and more inclined to give in to utter despair. Yet she refused to give up hope that she might be able to escape, remote though the chance seemed. Perhaps rescue would come when she least anticipated it. By digging deep into her inner resources, she was able to keep alive her hopes for the future.

One day, they quit early, and after a meal of roast venison, wild corn, and berries picked from a nearby vine, Emily felt even more tired than usual.

Saying nothing, she stretched out on the near side of the fire they had made to keep the bugs and mosquitoes away, and soon she began to doze. The desperadoes were about to begin their usual evening bout of drinking and horseplay, but they were told by Whipple to scout around the encampment first. One by one they withdrew, after a swallow or two of their hard drink.

Emily dreamed that she and Renno had been reunited and that he was making love to her. He kissed her, and she returned his embrace, winding her arms around his neck and pressing the back of his head closer as she clung to him.

She sighed, opened her eyes, and was horrified when she saw the despised features of Ben Whipple only inches from her face. Emily began to struggle valiantly, pushing him away with all her strength and jerking to a sitting position.

"Go away!" She spat out the words. "Don't you dare come any nearer!"

Whipple reached for her and pulled her even closer, in spite of her struggles to free herself. "You really are my woman now," he said. "I've waited long enough for you, and I'm not waiting another day."

In a viselike grasp, he held one of her wrists, and she lowered her mouth to the back of his hand and sank her teeth into his knuckles.

Whipple released her immediately, cursing her under his breath.

"Leave me alone!" she shouted.

He glowered at her. "I warn you," he muttered. "You give yourself to me freely and voluntarily, or I'll turn you over to the lads. You can imagine what they'd do to you with a few drinks under their belts."

"You say that's what your intentions are," she told him boldly in an attempt to put him off, "but you'll never do it. You wouldn't want a woman that such scum have had, and you know it."

Whipple stared at her in openmouthed astonishment.

"You're too proud to share me with others, Ben. Your arrogance is too great for you to take the leavings."

"So you think I won't hand you over to them?" he demanded.

"I know it," she replied courageously. "You want me too badly yourself."

He stared hard at her, cursed her again, and then raised a hand, intending to slap her face.

But Emily was too quick for him, and catching his wrist, she dug her nails into his flesh as hard as she could.

Grimacing in pain, he flung her hand aside. Wildly angry, he was prepared to use whatever force was necessary to subdue her.

Emily made ready to resist with her whole being but realized her strength was far from equal to his. She was afraid that he would take her against her will, and she could do nothing to keep him at bay.

Suddenly, when she had abandoned all hope of escaping or eluding him, he released her and grabbed for his rifle. His action was so unexpected that Emily was puzzled by it. But she very quickly understood that Whipple had not been motivated by decency or compassion, for the air overhead was filled with arrows. The party was being attacked by hostile Indians.

Durati and his men wasted no time, the majority concentrating their full attention on the desperadoes who were returning to the campfire after their scouting around. A few Indians devoted their attention to the elusive Whipple. All heeded the warning of Durati, who called out, "Spare the woman! Kill only the men!"

Whipple's freebooters refused to submit meekly but fought courageously, reloading after each shot, taking careful aim, and firing again. But they were badly outnumbered, and the odds against them were overwhelming.

The Seminole had dipped their arrows in a thickened mixture of the venom of poisonous snakes from the great inland swamp. An arrow needed only to puncture the skin to be lethal.

One of the two desperadoes who had the militiamen's long rifles managed to bring down a warrior with a single shot. His death only infuriated the Seminole, and they increased their efforts, pouring still more arrows into the clumps of high grass where the corsairs were trying to conceal themselves.

One by one the defenders were nicked by arrows and suffered agonizing cramps that shot through their entire bodies as they died. Their muskets and the rifles were silenced, and the Seminole moved in on the bodies of their victims, scalping each with practiced skill.

Meanwhile, Ben Whipple and Emily had been able to elude the attacking warriors. Emily sought cover in the tall grass, while Whipple hid behind the trunk of an old oak, from where he fired at the raiders again and again.

Emily was impressed with his fighting skills in spite of herself. She saw Whipple bring down a warrior, but when another stumbled and fell, she felt a sudden new alarm. If the attackers withdrew, she would again be left at the mercy of Whipple.

She looked around for a weapon of some sort and saw what she was seeking: a short, thick piece of tree branch in the grass just beyond her reach.

Emily crept forward through the grass, moving with maddening slowness, an inch or so at a time. She had no desire to attract Whipple's attention.

At last, by stretching out one arm as far as she could, she was able to touch the branch with her fingertips, edging it toward her. After what felt like an eternity, she was able to get her hand around it and to draw it to her. She grasped it tightly and waited for her chance.

She could not forecast what her fate might be if the Indians took her captive, but she knew that her life would be a bleak hell on earth if she remained with Ben Whipple.

Assuring herself that he was totally preoccupied, she held the clublike branch with both hands, raised it high into the air, and brought it down onto the back of Whipple's head with as much force as she could command. He moaned, slumped forward, and dropped his rifle as he lost consciousness.

Emily was immediately pulled to her feet by several gesticulating, laughing warriors, men darker and even huskier than the Seneca and Cherokee. Face to face with the man who appeared to be their leader, she quickly realized that he was of a tribe with which she was unfamiliar. His yellow and red war paint meant nothing to her, nor did the three feathers protruding from his headband. The brave seemed to be quite young. His features were chiseled, and he was good-looking. She spoke to him in the language of the Seneca, but he looked at her blankly and replied in what to her was gibberish.

Next she tried speaking Cherokee, the only other native language that she knew.

The warrior's face cleared. "I am Durati, war chief of the mighty Seminole," he said. "I offer my thanks to the squaw for her help in subduing this white devil who has killed some of my braves."

"I am Emily, daughter of the war chief of the settlers of Tennessee," she said. "I was the prisoner of this man, whom I loathe."

"Thanks to your help, he is now our prisoner," Durati told her. "But I cannot set you free, even though you helped us to capture this man. You were captured in a fair fight, and you must come with us. If you will come of your own free will, I will find it much easier to deal with you. If you object, however, I am required to take you by force as our captive."

Emily could see what she must do. "I will come with you freely," she told him promptly.

Durati immediately called out to his braves, informing them of her decision.

The warriors seemed pleased. Most of them nodded, and several grunted what appeared to be approval.

Durati continued to strive to make amends for depriving her of her freedom. "Are the thundersticks and the other belongings that the white braves carried your property?"

Emily understood the ways of the Indians sufficiently well to comprehend that, as best he could, he was trying to explain the customs of his people that caused him to make her a captive. "The property is mine," she assured him gravely, but felt compelled to add, "I freely make a gift to the Seminole of the thundersticks."

While speaking, she bent down and picked up a rifle that lay near the still-unconscious Ben Whipple. Although she did not recognize it, she was handling her father's own weapon.

Again, Durati explained her words to his men, and this time Emily could have no doubt of the Seminole

warriors' pleasure. Several of them grinned, and three
raised their voices in war cries of exultation. Possession of firearms, objects endowed with a rare and
potent magic, was the dream of every warrior. Her
generosity had won the entire band to Emily's cause,
and without exception they showed their readiness
to be of assistance to her.

Before they left the scene, the braves, at their war
chief's instigation, handed Emily two shiny metal
objects. She recognized them as gold pieces minted
for Franklin. *How could these coins of the new state
have come into the possession of Whipple and his
followers?* she wondered. Certainly they could not
have acquired them by robbing ordinary settlers,
who would have had no access to such money. Only
the highest officials, men like Governor Sevier and
her own father, would have the coins, especially in
large denominations or quantities.

Uncertain of what the future held, Emily quickly
braided the coins into her hair for safekeeping. Then,
trying to put from her mind all disturbing thoughts
and questions, she followed Durati's orders and, together with the braves, prepared to move on.

Leaving the bodies of the dead and dragging Whipple, the Seminole marched for several miles to the
near bank of a large, swift-flowing river. There they
paused for the night. While the men went fishing,
Emily, conscious of a squaw's duties, busied herself
gathering wood, then building a fire, which was blazing by the time the braves began to bring her fish,
which they had cleaned. Thanks to her recent training, she fried the fish in some wild herbs she col-

lected, serving them with a tubular root vegetable provided by Durati. The Seminole ate avidly, evidently much pleased by her unexpected expertise.

That night Emily slept well, her slumber untroubled for the first time since she had been taken captive by Whipple. She pictured the Seminole as a gentle people, warriors considerate of other nations, and demonstrating no belligerence toward former foes.

In the morning, she discovered how badly mistaken she was. She awakened to the sound of a whip cutting through the air and lashing some object. When she opened her eyes, she was astonished to see Ben Whipple, stripped to his waist, on his hands and knees, being beaten. A Seminole warrior stood over him with a rawhide whip made of several lengths of leather. He was wielding it viciously on the captive's bare back and shoulders. The Seminole had taught Whipple an unforgettable lesson; the less discomfort he showed, the less severely he would be treated. He gritted his teeth during the flogging, and when the warrior tired of his sport, Whipple kowtowed before him, pressing his face into the dirt. Ordered to rise, he immediately busied himself gathering firewood under the watchful eyes of his tormentors. Moving at a trot, he accumulated a large pile of limbs and brush for the fire that a brave had started.

By the time Emily approached the fire, flames were leaping high, and a body of coals was building up. She would have no need to make a fire that morning.

She prepared a breakfast of fried fish. It amused the warriors, while eating, to throw their scraps to

Whipple and watch him pick up bits of fish from the
ground and eat them, dust and all.

Whipple glanced at her, and she flinched before
the blazing hatred she could read in his eyes. *If looks
could kill*, she thought, *my life would be at an end!*

When they broke camp, resuming their march
toward the south, Emily assumed they were heading
toward their own homeland, although nothing was
said to her about their destination.

The warriors' blankets and other gear were placed
in several large bundles. Whipple, relegated to a
place near the rear of the column, was forced to
carry most of them.

Emily was pleased and somewhat surprised when
she was assigned a place near the head of the column, directly behind Durati. She could not see Whipple far to the rear, but she could hear the occasional
crack of a whip wielded by the brave who followed
close behind him, encouraging him to keep up the
pace. She shuddered when she heard Whipple's
screams.

Only now did she begin to appreciate the choice
she had made. If she had rejected Durati's offer of
friendship and had been less generous in her treatment of the Seminole, they would have responded in
kind, subjecting her to the harsh treatment accorded
to Whipple.

It occurred to her, not for the first time, that vast
differences existed between tribes. The Seneca, by
far the most advanced in making war, which they
had raised to a science, thought instinctively in terms
of strategies and tactics suitable for their terrain;

their knowledge compared favorably with the methods of renowned generals in Europe with centuries
of military tradition behind them.

The Cherokee, progressive in the peacetime agri-
cultural pursuits, grew a large variety of crops but
were always experimenting to find others that would
grow well in their soil and return the greatest yield.

As nearly as Emily could judge, the Seminole
were still a primitive people who relied on brute
force. Perhaps, she mused, the Seminole were less
advanced than other nations because they were so
isolated, living in a remote region, where vast swamps
cut them off from other civilizations. Whatever the
reason, she knew she had to exercise great caution to
maintain their goodwill. She could feel little sympathy for Ben Whipple, yet she could not help but
regret that any human being was subjected to such
cruel treatment.

Chapter III

Far to the south, Ben Whipple's cousin Emil was making a swift overland journey up the Florida coast. He followed a trail that ran northward until he reached St. Augustine, the walled community that had resumed its old status as the capital of Spanish Florida.

Presenting a gold medallion that identified him as the master of a ship that preyed on English, French, and American merchant vessels, he received immediate admission to the city. Increasing his pace, he made his way past the palace of the new Spanish governor and at last came to a compound that faced the ocean. Inside its walls of sun-baked clay was a lush semitropical garden, with a house that looked out over the water. A severe, thin-lipped woman, her hair pulled back into a bun, answered the summons of the bell. She regarded him unsmilingly.

"Good day, Señora Abilda," Whipple said in crude but passable Spanish. "The master sent for me."

She was a woman of few words. "You will wait," she said, and retreated into the interior of the house. He shifted his weight from one foot to the other while he marked time. At last the housekeeper reappeared and curtly beckoned.

After crossing a labyrinth of rooms, she led him into an inner court filled with flowers that were oddly choked with weeds. Seated in a high-backed wicker chair was a slender yet vigorous man with a fringe of black hair around his bald head. Without bothering to look up, he commanded, "Sit down, Whipple." The housekeeper disappeared, as Emil Whipple did as he was told, seating himself opposite the man.

Whipple had rightfully acquired a reputation as a courageous freebooter, the hard-driving master of a pirate vessel, scourge of merchant ships that dared to ply the waters between American ports to the north and the West Indies to the south. Even so, he was badly frightened by this man, his superior, overlord, and undisputed master of an entire corsair fleet. Known as Admiral Riley, he occasionally appeared in the uniform of an admiral in the Spanish navy. Whether he actually held such a rank or had made a private agreement with the governor was unknown, and no one dared inquire. Riley was too ferocious, and he was reputed to kill anyone who became unduly curious about him or his affairs.

The tension rubbed Whipple's nerves raw. He knew the rules, however, and silently concentrated on observing them. Anyone who crossed Riley had good cause for regrets.

Suddenly Riley raised his head, exposing a long scar down the length of his left cheek to the corner of his mouth. The scar caused his lips to droop in a perpetual sneer. The sight of it now suffused Whipple with dread.

"You took your time getting here, Whipple." Riley's voice was harsh. "What delayed you?"

"Unfortunately," the captain replied, "I had to come by an overland route."

Riley's eyes were pinpoints of light that drilled into him. "What happened to your ship?"

"The ship is intact, sir. But I was lacking several of my crew, the most important ones. Some of my petty officers and my most experienced helmsmen were otherwise occupied."

Riley rose to his feet and began to stroll with seeming aimlessness down a path between two banks of flowering shrubs. As he walked he swung one arm idly, seeming to be paying no attention, but in fact delicately lopping the heads off weeds with the sharp, short, slightly curved blade that replaced the hand on that arm.

Whipple shuddered. In more battles than he could recall, he had seen Riley lightly and deftly cut the jugular vein of an enemy with a backhand sweep of that blade. More to the point, he had known Riley, with an equally delicate swing, to dispose of a subordinate who displeased him.

"Where are your men?" Riley asked softly.

The menace in his voice was unmistakable, and Whipple hesitated before he replied, "They have gone north with my cousin on an overland treasure hunt."

"I expect crewmen in my fleet to earn their keep," Riley retorted icily. "Discharge them at once and sign on new men to replace them. Juggle your crew so that the more experienced hands will take over for them. Promptly!"

"Yes, sir!" Whipple was fascinated by the sight of the top of one weed after another disappearing under the sweep of Riley's arm.

"I shall expect you to take up your sea station ten days from now," Riley ordered. "You are to report for duty with a full crew at that time. I trust you notice I am being very generous. You should have ample opportunity to return to your home and sign on a new crew in ten days."

"Yes, sir!" Whipple replied again, doing his best to conceal his dismay. He would be obliged to travel day and night and then feverishly devote every hour to recruiting a crew. But he did not dare protest, and he accepted the admiral's dictum as law. Any deviation from those orders could result in his losing his own head as quickly and as easily as weeds were being beheaded in the garden.

A party of hunters chanced to find Roy Johnson, who had regained consciousness but was too weak to move unaided. They fashioned a pallet for him and carried him to the fort.

Under the care of his wife, he began to recuperate. Asked about the attackers who had injured him and killed his two escorts, he could remember little, possibly because of the blow on the head that he had received. He had never actually seen them, he said, and in response to repeated questioning, he could not even describe them as white men or Indians.

Governor Sevier responded promptly to the emergency by calling a platoon of the Franklin militia to duty. Dispatched into the wilderness, their instructions were to find the culprits who had stolen Colonel Johnson's money and killed the militiamen with him.

The scouts, all long experienced in wilderness travel, moved southward into the region where the colonel had been found. Under forced march, they spread out over a wide area as they scoured the woods for any sign of the attackers.

A scant seventy-two hours after they left the fort, one team of scouts spied a trail just left by Rusog. The Cherokee war chief was wandering dazed and aimlessly through the forest. Overtaken by the militiamen, he offered no resistance.

When the lieutenant in command of the militia-men opened his leather pouch, Rusog was astonished to see the contents: two newly minted gold coins, as well as a pipe and knife bearing Roy Johnson's initials.

Rusog's command of English was rudimentary at best, and he found it impossible to explain how these objects could have come into his possession. Placing Rusog under arrest, the scouts escorted him as a prisoner under close guard back to Knoxville.

His arrest created a sensation in Knoxville. The tide of public opinion immediately turned against the Cherokee, largely because most frontier dwellers were ready to believe the worst they might hear about any Indian. Rusog's inability to speak English was matched by his captors' equal unfamiliarity with the tongue of the Cherokee.

Not sure how to deal with the prisoner, Judge Benjamin F. Hill, a magistrate acting in the continued absence of Judge Roy Johnson, heeded advice from Governor Sevier and ordered Rusog confined to a cell. Governor Sevier and the judge visited the Johnsons' home and called on the invalid in his sickroom. Sevier wasted no time. "Roy," he said, "I know your doctor would raise holy hell with me for bringing this up at the present time, but we're in one awful fix because of that attack on you."

"I hope," Johnson replied in a voice that revealed his weakness, "that you haven't come to ask me to testify against Rusog, because I plain cannot do it. I didn't see any of my attackers, and I don't even remember being knocked unconscious. I have no idea why my pipe and knife were in his leather bag, or for that matter, how any of the coins came into his possession. As for the money, of course none of it reached the Choctaw, so we'll need to mount another expedition to them as soon as possible."

"As nearly as we can make out," Sevier said, "Rusog himself has no clear explanation of why he had your property. In fact, he seems vague as to what he was doing in that vicinity in the first place. He keeps saying something about Renno and the squaw of Renno—by which he must mean your daughter—but we can't understand him well enough to be certain.

"There's a whole passel of questions that nobody has answered, and until they do, we have no solution in sight. What strikes me right off is, assuming that Rusog did take your coins and your personal property, Roy, who was it who then bashed in his head and left him for dead? And why did they do it?

"All I know for certain is that we're playing with fire on top of a pile of gunpowder. Rusog is not what you would call just another brave. He's married to the sister of Renno, who is about to become your son-in-law. And if that isn't enough, he's the son of Wegowa, the principal war chief of the Cherokee, and the grandson of Loramas, their supreme leader."

Judge Hill shook his head. "Very recently, Jack," he said softly, "you signed a treaty of friendship with the Seneca and the Cherokee. How are they going to react when they find out that the ink was hardly dry on that treaty when we threw one of the most prominent of all Cherokee into prison?"

"This whole discussion," the governor said, "leads to only one conclusion. And that conclusion is inevitable. Unless a thorough investigation points to someone else as the guilty party, I don't see how we have any choice but to put Rusog on trial."

"True," the magistrate agreed. "Investigations do take time, and we don't want to turn the Cherokee and the Seneca against us between now and then. We will have to try to work out some solution that would not cause Rusog and the Cherokee to lose face."

Renno knew nothing of the misfortunes that had befallen his beloved Emily, her father, and Rusog, his brother-in-law. Therefore he was in high spirits when he returned to the main town of the Cherokee after his visit to the fort town of Knoxville. He carried a copy of the treaty that he had signed with Governor Sevier of Franklin. Loramas, the Grand Sachem of the Cherokee, was pleased with the result of his efforts.

"You have done well in your negotiations, just as you did well when you waged war against the Choctaw," Loramas told him. "Continue to serve your people faithfully, and the day is not far distant when it will not be necessary for Casno to act as regent of the Seneca. You will take his place."

Renno thanked him and then tendered Mrs. Johnson's formal invitation to his and Emily's wedding, which was now scheduled to take place within a few weeks.

Loramas was delighted to accept, as was Wegowa. As for the members of Renno's own family, he found their plans were already well advanced. Ah-wen-ga and Toshabe had arranged to lead a large delegation of Seneca.

"It was agreed with the mother of Emily when we last visited the Johnson family," Toshabe said, "that the Seneca who will attend the wedding will be too numerous to live in the homes of the settlers. We will establish our own camp across the river from Knoxville, and we will live there until it is time to return here."

Renno's older sister, Ena, had plans of her own. "Rusog will wish to stay in Knoxville after he has delivered Emily safely to the home of her parents," she said. "Before he left, we agreed that for him to come all the way to this place and then go right back to Knoxville again would mean needless travel, so I will meet him there. He did not take the headdress of his rank with him on his present journey," she added, "therefore, I will take it to him in order that he may be dressed properly when he attends the wedding."

Her mother and grandmother applauded her foresight.

The women were busy preparing delicacies that they would take to the wedding. In their spare time, they were sewing new dresses of doeskin or cotton cloth they bartered for at Knoxville.

Renno was somewhat bewildered by the activity. Not long before the party of Seneca and Cherokee was to depart with an honor guard of forty warriors, he began to feel a great sense of relief. Drawing his younger brother, El-i-chi, to one side, Renno confided in him.

"Take heed of what you see taking place around you, my brother. Know this also: all women love weddings, regardless of whether they are aged, like our grandmother, or are brides like Emily. The day will come, my brother, when you, too, will take a wife. Heed what has happened to me and be warned by it. When the day comes, go alone with your bride before a medicine man and marry her. Then go off with her into the wilderness on a trip where you will see no other persons for as long as you desire to be alone together. Then you will be free to return and begin your new life as husband and wife. During all this time, pay no heed to the wishes of squaws. She who will become your bride will be deaf to the sound of your voice and will listen only to the words of her mother and your mother. Remember they, too, are squaws, but you cannot reason with them. If it should be necessary, abduct your bride and elope, or else you shall be forced to endure the agonies of a large wedding, and that is a torment I wish on no warrior."

The march through the wilderness to Knoxville was uneventful. The honor guard guaranteed that no attack would be made by warriors of lesser tribes.

As soon as they reached their destination, Renno realized something was amiss. The sentries assigned to duty at the fort had been doubled. No explanation was offered, however, and he was admitted to the town, while the rest of the party set up camp, according to plan, across the river.

Excited by the prospect of his reunion with Emily, Renno went off happily to the Johnson house. He was surprised when Emily did not come to the door to welcome him; instead Mrs. Johnson greeted him somberly and promptly led him into her husband's bedchamber. A pale Roy Johnson was sitting up in his four-poster bed.

Judge Johnson shook hands with Renno, then waved him abruptly to a chair. "I have some bad news for you," he said, "and I don't aim to varnish it when I tell it to you. Emily has vanished. She disappeared on her way home. And if your friend Rusog was her escort—which I don't rightly know because we can't communicate properly with him—he appears to have no idea of what has become of her. I myself was ambushed and robbed in the forest, and left for dead. The finger of suspicion seems to point to Rusog." Speaking rapidly, he filled Renno in on the details.

The room spun, and one fact above all others impressed itself on Renno's bewildered mind. "What can have become of Emily?" he asked.

"The militia scoured the wilderness for miles in every direction from where Rusog was found," Johnson replied, "and they found no sign of her. Personally, I doubt that she has been killed or injured," he added. "I am inclined to believe that she has been taken as someone's captive, either by Indians or by renegade whites."

Renno bowed his head.

"She's resourceful and clever." Her father went on, "I have every hope that we will see her again. If her captors are renegade white men, they probably will be in touch with us eventually, as they will be holding her for ransom. If they're Indians, however, they might try to integrate her into their tribe. You'd know more about that than I do. But we shouldn't despair. Emily will figure a way out to escape and get back here. It will just take some time."

Renno dug his nails into his palms in frustration. "I know of only one way to determine what may have become of her," he said. "I will go to all the small tribes of the entire area and ask for information. Even if they are not holding Emily, they may have learned something about her."

"Will they speak freely to you?"

Renno looked grim. "The braves of any Indian nation," he said, "would be either exceptionally courageous or very foolhardy to refuse to give information to a war chief of the Seneca."

Their eyes met, and both refused to acknowledge discouragement. It was necessary, they agreed silently, to maintain hope that Emily would be found.

"I must waste no time," Renno said. "I shall begin my search today."

"Before I must leave you," Renno said, "can you please tell me anything that Rusog has said in explanation?"

"Unfortunately, very little. I am sorry to report that we've been unable to communicate because of the language barrier."

"Knowing only what you have just now told me," Renno said, "I am nevertheless willing to stake my own reputation on Rusog's innocence. He is guilty of no wrongdoing because he is not capable of doing wrong. Never would he do harm to a friend and ally. And never would he steal possessions not rightfully his."

Johnson shrugged helplessly, not knowing how to respond.

"I envisage many difficulties and complications arising in the relationship of the Seneca and the Cherokee with the people of your land," Renno went on. "Holding Rusog in prison indefinitely is a mistake."

"What choice do we have? Our country was founded as a nation of laws, and those laws must be obeyed if we are to have a civilized and peaceful society. You say that Rusog isn't guilty, and perhaps you're right. But many questions remain to be answered."

"A vast difference exists in the forms that justice takes among white men and among Indians," Renno replied, "even though the substance of justice is ultimately the same. If you insist that the forms be obeyed in this matter, I can predict that the new treaty will be in jeopardy, and your state may well find itself at war with the Cherokee and Seneca."

"That tragedy must be avoided at all costs." Johnson propped himself on one elbow, so agitated that he shouted the words.

"I entirely agree," Renno told him.

"How can it be averted?"

"First, I must speak with Rusog and learn whatever he may wish to impart. This will guide me in the actions that I will take. In the meantime, I urge you to use your influence to have him set free."

"That is easier said than done."

Renno frowned. "You think he will be tried for crimes that he has not committed?"

"In all probability that's likely to happen, I fear."

"Then let him be told the date when that trial will

take place. He will return here in time to stand up in court and defend himself."

"How can you be sure that he would show up?"

"Because I know Rusog!" Renno replied forcefully. "In fact, I am so certain he will be here that I willingly offer myself as a prisoner in his place if he does not appear!"

Renno was admitted to Rusog's cell, a tiny, cramped room with thick walls, a heavy oak door, and a single barred window. The door closed, and the brothers-in-law were alone.

They greeted one another formally, each raising his left arm in a salute, before Renno quickly got down to the serious questioning.

"Tell me all you can about the attack."

"I have not much to tell," Rusog said. "We were attacked with little warning, though I did fight back, and everything might have been different if I had not been hit from behind. I had told Emily to hide. When I awakened she was gone. I staggered away. That is all I know. The men who found me brought me here and accused me of terrible crimes because of the things they found on me. But I didn't take those things!"

Renno curbed his impatience. "You did see some of those who attacked you?" he asked.

"I saw four or five," Rusog replied.

At last Renno was getting specific information, and for the first time he felt slightly encouraged. "To what tribe did they belong? Surely you saw their war paint and could identify them by it."

"They wore no war paint," Rusog said stolidly. "Their faces were bare, and if they had paint on their chests, I did not see it because their bodies were covered by their shirts."

"They were not Indians, then?" Renno was leading him gently now.

"Their skins were pale like those of the men who dwell in this town," Rusog answered innocently.

"Ah! In that case they carried firearms rather than bows and arrows."

His brother-in-law seemed to consider the question was rather foolish. "Of course they carried firearms," he said in a nettled tone of voice.

"Were their firearms modern rifles, such as the weapons that Casno and I carry, or were they muskets, like those that some of the Cherokee use?"

"They had muskets, and rifles too. They did not conceal themselves well in the forest."

"Is it possible they lacked experience in wilderness warfare?" Renno's eyes were shrewd.

The question was too complex for Rusog, and he shrugged.

"Think well before you answer this next question. Did you know any of your attackers? Had you ever seen any of them on a previous occasion?"

"I have asked myself that same question many times since I have been in this room," Rusog said. "And I cannot tell you that I ever saw one of them before that day."

"You did not see the man who deprived you of your consciousness?"

Again Rusog shrugged. Clearly, he had no real idea of what had happened.

Satisfied that his brother-in-law had exhausted his knowledge of the attack, Renno asked no more questions. "Do not lose heart, my brother. Soon you will be released from this place and be free to go back to our own town. You will be obliged to return here only if they ask you to stand trial. Then you would answer about the same questions that I have just asked you."

Crossing the river in a boat provided by a guard at the fort's gate, Renno went straight from the jail to the quarters established by the Seneca and Cherokee. There his news created an uproar.

Learning that her husband was in jail, Ena became greatly distressed, and she began fanning the flames of anger and indignation in Loramas and Wegowa.

"If you make a show of strength against the people of Knoxville," she declared, "it will not be you who have broken the treaty. They broke it when they took my husband into custody. They have demonstrated a lack of faith and a lack of honor."

Wegowa, distraught, was willing to heed Ena's words, but the elderly Loramas was more cautious. Although he did not refuse to entertain the prospect of violence, he nevertheless wanted time to think it over.

Renno intervened immediately to put an end to such inflammatory and dangerous reasoning. It could destroy the alliance that he, like his father before him, had been so anxious to nurture with the white

American settlers. "I see no need," he said, "for blood to be shed against those who are still our close allies. The insult to Rusog will be no more."

His listeners grew quiet, and even Ena stopped sputtering long enough to take a deep breath.

"I shall go now, at this very moment, to Judge Hill, the magistrate who will hear the charges against Rusog," Renno informed them. "There, I will ask him to release Rusog immediately, and let him be free until he is put on trial."

"Are your powers of persuasion so great," Wegowa demanded, "that this chieftain will heed your voice and do as you have bidden him?"

"He will agree," Renno said, "because I will offer to become a prisoner myself if Rusog fails to appear in time on the appointed date for his trial. And we do not even know for certain that that day will ever come. We will meanwhile try to establish his innocence."

The Cherokee were startled, but the Seneca in the group, particularly Ah-wen-ga, were pleased by his decision, made in the true tradition of the elder Renno.

Ena and Wegowa accompanied him back to the courthouse. The court had adjourned for the day, but Judge Hill was in his private office. Renno lost no time getting to the point of his visit. "I request that Rusog of the Cherokee be granted his freedom until his trial for the crimes you say he committed. Rusog is an honorable and good man, and I consider it unthinkable that he could be guilty. I am so thoroughly convinced of his innocence that I freely offer to take his place and suffer the consequences if he does not appear when summoned."

Judge Hill was impressed by Renno's generous offer. Already, the suspicion had entered his mind that Rusog quite possibly was innocent. He saw no other logical explanation for his having been knocked unconscious by someone and left for dead. Under the circumstances, the magistrate was ready to take advantage of Renno's offer. He drew up a legal agreement, writing rapidly with a quill pen on parchment, then silently offered the pen to Renno, who signed his name with a flourish.

Rusog was ordered released without delay, and by the time Renno, Ena, and Wegowa reached the jail, he was already on his way out the door. Forgetting the traditional Indian reserve, Rusog swept Ena off her feet, enveloping her in a crushing bear hug. Then his usual calm returned, and he greeted his father quietly and thanked Renno with a long and deep look in which their eyes met.

That night, all the Indians celebrated Rusog's release by eating a special meal around a huge bonfire near the bank of the river.

Afterward, Renno, more silent than usual, announced that he would not be returning with the party to the land of the Cherokee. Instead, he would begin a search that he hoped would lead to Emily Johnson. He did not mention that some instinct told him that Ben Whipple, his father's murderer, was responsible for the abduction of Emily. Whipple had long coveted her and made no secret of his attraction to her. If his hunch was right, Renno thought, he

could kill two birds with one stone, obtaining the
release of Emily and, at the same time, taking vengeance on his father's killer. Then the gods would
relent and allow Ghonkaba to cross the Great River
and join his ancestors for all time.

Toshabe and Ah-wen-ga did not know what was
going through Renno's mind, but when he described
the plan to them, they agreed it made sense, and
they were satisfied. After looking intently at each
other, they caught the eye of Casno. Ah-wen-ga nodded, as did Toshabe.

Since Renno's grandmother and mother were agree-
able to his plans, Casno saw no objection, and he
promptly announced his formal approval. Renno then
disclosed that he would leave early in the morning,
and the brief discussion came to an end.

Almost immediately, Rusog, accompanied by a
proud Ena, materialized at Renno's side. "Thanks to
you and only to you, I have my freedom now," he
said. "I would be remiss if I did not now offer my
services in your hunt for Emily. I was responsible for
her safety, and I failed her. I hope that you will
accept my help so that I can try to make up for any
mistake I made."

Renno had no need to weigh the offer and responded instantly. "I am happy to accept, Rusog,"
he said, "and will be pleased to have your company
on the trail. Perhaps between us we can determine
what happened to Emily and rescue her."

"Where Rusog goes, I also will go," Ena announced.
"I have no wish to be separated again from my
husband."

Renno was willing to concede that his sister was highly expert in the forest and that she knew more than most men about tracking and wilderness survival. All the same, he could not predict what dangers might threaten, and he felt that a woman, even Ena, could hinder him and Rusog.

"You are needed at home, Ena, as help and support for Ah-wen-ga and Toshabe," he said. "I would not ask this of you if it did not seem to me to be absolutely necessary."

Rusog waited anxiously for his wife's response. Ena considered for a moment and then bowed her head. "I heed your words, my brother, and I will do as you ask." She prepared to join the others in the party of Seneca and Cherokee as they began the return trek to the land of the Cherokee.

Later, Renno went to tell Colonel and Mrs. Johnson of his plan, and at dawn he and Rusog departed. Their first stop, as they had agreed, would be the spot where Rusog had been attacked.

They made excellent time through the forest, and when they arrived at the scene, they inspected it with great care, gradually expanding their search to cover more and more ground in every direction. Ultimately, Renno found the heel print of a man's boot in soft earth due south of the site, so they concentrated on that sector and slowly moved farther south.

When they drew near a small stream that ran through the area, they discovered a clue in the tall grass—two dainty footprints, obviously those of a woman, and one large footprint, that of a man. The latter was of a boot, presumably that of the same person whose print Renno had found previously.

"Those who abducted Emily forced her to accompany them in this direction," Renno said, "and we know that she was able to walk under her own power."

Rusog nodded grimly, and they continued south.

Curbing their natural desire to move swiftly, they traveled at a cautious pace, making certain they followed the trail that was distinct, although seldom used, and would lead them in the right direction.

They lived off the land; game and fish were plentiful, and in the forest they found many berries and edible roots. Whenever they came to another river or creek, they paused and meticulously studied the land on either side of the stream. Their search was invariably rewarded by more footprints.

One day they came upon the scene of what had been a battle to the death: the bodies of five white men, scalped and decomposing on the ground.

Ignoring the stench, they examined the bodies but found all had been stripped of their belongings, including identification, and any firearms and ammunition. The Indians quite evidently had been the victors in the struggle.

Then Rusog discovered the body of an Indian warrior who appeared to have had a darker skin than most Indians. In spite of the decomposition, they could still make out his yellow and red war paint.

"I am not familiar with the tribe that wears those colors," Renno said, perplexed.

"They are Seminole," Rusog informed him.

"You are sure?" Renno demanded.

"Of course!"

"Look here!" Renno went down toward the bank of the little river adjacent to the scene of the battle. He pointed to the now-familiar woman's footsteps. With them were many other marks, all created by Indians' moccasins. Renno pointed out heavy marks that blurred some of the footprints, and observed that the Indians had been dragging something— probably a man or his dead body.

"What happened here is plain," he exclaimed. "All the abductors of Emily were killed, except for one man. Emily and that man were made prisoners by the Seminole, who continued on southward with them."

In silence, Rusog studied the prints in the soft earth, and finally he nodded his agreement. "You must be right," he said. "I can see no other interpretation."

"I thank the manitous for their protection of Emily," Renno said, "and I rejoice because she is alive and appears to be well enough to travel. And now our own travels have only begun. We must follow the Seminole to their land and obtain her release!"

That night, after he and Rusog ate a hastily assembled meal, Renno was discouraged and could not sleep. His search for Emily, already burdened by his vow to find and punish Ben Whipple, was becoming increasingly complicated, and the end nowhere in sight. At least, he thought, he was making progress in finding Emily. Freeing her was another matter.

Eventually, weariness overcame him and he dropped off to sleep.

All at once he realized that he was in a forest clearing, a glade unfamiliar to him in every way. For one thing, the trees surrounding it were strange to him, and from them hung a substance that looked like heavy fringe from a woman's shawl.

A dazzling light appeared at the far end of the clearing, so strong that it hurt Renno's eyes. In spite of his exceptional vision, he could not see clearly. He blinked several times and at last made out what he thought was a human shape.

Even as he stared at it, however, the shape seemed to turn into a brown bear. And then, to his astonishment, it changed once again and shrank into the size of a hawk. For many generations, the manitous had used bears or hawks to communicate with Renno and his ancestors, and his heart beat more rapidly as he looked at the apparition. Any fear vanished. He shielded his eyes from the glare but still could not make out the figure clearly.

Suddenly a deep voice emanated from the bright light, echoing endlessly through the vast recesses of the wilderness. "Renno," it called, "heed my voice, Renno."

"I am listening, O manitou," he answered, "and I will remember your words as though they were engraved for all time on tablets of stone."

"The gods rule the world in which you live and the world into which you enter when your time in this life expires. Your actions will be controlled by the manitous who serve the gods and who act as their intermediaries with men. I am authorized to inform you that the gods are pleased by your diligence in your search for Ben Whipple, who foully murdered Ghonkaba, your father. Remain diligent in your search for him, and you have the assurance of the manitous, and beyond them, of the gods themselves, that this search will also lead you to the woman you intend to marry."

Renno began to stammer his thanks.

But the dazzling apparition, which began to change shape and again bore a resemblance to a bear, cut him short. "Do you not know why the gods have favored you and your ancestors before you? You are like the great Ghonka and Renno, the white Indian, his son. You are like Ja-gonh, your grandfather, and Ghonkaba, your father. All of you have put the good of the Seneca nation first in your hearts and in your minds. You have served all the people of the Seneca, regardless of the time and effort that you have expended. Personal gain has meant nothing to you. For this reason, the gods intend to help you now in your search for the murderer of your father and for the woman whom you would make your wife. Pay close attention to my words, because I am able to speak them only once."

Straining so he would miss no sound, Renno merely nodded.

The white light became brighter and more intense. "As you make your journey southward into the land of the Seminole, keep your eyes wide open for a tall tree that has been struck by lightning. You can find it at a bend in a major river. In a field just beyond the tree you will find a white buffalo calf. Do you understand what I have told you so far?"

No longer trusting his powers of speech, Renno again nodded his head.

"You will kill the calf," the vision continued. "It is of the utmost importance that you kill it with one shot, which you will put into the head of the beast. You will take great care not to harm the coat. You will cook the flesh of the calf over a fire, and you will eat of it. That which you do not eat you will offer as a sacrifice to the gods and will let it be consumed in the flames. Under no circumstances will anyone share this meal with you. You will cure the white skin of the calf and you will prepare it so it can be worn as a cape. Because of your valor in combat, the cape is offered to you as a shield that can serve you well when you take arms against a foe, whether in battle or in hand-to-hand fighting with a personal enemy. We are confident that, as always, you will conduct yourself as a true Seneca warrior, ever ready to act on your own in all circumstances. The cape, however, will provide protection when you least expect it, in ways that the gods shall decide."

Questions crowded into Renno's mind, but he ignored them. Experience had told him to listen with great care to what he was told in a dream. Much as he had anticipated, the apparition began to fade, just as his mind was whirling. All the same, he bowed his head and murmured, "I have heard your words, and I shall obey your will, O manitou."

When he raised his head again the vision had

vanished. At no time had he determined whether a
human, a bear, or a hawk had spoken to him.

Utterly exhausted by the vision, Renno saw the
clearing begin to fade. He knew that this meant his
dream had come to an end. He was so tired that he
fell into a deep sleep and he did not dream again for
the rest of the night.

When he awakened in the morning, however, the
entire dream remained vivid in his memory. He
recalled the strange appearance of the dazzling, changing shape and remembered every word spoken to
him. He intended to obey to the letter the instructions, and he knew that the protection promised him
was real and would materialize.

As the Seminole traveled southward to their home
deep in Spanish Florida, the braves in the party
amused themselves at the expense of Ben Whipple.
Claiming his boots, clothing, and weapons, they forced
him to wear only a loincloth even smaller than their
own, and they drove him unmercifully on their daily
journey. When he failed to walk fast enough to please
them, he was whipped. Even during halt periods
when he otherwise might have rested, they forced
him to perform innumerable menial tasks for Emily,
treating him as her slave and rewarding him for his
effort by abusing him roundly. He gathered firewood, he cleaned fish that she cooked, and he brought
her roots and berries from the wilderness. He was
made to abase himself by falling prostrate on the
ground before her, and she was repeatedly commanded to press a foot into the back of his head,

grinding his nose and mouth into the dirt. When she relaxed her pressure and he raised his head several inches, revealing a dirt-smeared nose and mouth, the warriors laughed wildly.

Emily would have preferred to treat him more gently, but she was afraid of offending the braves on whose goodwill she depended. Although she knew Whipple was responsible for his own situation, as well as for her predicament, she could not help but recoil from inflicting cruel punishment.

Whipple hated her for her part in his humiliation, and although he was afraid to voice his feelings, he glowered at her silently, and she knew that if he had the chance he would kill her.

When the party reached the Atlantic coastline and began to follow the shore southward, the braves' treatment of their captive became even more vicious. They often forced him to crawl on his hands and knees through shallow water just off the beach, looking for mussels and clams. They pushed him when he tried to rest, and were amused when he fell flat on his face and swallowed salt water.

Emily was pleased that she continued to hold a place directly behind Durati in the line of march. In the company of their chief, the braves were relatively subdued.

Gradually Emily realized that Durati was greatly pleased by her efforts. He approved of her cooking, and when she repaired a rip in a warrior's garment with a bone needle and rawhide thread, he smiled approvingly. She was dignified at all times and aloof, refusing to participate in the rough teasing of Whipple, which seemed to please him.

Above all, what gratified him was her rapid progress in learning to speak his language. She discreetly refrained from mentioning to him that she had studied the languages of the Seneca and Cherokee and that she found the tongue of the Seminole not unlike that of the Cherokee. She would use it as she waited for the moment to escape and try to make her way back to Tennessee.

One day Durati brought down a deer, which meant that for the first time in more than a week they could have an ample supply of meat. At his direction, the carcass was butchered, and he was quietly impressed by the spit Emily made and used. He watched her as she roasted the meat and continued to scrutinize her when she expertly carved it with a hunting knife.

His steady gaze made her uncomfortable. If she had been unattached, she might have enjoyed such attention, but since falling in love with Renno, she had lost interest in all other men, even one as attractive and magnetic as Durati.

After supper, the braves forced Ben Whipple to clean up. Free to do what she pleased, Emily wandered a short distance from the camp. Climbing a sand dune, she sat at the peak and gazed pensively out at the moonlight shining on the breakers.

Behind her, she heard a faint sound, and out of the corner of an eye she could see that Durati had also climbed to the summit of the dune. He sat down near her. Afraid that she might have caused him to feel encouraged about the prospect of becoming intimate, Emily made the best of a potentially difficult situation and smiled at him.

Durati responded by inclining his head a fraction of an inch in the manner of a preoccupied senior sachem. It was evident that his mind was filled with serious thoughts. She made no further response and continued to watch the moon-dappled breakers.

At last Durati broke the silence. "Has Emily slept with a man at some time in her life?" he asked.

Emily felt as though she had received a hard blow in the pit of her stomach. She was many hundreds of miles from home, beyond where Renno or her father or anyone else could help her. If Durati wanted her—and he sounded as though he did—she could do nothing to stop him. Her physical strength was not equal to his, and if she put up a struggle, he might become angry and turn her over to his men. Aware of what Ben Whipple had been suffering at their hands, she had no illusions as to her fate if they had their way with her. Realizing that she was taking her own fate into her hands, she felt compelled to reply honestly. "I have gone to bed with no man," she said simply.

Instead of replying, Durati smiled broadly.

"You are much on my mind," he said. "I am deeply pleased by all that I have seen of you, and I am impressed by your knowledge of Indian ways, your use of the herbs of the forest in the food to make it better to eat, your familiarity with the sewing needle used by our people. And I am awed by the attitude you display as we walk. You behave like one born into the Seminole. You walk all day without complaint, and never is it necessary for warriors to slacken their pace so that you may keep up with them. You do your fair share of work, and you are always ready to accept more."

She thought his compliments unnecessarily extravagant but accepted them by bowing her head in acknowledgment.

"Soon," he said, "we will arrive in the land of the Seminole. There Emily will be placed in the charge of Ladira, the sister of Durati. Ladira will instruct Emily in those things that will make her a suitable squaw for a sachem of the Seminole."

Emily's blood ran cold. She wanted to protest that she was betrothed, but she did not dare to reveal this. It was evident that Durati, in observing her, was weighing her conduct and had concluded that she would be a suitable wife. In true Indian fashion, he had found it unnecessary to ask her to marry him. Having decided that he wanted her as his squaw, he was taking it for granted that she would obediently agree to their marriage.

Realizing that her status could change instantly from one who enjoyed the favor of a sachem to one whose life could be made miserable as a slave, she did not dare to express her true feelings. Instead, she pressed the fingers of both hands together and lowered her head in a typical feminine gesture of submission to the will of a conquering male. At least, with her head down, Durati could not see the dismay in her eyes.

He grunted to display his pleasure, and he beamed

at her to show that he was pleased the issue was settled to their mutual satisfaction.

Emily knew she would need to revise her plans immediately. She could not take her time, accepting her place with the Seminole and waiting until a favorable occasion to escape. To avoid being married to Durati and spending the rest of her days as a squaw in one of the most primitive tribes in North America, she would have to try to find some way to make her escape as quickly as she could—but that was only a dim hope at the moment.

Chapter IV

Renno and Rusog made rapid progress as they traveled south, using the Seneca trot, the special way of running taught to all Seneca when they were young. With a destination in mind, they no longer stopped to search for footprints on either side of the brooks and rivers they crossed. They tarried in the

forest only long enough to pick edible berries and to
unearth roots that they could use as food. They shot
only game that happened to cross their path. Similarly, they confined their fishing efforts to the streams
on whose banks they halted. If they had set out from
the main town of the Cherokee, they could have
taken ample supplies of parched corn and sun-dried
strips of meat, but such food was not available at the
fort.

During one of their hurried meals, Renno gave
renewed thought as to how much of the vision about
the white buffalo he should relate to Rusog. Finally,
he decided that he must tell the story, without needless detail, to his companion. Rusog exhibited little
surprise, for he had come to expect most unusual
deeds performed by the manitous for the favored
Seneca. He assured Renno of his complete willingness to be of assistance in the search for the land-
marks that would lead to the white buffalo calf.

When they crossed to the land claimed by the
Choctaw, they exercised caution, aware that the
Choctaw used a sentry system that was a modified
version of the system the Seneca employed in Renno's
own native habitat in New York State. The entire
territory was divided into separate zones, with a
single sentry responsible for finding any intruders in
his own zone. The Seneca used a system whereby
the sentries overlapped, thereby making it almost
impossible for them to miss an intruder. The Choctaw
did not go that far, and consequently the borders of
each zone were something of a no-man's-land. There,
the daring could find safety.

Renno had figured out the Choctaw system on a
previous journey into their territory. All he needed
to do now was to establish the boundaries of individual zones. This he did late on their first afternoon in
the land of the Choctaw, when the sentries on daylight duty were replaced by the sentinels who would
serve throughout the night.

He watched two braves as they traveled through
their respective domains. From this it was easy to
find the open spaces or "no-man's-land" between
zones. Thereafter Renno and Rusog confined themselves to these areas between zones. They seldom
needed to reduce their pace, and for that reason they
were able to prevent lost time.

The domain of the Choctaw lay adjacent to that of
the Creek, the largest and most belligerent of all
Indian nations in the South. They fiercely protected
the territory they claimed, guarding it against incur-
sions by any outsiders, regardless of their identity or
nationality.

The Creek, staunch allies of the British throughout
the American War of Independence, had remained
undefeated until decisively beaten by a force led by
John Sevier of Tennessee, Ghonkaba of the Seneca,
and Wegowa of the Cherokee. When they were
crushed they lost the right to call themselves the
"Seneca of the South." Since that time, they had
been more diligent than ever in guarding their borders. They relied for their security on teams of sentinels, each unit numbering from three to a dozen
warriors. These units traveled in irregular crisscross-
ing patterns known only to their leaders.

Renno and Rusog prudently slowed their pace and took precautions such as never building a cooking fire after sundown. Their advance was cautious, but they pushed deeper without difficulty.

They both knew that if, as members of the two tribes that had humiliated the Creek in battle, they fell into the hands of their former enemies, the Creek would be merciless. Without doubt, both would be tortured and then put to death in elaborate ceremonies in which many men, women, and children of the Creek nation would joyously participate.

At noon they halted in a small meadow surrounded by high foliage and thick, almost impenetrable bushes. A little stream ran across one edge of the open space, providing them with drinking water and two fish, which Renno caught. A strong westerly wind was blowing, so they decided to risk lighting a small fire, using very dry wood, believing that any smoke the wood might make the wind would quickly dispel.

Rusog, in charge of preparing the meal, allowed the flames to flare only briefly, and when they began to die down, he put the two fish onto the ends of sticks, placing the other ends of the sticks into the ground at an angle, so that the fish would be held over the coals for cooking.

Meanwhile, Renno rested, stretching out on the ground with his eyes closed. He relaxed completely, allowing his partner to take over responsibility for their security.

Suddenly, Rusog's trained ears picked up an almost inaudible sound in the distance. A rustling in the underbrush that could mean the presence of someone or something—either humans or an animal larger than the small game that sometimes were driven by curiosity to come close to man's settlements in order to inspect them.

Rusog reached out silently and squeezed Renno's knee twice, a signal that possible danger was near.

Renno awakened from a sound sleep instantly, wide-eyed and alert. Realizing that his companion was straining to hear something, Renno placed his ear to the ground and listened intently. He could hear cautious footsteps nearby, and he counted the presence of perhaps eight to ten braves.

In sign language, Renno told Rusog what he had learned and suggested a course of action. The Cherokee flashed some signals in return, nodding agreement, and they left the fire and crept in opposite directions around the clearing, with Renno veering to the left and the Cherokee to the right.

The fish, untended, continued to cook, the odor of their roasting unmistakable.

The rustling sounds became louder, and seemed to surround them. The strategy of the Creek patrol was evident to Renno. The enemy had fanned out and intended to attack simultaneously.

Renno checked his long rifle to make sure it was loaded, ready for instant use. He emptied several additional bullets on the ground, close at hand, and beside them laid a small bag of gunpowder. In a spirited action every second would count. He was glad that Rusog was his companion in the combat to come. The Cherokee, somewhat slow-witted in complicated matters, was a perfect companion in battle.

He, too, was armed with a long rifle. He had learned
to use it with devastating effect. Utterly fearless, he
never would give in to a foe, no matter how great the
odds against him. Together, they would give a good
account of themselves, and that was all Renno could
ask. He had nothing personal at stake in the battle.
He bore no grudge against the Creek, but they wanted
his scalp, and that stiffened his back. He would resist
with all his strength and cunning.

Tactically, he could let the Creek initiate the battle, but the Seneca were not like any other tribe.
From boyhood, Renno had been trained to take the
initiative whenever possible.

Peering through a tiny opening in the undergrowth,
he saw the black-painted torso of a Creek brave. Not
hesitating, he took aim and squeezed his trigger.

Geese in a nearby pond were disturbed by the
sudden noise. Squawking and honking, they rose,
beating their wings as they circled above and hastily
departed.

Rusog, too, drew a bead on an enemy and snapped
off a shot. His aim was as good as Renno's and a
second Creek died.

The remainder of the Creek patrol, badly rattled
by the sudden loss of two comrades and uncertain as
to the precise location of their hidden foes, fired a
volley. Their muskets, obsolescent two decades earlier, were incapable of accuracy. Their volley went
wild, giving Renno and Rusog time to reload and fire
a second time. Again both made their shots good.

Renno knew he was fortunate that a Creek had not
yet discovered him and made him a target. Picking

up his bullets and bag of gunpowder, along with his rifle, he wriggled through the tall grass on his stomach like a snake. With deliberate boldness, he did not go either to the left or the right but instead moved forward. This brought him several yards closer to the confused enemy.

Rusog was on the move too. Not knowing in what direction Renno had gone, he inched to his left, occupying almost the ground Renno had held. They needed more time to even the odds. Renno got off three shots before he killed another warrior. Rusog, much to his own disgust, had to fire four more times before he succeeded in killing one of the foe.

Four of the Creek remained, and for the first time Renno felt able to consider the possibility that he and Rusog would emerge victorious. He reloaded again, and while he searched cautiously for the foe, he was startled to hear Rusog begin the spine-curdling war cry of the Cherokee.

Jumping to his feet and rising to his full height, Rusog brandished his tomahawk over his head as he charged toward the startled remnant of the Creek war party.

If the Creek had kept their heads and remained cool, Rusog would have been an easy target, but they were completely unnerved by the sight of the ferocious giant bearing down on them. Giving in to sudden panic, they leaped up and began to race off in various directions, anxious to leave this battle-maddened Cherokee far behind.

Badly frightened, the fleeing survivors were clear targets. Renno leaped to his feet to support Rusog and screamed the Seneca war cry as he brought down first one and then another with two throwing knives. A strong chop of Rusog's tomahawk disposed of a third. He threw his tomahawk at the last man, almost decapitating him.

The battle ended as suddenly as it began. Ten Creek attackers had been killed, and the defenders were untouched.

Rusog and Renno began to scalp the dead. Each took five scalps, which they added to the collections in their belts. As they walked to the stream to wash blood from their hands, Renno said, "We did well. That was a good afternoon's exercise."

"Yes, it was," Rusog agreed. "I worked up quite an appetite for dinner." Drying his hands on his buckskins, he walked back to the fire. Then he stopped, looked down at the flames, and began to curse, softly but emphatically.

Renno, who followed at his heels, guessed what had happened but managed to keep a straight face.

"How do you like that?" Rusog demanded bitterly. "I'm so hungry I could eat almost any food now, and the fish for our dinner has burned up." He pointed down at the shriveled remnants of their meal, blackened and curling over the fire.

"I daresay we will have to miss a meal," Renno told him, still not daring to laugh for fear of hurting the Cherokee's feelings. "We must put some distance between ourselves and these bodies. The gunshots might bring a war party down on us. Perhaps we will be fortunate enough to see a deer and it will provide a meal more to our liking tonight."

* * *

Ah-wen-ga customarily did her cooking in the stone-lined pit near the center of the floor in her living quarters. Now, however, a fire burned in it to remove a chill from the air, and the smoke rose through a hole in the roof. Young Seneca might have found the room oppressively warm, but the two elderly people sitting companionably on opposite sides of the fire were comfortable.

Ah-wen-ga, cross-legged on the floor, was modestly dressed in deerskin cut with a high neck and long sleeves. As the widow of Ja-gonh, Great Sachem of the Iroquois, she was a living symbol of the glory and pride of the Seneca, a link to their illustrious past. Every member of the nation still revered her.

Her guest, puffing complacently on his pipe, was white-haired Loramas, Grand Sachem of the Cherokee nation. He had discarded his elaborate feathered headdress and his ankle-length cape of feathers, the symbols of his authority. Like his hostess, he was very comfortable. Both had known supreme authority all their adult lives, and their familiarity with it caused them to relax in each other's presence. Almost all younger people in the land, regardless of whether they were Seneca or Cherokee, were in awe of the couple. But their mutual relationship permitted no awe between them.

All the same, Loramas was nervous. He understood the reasons for his state of mind, and he was amused at himself, but this could not alleviate his condition. Months earlier, he had subtly proposed marriage to Ah-wen-ga, and she, with equal subtleness, had hesitated and suggested a delay.

Now, with the period of mourning for her son, Ghonkaba, having passed, he believed it appropriate to open the subject again.

When he spent a full minute clearing his throat before speaking, Ah-wen-ga glanced at him, then knew instantly that because of what was on his mind he was having a difficult time trying to express himself suitably. And he, in turn, was quick to recognize her ability to read his mind.

Both knew that if she wanted to avoid an intimate conversation she could easily launch into some impersonal topic. That would be a clue to him to avoid the subject after all. Ah-wen-ga merely smiled, however, and made no attempt to speak. Loramas concluded that she was encouraging him.

"I have a matter," he said delicately, "that is much on my mind, as it has been for months."

"I, too, have thought of it," she admitted unexpectedly.

Loramas was surprised by her candor. "Has your thinking been positive or negative?"

He was so direct that Ah-wen-ga had to curb a desire to laugh. "I did more than think about it," she said. "I offered prayers to the manitous and requested their help. I asked them to ascertain the state of mind of Ja-gonh, my late husband, and to obtain his approval of any action that I might deem desirable to take. I thought for a while that the messengers of the gods were indicating that Ja-gonh disapproves of the plans that I am making."

Loramas sat with his arms folded, his face set and expression inscrutable. He was bracing himself for her possible rejection.

"You may remember," she went on, "the night of the great storm, when the weather changed and became colder. That night thunder sounded in the heavens and the sky was illuminated by great streaks of light that snapped and cracked. During that storm I suddenly realized where I stand."

"Did the manitous speak and deliver a message from Ja-gonh?" Loramas inquired softly.

"No, they did not," Ah-wen-ga replied earnestly. "Even in such a great storm they remained silent. This is unusual, because the manitous often elect to deliver messages to mere mortals when the thunder roars and the skies are illuminated."

Loramas nodded to show that he understood and agreed.

"It was their continuing silence that convinced me that I was wrong to be seeking a sign or a word from Ja-gonh to be expressed through them. I am ashamed to admit that even after many, many years of marriage to Ja-gonh, I was ignoring something fundamental to his nature. Throughout the years of our marriage, he kept silent whenever he approved of an act or a decision. He raised his voice only when he disapproved. From the little I know of the land of one's ancestors, an individual's nature does not change when he crosses the Great River into that land. His nature remains what it always was. Therefore I know that Ja-gonh approves of my decision in this matter. If he did not approve, he would speak up sharply and would find many ways to communicate with me. He knows how I feel, and he agrees that it is right, just as he knows many other things about my present and my future."

Loramas was perplexed.

"I was wondering whether, when you and I die," Ah-wen-ga explained, "we would go together to the land of our ancestors. Would I live there with you or with Ja-gonh? Would you live there with me or with Mirala, your first wife?"

"Those questions and the answers to them did not cross my mind," Loramas admitted.

"They surely entered my mind," Ah-wen-ga said, "and the answers were not difficult to find. Any union you and I might enjoy will be temporary, confined to our lives in this world. It will be a union based on companionship and mutual understanding, on a mutual desire to share burdens and the responsibilities of high office. When we depart from this life it is only natural that we resume our places with our original mates. As a young woman I loved Ja-gonh in a way that I could never love you now, in my latter years. By that same token, you undoubtedly loved your wife in a way that you could not now give your heart to an old woman who would become your squaw for the twilight time that we hope to share here."

"The gods have endowed Ah-wen-ga with great wisdom. You are right."

She inclined her head, accepting his praise. "The thought occurred to me," she said, "that perhaps we should wait, that our union should be postponed until our grandsons return from the dangerous mission in which they are engaged."

The mere mention of another delay caused Loramas to frown.

"But I was mistaken," Ah-wen-ga continued cheerfully. "When people are our age, they cannot afford delays. Only the young can enjoy the luxury of postponements. What you and I do, or refrain from doing, will have no effect on the success or failure of the mission that our grandsons have undertaken. All we can do is wish them well in their enterprise and hope they succeed."

She was giving her consent to an early marriage, but because it would have been unseemly for him to rejoice, his face continued to betray no emotion.

All at once Ah-wen-ga became demure. "It would be forward of me to suggest a date when we become united," she murmured. "I will leave the decision to Loramas to determine. It is appropriate that a warrior decide such a matter."

He knew her coyness was artificial, an attempt to flatter his masculinity. Even so, it pleased him to think that a woman of Ah-wen-ga's stature would stand aside and allow him the privilege of determining their wedding date. He smiled at her. "The hunters," he said, "will need only a few days to bring in the meat for the wedding feast, and the squaws will require very little time to prepare it. The medicine men of both our nations are ready to serve us whenever we call on them. I suggest that we set the date for our wedding as one week from today."

Ah-wen-ga bowed her head to show her acceptance of his choice.

There was, she realized, one further task for each of them to accomplish. He would need to notify his son, Wegowa, of their plans, while she would have to inform her daughter-in-law, Toshabe. For reasons she did not understand, this prospect made both of them apprehensive.

"I will call a meeting of all our people at sundown this day," Loramas said, "so they may hear our news."

Word to Wegowa to attend his father without delay was relayed promptly thereafter.

Disturbed by the messenger's tone, and anticipating a crisis of some sort, Wegowa hurried to his father's side.

"I want you to know," Loramas said abruptly, "that Ah-wen-ga of the Seneca and I are going to be married in seven days from this day."

To his astonishment, Wegowa began to laugh.

Thinking his son was mocking him, perhaps out of a sense of loyalty to his own mother, Loramas hastened to reassure him.

"I was careful to follow the formula prescribed by our ancestors. Three times I went off alone into the wilderness. There I called out to the spirit of your mother, who was for many years my wife, to hear me. I told her it was my wish to marry Ah-wen-ga because we are both old and lonely, and we offer each other the solace of mutual understanding. On each of these occasions I asked her spirit if she objected to such a union. At no time did she raise her voice or signal me in any other way that she was displeased."

Wegowa laughed even harder.

His father glowered. "Why do I appear absurd in the eyes of my own son?" he demanded fiercely.

"You are not ludicrous," Wegowa replied, still chuckling, "but you should know the cause of my laughter. I made a wager with Toshabe of the Seneca many days ago. I predicted that you and Ah-wen-ga would marry soon, but she doubted you would. I laugh because I could see so clearly your feelings and Ah-wen-ga's."

His father's offended feelings were not easily assuaged. "Are my feelings and those of Ah-wen-ga so simple to know, then?"

"You have proved that you can readily conceal a decision on whether to go to war against a potential enemy or to keep the peace," Wegowa told him. "You have also demonstrated that you are able to hide your decision as to the guilt or innocence of one who comes before you charged with a grave crime. But affairs of the heart are not easy to conceal. We reveal our feelings in the way we look and act more than by what we actually say."

Wegowa paused and, reaching out both hands, clasped his father by the shoulders. "I rejoice for you, my father," he said huskily, "and I am certain that my mother looks through the veil separating her from the living and that she, too, is pleased. You have long served the Cherokee faithfully and well, asking no reward for yourself in return. Ah-wen-ga similarly has devoted herself to the welfare of the

Seneca. May both of you benefit from the rewards you deserve."

Loramas was known among the Cherokee for his ability to conceal his emotions, but if his people could have seen him with Wegowa, they would have been surprised by the tears that came to his eyes as he embraced his son.

"You can hardly know," he said, "the relief that you offer me now. I dreaded telling you my intentions about Ah-wen-ga because of your feeling for your late mother."

"Of course I am loyal to my mother's memory," Wegowa replied. "But you forget, my father, that I am equally loyal to him who sired me."

While father and son talked, Ah-wen-ga was finding it far simpler to communicate with her daughter-in-law. Toshabe understood what she was trying to tell her and spoke up immediately to put her at her ease.

"Wegowa told me this day was coming soon," she said with a smile. "But I expected that you would need more time to permit yourself to find the happiness you deserve. I am happy for you, my mother. And I know that wherever Ghonkaba may be in the afterworld, he, too, hopes that the rest of your days in this world will be peaceful and filled with joy."

Ah-wen-ga was pleased by Toshabe's warmth; the younger woman's quick smile lighted her sensitive face, and she broke from Seneca tradition to hug her mother-in-law.

"I hope you and Loramas will delegate duties and responsibilities to those leaders who are younger,"

Toshabe said, "so you may have more time to yourselves."

When Loramas, with Ah-wen-ga seated demurely beside him, publicly announced their forthcoming marriage, their people reacted spontaneously and enthusiastically. Braves let loose with loud war cries of the two nations, and women jumped to their feet and began to dance. Small children, infected by the excitement and left without supervision, ran around noisily, and even the dogs barked loudly as they followed. Approval of the forthcoming marriage, it appeared, was universal as people came to congratulate the couple and to wish them happiness.

One of the last to step up was Ena, Ah-wen-ga's granddaughter and Rusog's wife. She raised her left arm in formal greeting but spoke in stilted phrases, her voice mechanical as she expressed her good wishes. Then she lowered her head and, folding her hands over her breasts, fell silent.

Ah-wen-ga looked at her askance but said nothing. She looked at Loramas, but he seemed to find nothing amiss.

Deciding nonetheless to try to clear up the questions newly raised in her mind, she asked quietly, "What is wrong, Ena?"

Ena looked at her grandmother almost defiantly. "The whole world has forgotten Rusog, but I have not forgotten him. I have waited and prayed daily to the gods for enlightenment. But they have not visited me. They have given me no messages and have outlined no course of action to follow. We will become the victims of the white man's sense of justice. Rusog will be sent to prison for many years, and he will languish there in disgrace while he is entirely innocent of wrongdoing."

"You have no faith in the gods' sense of justice," Ah-wen-ga said chidingly.

"I have none left," Ena replied stridently. "Rusog is a good man, a decent man, an honorable man—as no one knows better than his own grandfather. But he has been branded as an outlaw, and the people of Knoxville will not be satisfied until he is doomed for all time."

"You exaggerate!" Ah-wen-ga said sharply. "You have allowed yourself to become hysterical because of your concern for him."

"I agree that you exaggerate," Loramas said. "No one can do anything until the gods have shown the way. If you believed, as we do, in the harmony of all creatures, you would realize that the truth soon will reappear, as indeed it will. Until then, we must wait."

"I am tired of waiting!" Ena said savagely. "I want to fight for the innocence of my husband, though almost no one else on earth seems to care except for Renno."

"Wait patiently for the gods to assert themselves," Ah-wen-ga said reprovingly. "Renno exhibited patience, and we must depend now upon him to find the solution to this strange predicament in which Rusog finds himself. It is plain that he, at least, is prepared to await the pleasure of the gods."

*   *   *

Day after day, Renno searched in vain for a tall tree that had been struck by lightning as they traveled toward Seminole country to find the white buffalo. Finally, one night, the thought occurred to him that he had been victimized by a false dream. But no sooner did the idea occur than he shook it off, silently begging the pardon of the manitous for such disloyalty. Never had he been led astray by any sign or any false information from them, and this was hardly the time to begin. No, he realized, the fault might be his, rather than the manitous'. He should have known that the gods— particularly the manitous, their messengers—would be extremely reluctant to reveal their power until conditions were exactly right. Perhaps they wished to speak to him alone.

By morning, he awoke convinced that his instincts now were leading him in the right direction. At breakfast, he mentioned the matter to Rusog. "Do not take offense at what I am about to relate, my brother," he said. "But after giving much thought to the manitous' silence, I am persuaded that I have not encountered the white buffalo that has magical qualities because the manitous wish that you and I part. For a reason that I do not understand and therefore cannot explain, they seem to wish me to experience the miraculous event alone."

Rusog nodded his large head and said slowly, "I believe you have spoken the truth. I trust in the manitous and in the great power they exert. Never once, though, have I witnessed a miracle by them, even though I would almost give my soul to see one."

"I am sorry," Renno replied, "but it seems that because of the manitous' reluctance we will be well advised to part and travel separately for several days."

Rusog looked as though he might weep. "So be it," he answered sorrowfully.

Renno frowned, hoping to get the unpleasant business done as rapidly as possible. "We will separate this morning," he said, "and travel apart for what may well be many days and nights. At a time appointed by the manitous, we will meet again. I somehow feel that I will next see you on a beach close to the great sea. The place will be distinguished by an unusually high sand dune. Near the top of the dune you will see three tall trees with very unusual leaf clusters. One of them has very large nuts covering sweet meat and good liquid to drink. Whoever arrives there first will wait for one day for the other to arrive."

"Good!" Rusog exclaimed, brightening. "I had thought that you never have been in this land, but I see you have traveled here before."

Renno was perplexed. "I do not know," he said slowly. "I swear to you I never have been in that area in my life."

"But you described the scene so fully," Rusog replied. "How do you know about the three trees standing near the crest of the hill on the beach? How can you describe them?"

A note of awe entered Renno's voice. "All I can tell you," he said, "is that I described the scene that I saw in my mind's eye as I was talking about it. I saw it for a moment as clearly as though I were looking up at the hill with my own two eyes while I stood with my own feet planted on that beach. I swear to you that this is true."

"It makes no sense," Rusog muttered.

"The gods are everywhere, you must admit," Renno said, "and those who represent them hear and see everything that happens in our lives. They heard you say moments ago that you had never before witnessed a miracle performed by the gods or by those who represent them. They were challenged, so they performed a miracle for you at that very moment. This you cannot deny!"

"No," Rusog muttered, his eyes round, "I can deny none of it."

"Very well, then," Renno said, "thus it shall be, and we shall meet where the three palm trees are gathered."

Rusog was overwhelmed. "Are you sure they will be in the place that you say?"

Renno was sure of his ground. "I am positive," he said, "that all will be exactly as I outlined it to you. Have no fear and keep your faith in the gods, my friend. They will never fail you."

They parted, each certain that the other would keep the rendezvous in the strange land. That afternoon, Renno was rewarded when he saw beside the river a fallen tree that had been struck by lightning. Noting where it stood, he followed that point inland.

He was not in the least surprised when he soon saw a young calf buffalo, pure white, standing alone, placidly munching some grass, as had been foretold. Renno felt instinctively that it would be sacrilege to shoot the animal with his rifle, so he took the bow from his shoulder and reached for an arrow from the quiver. Fitting it into the bow with an easy assurance born of long practice, he sighted down the length of the shaft and released the arrow. It flew straight and true, striking the calf between the eyes.

Renno raced forward, expecting to skin the dead animal, following his instructions, but suddenly he heard a loud, vicious snarl. Stopping abruptly, he raised his head. There, on top of a nearby outcropping, was a mountain lion, jaws parted, ready to spring at the enemy who was daring to take the prey that it had intended to devour.

Renno realized that, as always, the manitous were forcing him to fight for what was his. Nothing came to him easily, and he had to exert mastery before he could claim the reward.

He knew he must act with incredible speed. If he delayed, the lion would be on top of him.

He saw one—and only one—opportunity, and as quickly as the thought entered his mind he reached for the tomahawk in his belt. Aiming it more by instinct than by sight, he let fly with all his force.

The weapon sliced through the air so rapidly that it was almost impossible for the eye to follow. The blade struck, slitting the forehead of the snarling lion. Lunging forward, the animal fell at Renno's feet, the bloody tomahawk falling free.

Looking down, he saw that he had conquered and won. The manitous had required him to strive mightily against great odds for his victory.

Only then could he draw a knife and skin the small

buffalo, taking care not to damage the pure white skin. When this was done, he built a fire, cooked a small steak over it, then consigned to the fire all the rest of the animal. Acting on a strong impulse, he also cut up the dead lion and threw it on the fire.

Hacking out a chunk of salt from the cliff on which the lion had been standing, and mixing it with the brains of both animals, Renno started to work, rubbing the mixture into the buffalo skin. He worked hard through the night, and when the sun came up he spread the skin on top of the height and stood guard over it with bow and arrow. Only at nightfall did he relax his vigil to search for food.

For three days and nights, he devoted all his time and energies to making a cape. It was as soft and as pliable as the finest bolt of wool cloth made in England. Renno was pleased. He was satisfied that he had followed the manitou's instructions exactly, and felt confident that the cape would provide the promised magical protection.

Now he could resume his journey. But before leaving, he climbed a tall cedar to reconnoiter the land ahead. From that vantage point, he spotted a band that he later came to identify as Calusa Indians, a tribe prominent along Florida's west coast, and identifiable by its warriors' blue war paint. They were engaging in combat a single warrior whose dark brown and black war paint identified him as an Ais, a tribe prominent on the eastern shores.

Renno was fascinated by the unequal struggle. The one Ais warrior, nimble and quick-witted, held a half dozen of his opponents at arm's length. He found himself hoping the Ais could prevail.

While Renno watched, the tide gradually began to turn. The Calusa were too numerous and began to surround the Ais warrior. He soon would be overcome. That, however, did not stop him, even though he must have realized what was happening. He continued to fight with the same relentless fury.

Suddenly, Renno felt an overpowering desire to equalize the odds. He rapidly lowered himself to the ground and dashed forward silently through the forest toward the scene of the struggle.

Without stopping to think or weigh the consequences, he burst into action, emerging through the screen of trees on the run and wielding his razorsharp tomahawk as a Turk would wield a scimitar.

The Calusa fell back before the maddened attacker. Paying no heed to danger, he leaped into the midst of the fray, swinging his arm in a wide arc. Death rode at the end of the swing, and the Calusa warriors shrank before the impact of his assault.

Renno fought with the reckless abandon of a Seneca warrior caught up in the fury of an attack. He was inspired, never once stopping to consider that the white buffalo cape might be protecting him. Instead, he pushed ahead, intent only on driving the Calusa away from their target.

The Ais warrior, startled, stood silent for some moments, watching Renno attack the Calusa. Suddenly, however, he came to life, effectively swinging his tomahawk and a long-handled knife. While he made short work of several foes, Renno was able to increase the fury of his own attack. Not once did he find it necessary to use his bow or rifle. Never wasting a single motion, he was precise in every deadly move.

The blows that rained down on Renno had no effect. Again and again, the blunt end of a tomahawk came crashing down on Renno but only bounced off the white leather cloak. Even when the sharply honed edge struck him with enough force to gravely injure him, he was untouched. Remarkably, too, the white leather itself remained unblemished. It showed not even the slightest nick from the sharpest blade.

Suddenly the battle ended. The last of the Calusa were dead, their bodies scattered over the bloody ground.

The Ais warrior and Renno began to scalp the victims quickly and expertly. After they had divided the scalps, they looked at each other and grinned. The Ais, a slender man who did not stand higher than Renno's shoulder, raised his left hand formally and said stiffly, "I am Tobiko, the subchief of the Ais, who live by the ocean where the sun rises." Fortunately, Renno was able to recognize his words as being from a language common to many of the smaller tribes of the South. He had encountered it several times.

"I am Renno," was his brief, modest reply.

Tobiko's large, dark eyes opened wide. "I have heard many songs composed about Renno of the Seneca."

"That is my ancestor."

The Ais warrior was not to be put off. "Tell me,"

he said, "I could see that the cape of white buffalo hide that you wear seems to have extraordinary properties. When you were struck repeatedly with tomahawk blows you did not feel them. And when the skin would have been cut to shreds by a blade not a mark appeared on the leather. How could this happen?"

Speaking with great reluctance, Renno told him about the search for Ben Whipple and for Emily, as well as the dream.

Tobiko was impressed. "I will accompany Renno in all he intends to do," he said, "because that must be the wishes of the manitous. I owe my life to Renno, and so I am devoted to his service."

Ben Whipple was desperate and planning an escape. His days and nights were filled with great pain and suffering. Emily often wondered how he was able to tolerate so much abuse and punishment.

One evening he was there, taking abuse, being ordered about, being forced to humiliate himself. The next moment he was gone.

Every move, inch by inch, had been shrewdly planned. All through the endless hours of humiliation and suffering, Whipple had tested his plot, knowing that if he made one mistake he would be killed. He worked out a scheme, then put it in operation late one night after the Seminole camp had fallen asleep.

He moved five feet, then paused to listen and heard nothing. Inch by inch he crawled for another five feet, and again he stopped, straining his hearing and fearing the worst was about to happen.

Not until he had moved at least a dozen paces from the camp did he begin to relax slightly. And that was when catastrophe struck. He stepped down on an incline leading to the beach, and to steady himself, he lowered himself to his hands and knees. This brought his face only inches from a fallen tree.

As fate had it, he was disturbing a swarm of wild bees nesting in a hollow log. Alarmed and disturbed because they thought their home was being attacked, the bees swarmed out, covering Whipple's face, head, and arms and stinging him viciously.

He did not dare cry out or fling himself into the water because he knew the noise would disturb the guards.

He had no choice but to suffer the stings, brushing the bees off and clawing at his face and head to rid himself of the torment that was even worse than the hell he had escaped. Stumbling and falling, rising again and staggering onward, Whipple managed to get away from the bees. When he believed he was far enough away from the camp, he fell to his knees and scooping up wet, muddy sand in his bare, swollen hands, he plastered it on his face, head, and arms.

At last he was able to think again. Lifting up his head to the dark, cloudy sky above, he silently cursed Renno and Emily with all his heart. If only nature had been allowed to follow her normal course, he and Emily would have married. Instead, she had become fascinated by Renno, who had appeared out of the blue and created all of Whipple's problems.

Now Ben had become an outlaw and a renegade with a price on his head. He considered Renno and Emily personally responsible. They alone were responsible for all that had befallen him.

Later no one could figure out how Ben Whipple managed to cross the wilds of Florida alone and sick. Only a strong man could have survived, one with reason to live. Whipple had reason to live: he'd vowed revenge against Renno and Emily Johnson.

Chapter V

In keeping with the wishes of Loramas and Ah-wen-ga, their marriage took place quietly, with only close relatives on hand for the ceremony. Casno and the principal medicine man of the Cherokee presided.

But afterward came the time for the people of both

nations to celebrate. Warriors who had ranged into the field had been fortunate in bringing down several deer and a young buffalo. Women had prepared an elaborate meal, making certain that there would be enough for everyone.

The tables were piled with mounds of smoking meat, cakes of pounded corn, a half-dozen vegetables, several kinds of fruit, and a few sweets. Even the children were encouraged to eat all they pleased.

Because of the couple's distinguished roles, the byplay that often accompanied marriages was forgotten. Similarly, the dances and other festivities that ordinarily marked all weddings were ignored. Nevertheless, it was important that the occasion be set apart by fitting words, and Loramas recognized the need to make such a speech.

"My good friends," he said, "this is a memorable event. We have done more than participate in the union between a man and a woman. We are taking part in the merger of two great people, the Seneca, who have ruled in the North, and the Cherokee, who have held sway in this part of our great land. Together we shall continue to flourish, and together we shall stand preeminent among all the tribes in the portion of the world that is known as North America. In our own lifetimes you have watched British armies from across the sea vanquished in battle and forced to retreat to their own shores. We have seen the rise of a new breed of people who call themselves Americans, and we have watched them growing stronger as they have increased in numbers, in power, and in proficiency, claiming part of the land and its riches.

"We of the Cherokee nation chose correctly when we elected to side with the Americans because their love of freedom coincided most closely with that of our own freedom, which we have practiced since time immemorial. By the same token, those of the Seneca nation who came from the North to join us shook off the friendship of the British and elected, too, to join hands with the Americans because they also shared a vision of the present and of the future.

"I see a splendid tomorrow stretched out before the Cherokee and our brothers of the Seneca. I see us growing with the new United States, becoming strong with her and sharing in her glory. I see us, with them, becoming preeminent among all the nations on the face of this earth."

A murmur of approval arose, but not everyone present joined in. Some, particularly among the more mature warriors and their women, looked dubious. Similarly, some younger men, those inclined to be hotheads, raised their voices in only half-hearted approval. Not that they necessarily disagreed with what the Grand Sachem of the Cherokee said, but they were uncertain that his words were wholly true.

And of all who disagreed with the views he had expressed, the most obvious was his bride. No sooner did Loramas resume his seat than Ah-wen-ga was on her feet.

"Only the few Seneca who are my age will remember the occasion many decades ago when I was abducted from the land of the Seneca and was taken to

France as a prisoner. I learned on that occasion that although the English pay a greater lip service to the cause of freedom than do the French, they are both the same under the skin. It remains to be seen whether the whites who call themselves Americans also truly crave freedom as we insist upon freedom as our natural-born right. Or whether they merely go through the motions of pretending to love real liberty. If the Americans truly love freedom, they will find us valuable allies and good friends. If they merely pretend to worship liberty while pursuing acts that deny freedom to all, we shall be their enemies. Let them demonstrate to us what they will, so that we may judge accordingly and then make our choice. Whether or not they are going to be our friends they must determine!"

The Seminoles' journey back to their homeland seemed endless to Emily, who was surprised that the warriors showed no regret or annoyance at Ben Whipple's disappearance. Seemingly, they were relieved to be rid of him.

Days and nights melded and became one, but at last the homeland was close at hand, though, as Emily discovered, their community lay deep within the heavy forest and could not be reached except by a series of tortuous paths. Ponds and swamps, their still waters dark and menacing, offered seemingly impassable obstacles, but with Durati in the lead, the party easily found its way.

The area gave no indication of the land of plenty it had actually become. The Seminole occupied a part

of the country where food—always a problem for
Indians—created no difficulties. No matter how many
people had to be fed, there was always enough. That
was the great secret weapon of the tribe that welcomed all refugees, and made them at home.

The secrets of the tribe were many, and not the
least of them was the warriors' ability to seem invisible whenever necessary. The dense foliage made it a
simple matter for a warrior to conceal himself and
then act as the tribe's eyes and ears.

Now, these unseen eyes watched Durati's party,
and the heavy, insistent beat of tom-toms spelled out
a message for those at home. Every member of the
returning party was described in detail, and, predict-
ably, great curiosity was aroused by the white woman
who—as the message conveyed—walked freely, unat-
tended by guards and wearing no restraints.

At last the party came to a large, cleared space in
front of the village, where it was met by a welcoming
group. In its center was a woman clothed in doeskin
with a feathered band around her forehead, testifying to her rank. As Durati approached, she pros-
trated herself on the muddy ground. She rose and
they talked in low undertones for several minutes.
Durati did most of the talking; the woman nodded
occasionally, her expression bright, a slight smile on
her thick, sensual lips. Occasionally, she looked in
Emily's direction, studying her intently.

Durati beckoned, and Emily walked toward him
slowly. Uncertain how to meet the Indian woman,
she waited for a moment before raising her left hand

in formal greeting. Ladira finally smiled and raised her arm in brief acknowledgment.

"This is Ladira, the sister of Durati," he said to Emily. "You will be in her care while she teaches you all you need to know. Ladira will make you a wife fit for a sachem of the Seminole."

Although Emily did not understand, she knew not to ask questions. Indians disliked being pushed; and it was invariably desirable to let them arrive, in their own way, at whatever point they wished to make. Questions, interrupting the natural rhythm of developments, were to be avoided because they caused resentment.

Emily was irritated by Ladira's forced smile. No man would have noted anything even faintly wrong, and Durati clearly was unaware of a change in the atmosphere. Only another woman would discern that Ladira's lips parted unnaturally, that her eyes were too bright, and that anger boiled beneath her surface.

As soon as they were out of Durati's sight, Ladira took a knife from her belt, cut a long switch from a nearby shrub, and struck Emily's legs fiercely and without warning. The sharp blows raised welts and brought tears to her eyes.

A nightmare was coming true: she was being prepared for a marriage to Durati, and she saw no way to escape that fate. Her blood ran cold, the pain in her legs forgotten.

Another slash across the back of her legs brought Emily face to face with the harsh reality. "You go now!" Ladira ordered, pointing.

Emily trotted off, seething within as the switch

whistled overhead and struck her repeatedly on the back.

As they moved through the town, the people looked on with curiosity and evident satisfaction at the spectacle, believing that the beating was justified and that under the circumstances the white woman undoubtedly deserved the punishment.

Emily and Ladira came to a house before which a slender young woman was stirring the contents of a scarred iron pot over a stone-lined pit. She raised her head and watched Ladira and Emily approach with a dull expression on her face. Ladira called to her, speaking so rapidly that Emily could not keep up. All she knew was that the woman's name was Nalata.

Only when Nalata replied, speaking more softly and distinctly, could Emily make sense out of the conversation. What she heard shocked her. Nalata had been Ladira's candidate to become Durati's wife. The woman was mild, rather meek, and the way Ladira spoke to her made it clear that she was very much under the influence of the sachem's sister, who, like her brother, was accustomed to command.

Ladira had hoped that by persuading her brother to marry Nalata, she could continue to exert a strong influence over the sachem. Nalata was her creature, someone who would jump whenever Ladira cracked the whip.

Ladira now handed her whip to Nalata, instructing her to use it on Emily. But Nalata's blows were ineffectual, which annoyed Ladira.

Nalata struck again and again, trying to please

Ladira, and Emily, almost fainting from the pain, was forced to endure more and more blows until Ladira was finally satisfied.

That, however, was just the beginning. Ladira handed Nalata a knife, instructing her in a low voice how to use it. Emily thought that her last hour on earth had arrived. Instead of cutting her, however, Nalata slashed away her clothes, reducing them to ribbons. Then Ladira produced a small leather skirt and a pair of moccasins. These she ordered Emily to put on. There was nothing to cover the upper part of Emily's body, and the skirt was so short that most of her legs were likewise unprotected. There would be no escaping the relentless attacks of flies, gnats, mosquitoes, and other huge biting insects of the swamps. Permitting these creatures to dine on Emily's bare flesh was part of Ladira's plan to torment her as well as humiliate her by making her virtually naked.

The cruelty of Ladira's next scheme was worse yet. It amused her to make Emily prostrate herself on the soft ground. She laughed hysterically and told Nalata to drive her foot into the back of Emily's head and push her face into the mud. Sputtering and gasping for breath, Emily then had to endure the pain of being whipped once again. How long could she tolerate the brutal treatment? She knew that Ladira had a reason for her violence. She was encouraging Emily to revolt and seek to escape. If Emily succeeded in getting away, she would be easy prey for the alligators, snakes, and other venomous creatures of the swamps; she would not live long. Ladira would be rid of her and the way would be clear for Nalata to marry Durati.

Later, driven into the swamp to search for firewood, Emily was glad of the respite, even though her flesh crawled at the thought of the snakes and scorpions hidden in the dense foliage. At least she was not being whipped, and the change came as an enormous relief. Returning with the wood, she built a fire, then was told to cook the meal. It was clear that Ladira intended to use her as a servant while supposedly "teaching" her how to prepare herself for life as wife of the tribe's sachem.

When her chores were finally done, she threw herself down on a hard pallet of branches that scratched her bare skin. In spite of her exhaustion, she stayed awake for a very long time. As she stared up at the sky through thick vines, she knew she would need all her stamina, all her courage, to survive the vicious ordeal that lay ahead.

She would survive because she had little choice. If she ever wanted to see Renno again and fulfill her promise to marry him, she had to live through the tormented days to come that stretched out toward infinity.

The scene in the northern Florida wilderness could have been almost anywhere on the frontier of the new country. Out of the wilderness, land had been cleared and planted. At the center of the clearing was a small sturdy house of palmetto logs. A serviceable stone chimney rose above its roof. Chinks between the logs were filled with clay. Behind the cabin, a large, open-air cooking pit had been hollowed out of the ground and lined with stones. Beside it hung a deer carcass, skinned and gutted and exposed to the elements to age it properly. It was the home of a pioneer who had come to terms with the wilderness and by dint of exceptionally hard labor and courage was managing to stay alive and raise a family.

The scene, however, was far from peaceful. The family was barricaded inside. The heavy front door was shut and the windows were covered with shutters that had slots in them only large enough for a rifle. Occasional flashes of gunpowder igniting were visible even in the sunshine. Explosions matching the flashes contrasted eerily with the surf booming on a beach nearby.

Surrounding the house were dozens of Indian braves wearing startling red and blue war paint. They were armed with muskets and were firing at the house. From a safe distance, Renno identified them as similar to muskets issued by the Spanish to their troops. He quickly estimated the assault force to be approximately forty men. He and Tobiko hugged the earth, hiding themselves from view.

He looked questioningly at Tobiko. "They are warriors of the Apalachee," the Ais said, his voice seething with hatred. "They are the enemies of my people." He seemed ready to attack at once, despite the overwhelming odds.

Renno knew that a fight would be necessary if the pioneer family was to be saved, but he wanted to be sure that he understood the strength of the enemy. He waited, watching closely.

Shots were being fired by three guns from within the cabin. One gun was relatively accurate and hit its mark several times. Renno assumed that this marksman was a man. Other shots, spasmodic and difficult to predict, only occasionally came close to a target. From a third window, shots were even more unpredictable. Renno assumed that these random shots came from other members of the family, probably a wife and son. But no matter, he and his Indian companion were hopelessly outnumbered. Nevertheless, they had to attack and drive the Apalachee away.

Renno looked at Tobiko, who returned the stare steadily. He, too, would favor a sharp, hard strike.

A decision having been silently reached, Renno turned his attention to his rifle. He checked that it was loaded, primed, and ready to fire, then he moistened his fingertips, picked up some loose dirt, and rubbed the dirt onto the barrel of the gun. Now there would be no reflection of the sun when he looked down it toward his target.

He waited a long time before firing his first shot. When a flash in the undergrowth revealed where one of the Spanish muskets had been fired, he took a bead on the spot and gently squeezed his trigger. He was rewarded by a howl of pain. In a very short time he had killed a half dozen of the Apalachee.

Driven by his intense hatred for the Apalachee, Tobiko jumped wholeheartedly into the thick of the struggle. His shots with his bow and arrow were effective, and soon the two men were taking a heavy toll of the foe.

For a time the Apalachee did not even realize that an enemy was attacking them from the rear. Eventually, they turned, one by one, to study the ground behind them. But they were facing west, and the sun half blinded them. When one of them appeared to catch a glimpse of either Renno or Tobiko, Renno raised his rifle again. Four more Apalachee were killed.

At last, the remaining raiders lost heart and took to their heels. The retreating braves were sent on their way by volleys of shots.

Raising his rifle high over his head and holding it there with both hands, Renno leaped to his feet. "Don't shoot," he called in English. "The enemy warriors are gone now. Only friends are here!" He made his way slowly toward the house, followed by Tobiko.

When they drew near to the house, the door opened and a large, square-shouldered man and a red-haired woman came out. They were followed by a towheaded boy. All three were armed.

"That was the damnedest shooting I've ever seen," the man shouted. "Where in hell did you ever learn to handle a rifle like that?"

"I spent four years with General Washington's battalion of scouts," Renno replied proudly.

"Then we are doubly grateful to the general," the woman exclaimed. "He saved us from being killed by the redcoats up near Germantown, Pennsylvania, where we used to live. And now, thanks to you, he has done it again!"

The couple explained that they were Arthur and Marianne Rodney, who, with their son, had come south to Florida to seek a new life. Conditions in the north had been too unsettled for Rodney to make a livelihood as a trapper and farmer.

"Most days," he said, "I sure wish we hadn't come this far. Living here sure ain't easy."

"What do you mean?" Renno asked.

"First there was the British and now the Spanish, who sure ain't any too friendly to Americans," Rodney explained. "They're scared to death they are going to see a mighty wave of Americans come down from up north, so they pay bounties for American scalps. Any Indian who turns in a white scalp will get ten dollars in gold."

Renno had never heard of such barbarity and was shocked.

"It is true," Tobiko told him. "Any warrior of my people who goes to St. Augustine with the scalp of a white person is paid in fine gold, with no questions asked."

"The land is rich here, and almost all vegetables grow in this soil." Rodney waved expansively toward the kitchen garden. "And that reminds me. We are eternally indebted to you two, and the least we can do is to give you a meal that you'll not forget. Son, go find some crabs and oysters and other shellfish that will make good eating in soup. Marianne, pick up all the vegetables you can carry and throw them into the pot. I'm going to carve off a piece of the juiciest tenderloin of venison."

The family scattered, ignoring Renno's protest that he and Tobiko wanted no reward.

When they sat down to the meal, their soup contained crabs, oysters, and clams, mixed with a thick, rich venison stock. With the fillet of venison they ate potatoes, corn, and squash that just had been picked.

The Rodneys were curious about their Indian saviors and asked why Renno was so far from his home. He explained how he and a group of fellow Seneca had come into the Tennessee country and had settled down with the Cherokee, with whom they had made an alliance. Then he told how he had become engaged to Emily Johnson, who had disappeared, and that he was following her trail.

Tobiko, who listened attentively for the sense of Renno's words, noted that he apparently made no mention of his dream and the white buffalo cape that protected him against evil. Renno would not mention the magic to this family. It was strictly an Indian matter, nothing that a person raised in a white community could understand.

After dinner Rodney left the table and came back carrying several large, fluffy fur pelts. "I trapped these foxes on the edges of the Great Swamp. They're all matching, and sewn together into one garment they'll make a magnificent cape. I notice that you wear a cape of buffalo skin, so I'd like you to accept these four foxes as a gift. They are only a token for saving our lives from the Apalachee."

Renno shook his head decisively. "Thank you," he

said firmly, "but I must decline. The white skin of the buffalo is the only cape that I shall require."

The entire family looked disappointed, and Marianne turned graciously to Tobiko. "In that case," she said, "you must accept the gift."

Tobiko knew that a crisis was at hand. He realized that Renno had rejected the furs because he did not want to offend the gods who had given him the cape.

What was true for Renno undoubtedly was also true for his friend. Tobiko could not accept a valuable present from the trapper; he would be required by the gods to pay a penalty if he gave in to greed.

"Thank you," Tobiko said, "but I have no need for a cape. I am a member of the Ais tribe, and I have spent my whole life living in these parts, where the sun is hot and the winds also are very warm. I have no need for a cloak to keep my shoulders and my chest warm, so with many thanks I must reject your kind offer."

Renno and Tobiko exchanged a quick look, and both recognized that their mission had assumed an importance beyond their ability to understand.

They did understand, however, that the rescue of Emily and the killing of Ben Whipple would be good for all the Indians of North America. In one way or another, the gods would be satisfied, and the manitous would spread their bounty for all tribes in the years ahead. In the meantime, nothing must arouse the ire or the enmity of the gods.

Each day the horrors suffered by Emily grew worse. Ladira and Natala competed to see who could abuse her the most. Her lot was unbearable. She was forced to fetch firewood, carry water, and cook, and whenever she failed to work fast enough or hard enough to please Ladira, she was whipped across her bare back. She lived on slops and leavings, and when she dared to complain, she was threatened with an even worse beating.

The last straw was when Nalata began to "punish" Emily for alleged misdeeds by pinching her, screaming aloud with mirth when she forced Emily to jump in surprise and pain. Ladira began to do the same, and when Emily's entire body felt bruised she decided the time had come to call a halt. She had taken all the abuse she could tolerate. She made up her mind to find Durati and make certain that he would know what had been happening to her.

Emily created a stir as she walked through the village half naked. Squaws stared, as did warriors, most of the latter with lust in their eyes. Children followed her and dogs yapped at her heels. Nevertheless, she was determined that nothing would stop her until she found Durati's dwelling. But long before she could reach it and appeal for his help, Ladira and Nalata appeared. Each was carrying a vine whip, and they looked greatly annoyed.

When Emily saw the expressions in their eyes, she shuddered.

Ladira looked contemptuous. She muttered to Nalata, and at the same moment, both struck out with their whips, laying them across Emily's bare back.

The attack was so painful that Emily could only gasp.

Again Ladira whispered to Nalata, and they reached out at the same moment, with Nalata grasping Emily's upper left arm in a twisting pinch, and Ladira pinching her right arm. Their movements were particularly vicious, and as they pressed the skin tightly between thumb and forefinger, Emily squirmed and tears came to her eyes.

"Is the white skin so delicate that it must not be bruised?" Ladira said, sneering. "Is she such a fragile flower that no wind may blow in her direction? After all, Nalata and I are toughening her skin so she may become a worthy wife to the sachem of the mighty Seminole."

As Emily shrank back, she failed to see Nalata deliberately place a foot to trip her.

She fell heavily, and as she was trying to get up again, Ladira gave her two swift kicks in the ribs that sent her sprawling once more.

Ladira's whip then sang out again through the air, landing on Emily's back and reminding her that she was to start her return journey to the house of her tormentors.

Her ribs still aching from Ladira's kicks, Emily began to crawl down the path, the whips of the two women often biting cruelly into her flesh and leaving angry welts.

Others joined in the game. Women, apparently enjoying themselves, threw garbage. Children placed rocks and other obstacles in the path that made Emily's progress much more difficult.

Unable to see where she was going, she crawled on aimlessly, goaded by jeering shouts.

This was the last straw, the final humiliation of body and tormented soul. Now she must concentrate—regardless of the consequences—on finding a means to escape from this cruel tribe of semibarbarians and, unlikely as the prospect appeared, try to make her way to some semblance of civilization.

After days of traveling southward through Florida, Renno and Tobiko came to a huge inland swamp, the Everglades. Here, Tobiko warned, were many of the most deadly of all creatures: alligators and snakes and deadly insects. The heat was intense; Renno removed the cape and wrapped it around his waist.

The foliage was sometimes impenetrable; sometimes they could see no more than a few yards. There was water everywhere, from an inch or two in the "dry places" to bottomless troughs fifty feet deep. The smell of decaying vegetation often was overpowering.

They traveled on foot where possible and built a "water carrier," or canoe, to see them through the worst parts. If they kept their eyes open at all times, they could reduce the dangers greatly, Tobiko said.

Soon they felt the power of the Everglades. As Tobiko began to sink in the soft ground he muttered, "Quicksand!"

He lacked the footing to free himself, and the more he struggled, the more he became engulfed in the muck into which he was being drawn. His eyes revealed his terror, and he appealed urgently to

Renno, knowing that his rescue would depend solely on his friend. He was powerless to save himself.

Renno instantly recognized the peril and knew that he could not hesitate. Every moment made Tobiko's plight more dire.

Whipping the double-edged knife from his belt, he reached out and caught hold of a long vine, which he severed. He doubled it and threw the looped portion through the air to Tobiko.

Relief showed on Tobiko's face as he lunged for the vine, caught it in one hand, then grasped it in both. He stopped sinking and was now holding his own.

Making certain that he was on solid ground, Renno planted his feet far apart and began to pull on the vine with all his strength. As he struggled, he found it harder and harder to breathe in the moist heat. Nevertheless, he persisted, straining until the muscles in his upper arms and shoulders ached as though a knife were pressing into them.

The vines cut into his palms. Tobiko was slowly emerging from the quicksand, coming closer to Renno. Both men were breathing hard as they continued to struggle with all their might. At last Tobiko was able to free one foot and plant it on solid ground.

Renno reached out and caught Tobiko's hands, as bloody as his own, and pulled his companion's struggling body up. All at once, Tobiko came free and both of the men tumbled onto the ground. Renno wiped sweat from his head and gazed at his friend.

The moment was so solemn that neither spoke.

The expression in Tobiko's eyes showed his awareness that he was once again in Renno's debt.

They rested for a long time, neither speaking. The Everglades were already exerting their sinister influence on the two Indians, but that influence had been defeated on this occasion. Gradually, the effect of the long, harsh battle began to subside.

Suddenly, the silence of the Everglades was broken by a scream echoing through the stillness. Such terror was concentrated in the scream that Renno was on his feet and moving toward the sound the instant he heard it, Tobiko on his heels. As they came to an open area, they stopped abruptly.

A young black woman with long black hair flowing behind her was fleeing a sixteen-foot monster, an alligator with skin that resembled an aged tree trunk, and a long, powerful head. Its jaws were open and its teeth gleamed in the half-light. Its tiny, bloodshot eyes gleamed malevolently as it fixed its total attention on its prey.

Reacting instinctively, not pausing to think for even a single second, Renno snatched the knife from his belt and threw it with all the force that he could command. The blade buried itself in one of the reptile's eyes, penetrating so deeply that only the hilt showed. Still the alligator plodded forward.

Too horrified to think clearly, Renno threw himself at the mammoth, swishing tail, even though he knew that this could be the most dangerous part of the beast. Catching hold of the scalelike hide with both hands, he pulled, trying to slow the beast's progress. The powerful tail flicked with such force that Renno was sent flying and crashed into a palmetto tree ten feet away. He collapsed to the ground. As Renno lay dazed, the knife he had thrown finally did its deadly work, and the alligator collapsed just before it reached the young woman. It lay twitching at her feet.

Its death almost appeared to put to rest the malevolent spirit of the Everglades, but not quite. Dazed and unable to move, Renno did not see the rattlesnake closing in on him, but the rattle in the tail sounded the alarm just as Tobiko spotted the snake rising up, its tongue darting in and out as it prepared to strike at the helpless man. Not thinking of his own safety, Tobiko threw himself between the snake and Renno.

A shimmering burst of light appeared between them and the venomous snake. Tobiko saw a manlike form that kept changing from man to hawk to bear and then back to a humanlike form, but always indistinct, like wisps of brilliantly lighted clouds. He was quick to recognize the supernatural at work, and he watched in silent awe as the light formed a solid wall between him and the reared-up snake. Renno, dazed and seeing nothing clearly, blinked his eyes but could only shake his head in dismay.

The snake appeared to bow its head in resignation as it dropped to earth and slithered away.

The light faded slowly. Tobiko glanced at Renno and knew they had been doing the bidding of the manitous.

From a distance, the black woman stared at them with fright. Unsure of their intentions toward her, she nevertheless knew that they had saved her life. She also realized that a miracle of some sort had taken place. She could only ask in a quivering voice, "Seminole?"

Tobiko smiled at her to assure her that they meant no harm, and said, "No, but we will take you to them."

She listened in silence before she recovered her poise sufficiently to bow. "I am Venya," she said. "I am on my way to join my lover, who said he would go to the Seminole because they take in escaped slaves. His name is Quanto, and he is a blacksmith of good reputation. He killed a plantation overseer when the man was about to rape me. Quanto told me that if he could make contact with the Seminole, and if he found it possible to give me a good life among them, he would come back for me. If he stayed at the plantation, he would have been hanged.

"When Quanto disappeared, I was called before the owner of the plantation, and he ordered me to come to his bed that night. I put together a few provisions and started to follow Quanto. I got lost at the edge of the swamp, and now I need help."

"I swear to you, Venya, that you shall have all the help you need," Tobiko told her.

Venya bowed formally, and she continued to stare at Renno, her eyes bright and curious. "Why," she demanded, "did the snake that was ready to kill you suddenly glide away? What power do you hold over such a beast?"

Renno and Tobiko exchanged a quick, startled glance. Both realized that the strange vision had been for their eyes only, and that under no circumstances were they to disclose its significance to any other person. The special attention of the manitous and of the gods was theirs alone, and they were never to reveal it.

Renno, now recovering his senses, bowed his head in submission to the divine will. "Many questions cannot be answered in the words of men," he said. "Let it suffice that we will do all in our power to help you. You in return will ask no questions but will be confident in our abilities to see you safely to the end of your journey."

Traveling alone, Rusog was filled with grave doubts. Through no fault of his own, he seemed to have assumed second place to Renno, his brother-in-law. Renno made the major decisions, and Rusog merely acquiesced to them. Even Ena, his wife, seemed to favor Renno at all times.

Still, brooding on his fate, Rusog shot a small deer, and after butchering it and building a small fire on which to roast a portion of it, he stripped off his loincloth and ran to a nearby lake to swim until his meal was ready. When he emerged from the water, he returned to the fireside and squatted in the short grass. Looking into the flames, he examined the whole fabric of his existence. Much in his life satisfied him and gave him pleasure, he realized, but other aspects caused him to feel a great disappointment and made him unhappy.

While he sat with the sunlight streaming down on him, he heard a faint noise coming from the direction of the pool, and squinting, he turned to look in that direction.

A young woman seemed to be rising out of the water. Her hair, which was blue-black, streamed down past her shoulders. Her skin, glistening and wet, shone like copper in the sunlight, and although she wore no clothing, she walked with complete self-confidence.

Rusog was tempted to reach for his loincloth, but he refrained. As long as she remained nude, he did not want to be dressed, for fear of causing her embarrassment.

As she approached him on the narrow path from the lake, she raised her right hand in greeting. "Hail, Rusog," she called.

Not until long hours later, when he pondered the incident, did it strike him as very strange that this stranger met him in an unknown wilderness, yet somehow knew his name. At the time, he accepted her familiarity without question. "Hail," he responded.

She reached behind her and produced a long veil-type garment of soft woven material, which she draped across the front of her body to conceal her nudity. Then she sat decorously on the ground before him. "You have been contemplating your present and your future," she announced.

"That is so," he conceded, crossing his legs and filling his pipe. She made no objection when he lighted the pipe from a coal that he took from the fire.

He felt it only polite to be hospitable. "You will

stay and share my supper, I hope?" he suggested tentatively.

She nodded. "If that is your pleasure."

"I will take great joy in it," he assured her.

She looked at him steadily, and he could not decide whether her coal-black eyes were cold and shrewd or warm and sympathetic. "You take joy in few things these days, Rusog of the Cherokee," she said in the accentless Cherokee of a native of that far-flung nation.

"I have much that occupies my mind," he replied.

"Your life has been much changed in past moons," she said. "When the time comes for your grandfather to step aside as sachem and your father to advance to that responsibility, you were destined to inherit the mantle of chief warrior. Then all braves who take part in battle would bow their heads to you and obey you the moment they went into the field.

"But your place as the future first warrior of all the Cherokee," she said, her voice gently insinuating, "has been taken by one who claims kinship to you by marriage and by the exchange of a blood-brotherhood, which you have undergone with him. Renno of the Seneca rates first among all the warriors of your generation. He stands in first place among the Seneca, as well as among the Cherokee. In battle, his will be the authoritative word. You astonish me, Rusog. You show no jealousy of Renno, your brother-in-law."

"Why should I be jealous of one who is better than I am at the art of making war?" he demanded reasonably. "I am superior to Renno in the art of throwing a spear. I can throw one farther and with greater

accuracy than can Renno, or any other man. Therefore, in a contest in throwing a spear, Renno will
invariably give first place to me. By that same token,
I freely give him first place in the art of making war.
His thoughts develop with great rapidity and always
are accurate. He knows what needs to be done and
how to do it. I will gladly place myself under his
orders at all times in war-making."

The young woman sighed. "If you are content to
spend your whole life in the shadows of someone
who stands far above you, I cannot complain. If you
choose to take second place to someone who is really
your inferior, I will not object. Is it not true that you
are a tracker in the forest who is second to none?"

"So it is said," he replied modestly.

"Even in tracking," she said, a hint of scorn ap-
pearing in her voice, "you take second place. Your
wife has assumed a glory greater than yours and is
known among the Cherokee and the Seneca as the
greatest of living trackers."

"If she has acquired such a name," Rusog said
equably, "then I guess she deserves it. I do not
compete with my wife in such matters, any more
than I compete with my brother-in-law or with anyone else with whom I am on close terms. It is enough
that I am opposed to the enemies of my people and
will do everything in my power to annihilate them
and drive them far from their inland homes into the
great sea."

"Some will say that you lack ambition," she charged.

He grinned. "That may be true."

"It is said," she told him, "that you will be forgotten when the heroes of your nation are remembered."

"That well may be true," he said, "but I will nevertheless be remembered as one who fulfilled his destiny and who lived a happy life to the fullest possible extent. I will never be accused of having shirked in my desire for a true place in the annals of my people."

They sat in silence for a time, and then she looked at him with a strong hint of guile in her glance. "You are happy with life as you find it. Is that not so, Rusog?"

He poked the ashes, and the sparks rose in a brief shower, scattering onto the meat. "I am satisfied," he said, "that all that can be done by man for the sake of one's happiness is being done. I can think of nothing that could make me happier."

"Do you find contentment with your wife?" She was flirting with him now, making no secret of her intent to entice him.

In his embarrassment, Rusog stared at a rock near him where she had stepped. The rock was still damp with a perfectly visible footprint. As he looked at it, he thought it odd that the rock had not yet dried, even though the sun was beating down on it.

"You react to my beauty," she was saying. "You do not find me unattractive—of this I am certain. I can see by your attitude that you would not turn your back on me. Is this not the truth?"

He was compelled to admit what he could not deny. "Yes, it is true."

"You and I," she said softly, "are alone in this

endless wilderness. No one knows that I have visited
you. No person whom you know is acquainted with
me or has ever learned my name. I will never be
seen by those who are related to you or are close to
you. Your wife has never heard of me and will never
know that I exist. Do you understand all these things?"

Glancing again at the wet footprint, Rusog nodded
dumbly. He knew that every word the young woman
spoke was the absolute truth, and he had no reason
to question anything she said.

She reached out to touch him, and her hand felt
warm on his arm. "You and I," she murmured, "could
sleep together for the entire night. No one ever
would know. No one would even dream that you had
encountered me in this wilderness and that we became one here. As far as your wife knows, or others
who are near to you, you were alone the entire
time."

Rusog could feel her hot breath on his face, and
the moisture from her hand on his arm made it feel
as though he were receiving a series of sharp shocks.
He made no reply because he was so badly torn that
he did not know what to do.

She began to slide her hand up and down his arm.
"Come," she whispered. "Come. What your wife
does not know, she will never learn. You have an
opportunity that few men are granted in this world.
Come now, and you will experience joy that will
never be equaled as long as you live."

Waves of temptation washed over Rusog, and he
knew that never again would he face a crisis as
painful as this one. He could enjoy himself with

impunity; Ena would never know the difference. Nothing would influence their relationship. On the other hand, his common sense told him that if he strayed now something would be sacrificed that he and Ena would not be able to retrieve.

He knew only that he would be wrong to give in to temptation and accede to this woman's wishes. It was essential that he remain loyal to his wife, just as he had to remain loyal to the concepts of his nation and of the principles he held dear.

Slowly he pulled back and shook his head. "I'm sorry," he said, "but though you are not unattractive, and I thank you for thinking of me as you have, my life is so complicated that I cannot consider your proposal."

He drew back his hand and averted his face, finding it too painful to look into her doelike eyes. When he glanced in her direction again, she was withdrawing. She stood and started back toward the lake.

She moved only a few steps when the dazzling sunlight touched her again and made it difficult for him to see her. In a moment, Rusog heard a faint splash, and she was gone.

All that was left of her was the wet footprint that still marked the place where she had trod on the rock in approaching him.

Chapter VI

The short, sharp, glistening steel blade affixed to the stump of Admiral Riley's right wrist by a leather cuff swished menacingly as he brandished it beneath the noses of four volunteers for his new crew. "When I give you an order," he said, "you will obey it instantly. You will take no time to think about it, to decide if it makes sense and whether or not you will obey it. You are to do exactly what you are told when you are told to do it. Do I make myself clear?"

"Aye, aye, sir!" the quartet replied in unison.

Other seamen on the deck of the converted merchantman in the harbor at St. Augustine had set about their business in silence—swabbing the deck, polishing the teakwood and the bits of metal, painting the superstructure, and making the ship ready for her next voyage at sea. They knew from their own experience with the rites of initiation that soon this would end with the violent death of one of the quartet of volunteers. Now they were one by one finding excuses to take themselves elsewhere.

The lecture went on. The admiral's voice was as cutting as the blade attached to his wrist was sharp.

"When I give an order," the admiral reiterated harshly, "no matter how ridiculous it may seem to you, it could mean the difference between life and death for our entire company. Only those who jump to do what I order deserve to live. Now then, are you ready?"

The four heads nodded simultaneously, all the recruits doing their best to hide their apprehensions.

The admiral lived up to their worst expectations. "Overboard!" he ordered. "Into the water with you! Immediately!"

The four sailors jumped up onto the railing of the deck that stood between them and the water. Three of them promptly dove into the Atlantic.

The fourth man hesitated. That morning, when he

had assisted in throwing the garbage overboard after breakfast, the ship's cook had called his attention to a school of sharks circling near the ship. Remembering them now, he had no desire to jump into shark-infested waters. He stood indecisively on the railing, wondering if he could somehow avoid going into the water, but also wanting to avert punishment at the hands of the admiral.

The admiral was throwing lines to the three sailors, ignoring the one recalcitrant. Only when they had climbed up the ropes and stood on deck did the admiral turn to the fourth sailor, who had clambered down and joined his dripping companions. Riley pointed the ominous edge of the blade at him. "You!" he barked. "What is your excuse?"

His voice quavering, the young man explained about having seen sharks.

His colleagues shuddered when they recognized how narrow their escape had been.

But the admiral showed no mercy.

"You were given a direct order," he said contemptuously. "But you failed to obey it. You have no excuse! The lives of your entire company could be lost because you stopped to think of your own skin before worrying about the welfare of your brothers. You deserve only one reward!"

The words were scarcely out of his mouth when he swung his arm sideways. The blade, which he kept sharpened until it was as finely honed as a razor, caught the seaman on the side of the throat and slashed into his jugular vein. Blood spurted out, dripping from his body and staining the deck around him. He fell, his hands clawing ineffectually at his throat.

"Throw him overboard," the admiral commanded. "He is worth nothing now except food for those sharks he feared."

He waited until the three surviving sailors picked up the man, who was still alive, and heaved him overboard. The smell of blood immediately attracted four sharks. When the terrible churning of the water subsided, nothing was visible below. The admiral turned away, gesturing toward the blood-spattered deck. "Clean up the muck," he ordered, "and divide the contents of his sea chest among you. Never mention his name—whatever it was—in my hearing again." He stalked off, satisfied that he had successfully instilled enough fear in his new crewmen to last a lifetime.

The three new sailors hurried to do as he had instructed, convinced that they had signed up with a madman whose every command was to be instantly obeyed.

Casno, regent of the Seneca, paid a private call on Wegowa, war sachem of the Cherokee. Wegowa was expecting such a visit, and they walked together to a hut made of corn stalks that warriors guarded night and day. Here, in the sacred precincts of the most religious site in their land, they sat down to confer. Both men were extraordinarily grave.

"If I had greater authority, I would exert it immediately," Casno said. "But I have reached the limits of my power. I am helpless to swim against the strong tide of feeling that sweeps over the people of the Seneca."

"I understand what you mean," Wegowa answered. "My people, too, are up in arms, clamoring for justice."

"We cannot forget, as the people of Knoxville appear to have done," Casno continued, "that Ena, the wife of Rusog, is also the daughter of Ghonkaba, who was a direct descendant of Renno, the white Indian. She is no ordinary person. The fact that it is her husband who is unfairly charged with murder strains the patience of the Seneca, who are demanding justice. They broke the sacred treaty of the Iroquois with the British in order to side with the Americans, and they cannot understand why they are now being repaid for their loyalty in this manner. I have tried to explain that no connection exists between the American government and the government of the State of Franklin. But they cannot see a difference. They claim it is all the same people."

"I face much the same situation," Wegowa told him. "Rusog, my son, is the only grandson of Loramas, our Grand Sachem. Without exception, the people of the Cherokee were faithful to the Americans. Never once have we wavered. My people, too, do not understand how loyalty can be repaid so shabbily."

"Unfortunately," Casno said, "while our people are at peace, they have no need to prepare for war with any other nation, and this makes them restless. The forests are filled with animals and food, and the rivers heavily stocked with fish, so even the tasks of hunting and fishing are more limited than usual. Our

people consequently have time to brood. And this
brooding makes them dangerous. I fear for the
consequences."

"I tried to speak to my father about this," Wegowa
said. "He is so preoccupied by his marriage to Ah-
wen-ga that he allows nothing else to enter his mind.
The very idea of a war between our people and the
settlers at Knoxville is so horrible it truly cannot be
contemplated. We must go to Loramas and Ah-wen-ga
and together convince them that the situation is far
more serious than either of them is willing to admit."

After discussing various ideas, they decided that
they must report without delay. They went straight
to the dwelling that Loramas and his bride now
occupied. Ah-wen-ga was preparing dinner when they
arrived, and by common consent they sat near her at
the fire so as to include her in the conversation.
Speaking succinctly, Casno outlined the problem.

"I think the feeling of the people of both our
nations is truly justified," Loramas responded. "They
made many sacrifices to join hands with the Americans. I cannot blame them in the least for resenting
the attitude now shown by the Americans in Knoxville. They seem to lack appreciation of the aid we
gave them."

"I quite agree," Ah-wen-ga said forcefully. "The
lack of courtesy being shown to our people is
shocking."

Casno was startled that these leaders of the two
nations would be so shortsighted in their views and
disinclined to see the overall situation. He could see

that Wegowa, too, was struggling with a severe inner disappointment.

After considering the issue from every angle, Casno and Wegowa decided they had only one choice. With their leaders adamantly opposed to a compromise, they would be forced to confer with officials of the State of Franklin to avoid the possibility of a war that would only be detrimental to both the Indians and the state. Having made up their minds, they set out almost immediately, accompanied by an escort of forty warriors, enough to repel any stray hostile patrols they might encounter.

As they approached the ramparts of Knoxville, they raised a white flag to announce their good intentions. When their identity became known, the authorities were notified. A short time later, Governor Sevier arrived, accompanied by Colonel Roy Johnson, who had just returned to duty, pale and thin, but hardy in his speech.

"We have come the long distance from the land of the Cherokee to see you on a matter of great urgency," Casno announced solemnly. His demeanor and his words were sufficiently grave that the group moved to the governor's office. While they sat around a highly polished table, several women set about preparing a banquet suitable for the distinguished guests.

"We rejoice to see that Colonel Johnson has recovered his health," Wegowa said diplomatically. "Now that you have, perhaps we have made our trip in vain. Will your charges against Rusog for trying to murder you be dropped?"

Johnson and Sevier looked at each other quickly. Their suspicions were confirmed about the purpose of the visit, and they were unhappy that they could not comply with the naively worded request.

"I regret," Colonel Johnson said, "that it seems as though a trial will be needed to restore Rusog's good name. You do not believe him guilty of attacking me, and neither do I. But the evidence against him was deemed sufficiently strong that the court has ruled he must be tried in accordance with our laws."

"Our society," Governor Sevier added hastily, "is built exclusively on laws! It is the law that holds together the fabric of life as we know it. We judge all men and live in accordance with the law's dictates. We must administer it fairly and in justice to all persons, regardless of who they are."

"You do not understand," Casno remonstrated. "The warriors of the Cherokee and of the Seneca are very angry. They feel their allies have deserted them. They are ready to prepare to make war against the very people they believed to be their friends."

"We must ask you to have faith in our way of doing things," Colonel Johnson replied. "Trust us to treat Rusog fairly. I am personally convinced our court will find him not guilty of the charges being pressed against him. You must have faith in us, as we have faith in our system of justice."

"Your words," Casno said, "will only serve to convince our people that you are trying to confuse them and to make them subject to your will. If you want to avoid trouble that otherwise will plague you for all time, I beg you, dismiss the charges against him."

"If it were possible to follow your advice and to avoid a war that neither side could possibly win, believe me, we would do it," Colonel Johnson answered soberly.

"But we cannot perform an impossible act," Governor Sevier added. "You must please take my word for it. Either the Indians will trouble themselves to understand our ways and behave accordingly, or they, too, will become enmeshed in a war they do not really want.

"Believe me," he went on, "if it were possible to avoid further bad feelings, I would do it. It now appears that the only way the situation as you describe it can be remedied is for Renno to return in time, to persuade your people not to attack us. Otherwise, as sure as we all are sitting around this table, if your nations persist, we will resist and there will be war."

More dead than alive, Ben Whipple had staggered up to the Spanish sentries on duty at the gates of St. Augustine. The Spanish guards had promptly taken him into custody, and with little formality he ended up in their prison. His case was foreordained because he spoke only English. Eventually, word of his whereabouts drifted down to his cousin Emil, who made a point of visiting him on a trip to St. Augustine. He was able to persuade the Spaniards to set him free so he could be enlisted in the growing contingent of sailors on board the ships being outfitted in the harbor by Admiral Riley. Over several weeks, Whipple's body healed and he was able to regain his strength.

The scars that marred his mind remained unhealed, however, and were as virulent and inflamed as ever. He hated the Seminole for their treatment of him, and in his own warped way he blamed Emily Johnson for his downfall.

By the time the rigorous training period under Admiral Riley came to an end, he had made up his mind. He would lead an expedition to the land of the Seminole and wipe the slate clean by killing every brave who had participated in his suffering and humiliation.

He soon found it an easy matter to persuade some of the members of the admiral's buccaneer fleet to join in his mission of vengeance against the Seminole. Waiting until the recruits had a completely free evening, he called a meeting on the poop deck of the admiral's flagship. In the half dark of midnight, he addressed them.

"Men," he said to the group huddled in a semicircle before him, speaking softly so the officers would not hear him in the quiet night air, "every last one of us enlisted here for a purpose. We agreed to withstand many dangers, to put our lives on the line in the hope of winning substantial rewards from freebooting. My cousin has been a captain with Riley for years, and I know that he has prospered. But I can tell you of a far easier and quicker way to earn riches."

The men stirred, and a low, muttering sound showed the depth of their interest.

"Scarcely more than a week's march from here is the area of the Seminole, the most secretive tribe in North America. I have learned why they remain so secretive. I just recently made a trip there. Hidden in their territory is a mine with a rich vein of gold. The early Spaniards discovered this mine hundreds of years ago, but they were driven out of the area by the Seminole, who have allowed no white man to return. They guard the treasure with a special force of warriors and allow no strangers within reach of it. I propose that we mount an expedition, send it to the heart of Seminole country, and seize the gold mine. We will kill any guard who tries to stop us, and we will be rich forever! What do you say?"

A suppressed buzz of animation showed that the men were very much in favor of the idea.

Whipple was delighted. He had won them over and he gloried in the thought that his vengeance against the Seminole could be carried out.

Suddenly a sharp voice spoke up from the rear. "You say that the Seminole have a gold mine worth a fortune, eh? In that case, I will lead the expedition myself!"

Amid an ominous silence, Admiral Riley moved forward from the hatch from where he had been listening. The men shrank from him as he advanced.

Ben Whipple looked on in dismay. The one thing he had feared had come to pass: the admiral now knew of his scheme. But it was too late for any changes, too late to explain that the story was only a figment of his imagination, thought up to trick the seamen in joining him in his campaign.

Riley took his time as he came to the front and slowly looked Whipple up and down. "You are sure you have the facts straight, Whipple?" he demanded.

Ben faced him bravely. "Yes, sir."

"As I understand you, the Seminole have a secret gold mine they have been hiding for many years. You claim the Spanish authorities know about it. Is that correct?"

"Well, yes, sir." Whipple was glad that his voice did not tremble.

"How does it happen that in more than twenty-five years among the Spanish I never before heard a word of this gold mine?"

Whipple faced him boldly. "I would not think an outsider would be told a state secret of that importance."

His words had the ring of logic and stopped Admiral Riley short. "Yes," he admitted, "I suppose you're right." He hesitated for a moment and then went on. "Very well. I shall command this expedition myself, and you shall march at the head of the company with me to point the way toward the gold mine. If I have been tricked, or if you have lied to me, then may God have mercy on you, Whipple!" He raised his hand in such a way that a slender beam of moonlight fell on the sharp, curved steel blade.

Renno led the way slowly through the heavy undergrowth of the Everglades, his tomahawk gripped in his right hand as he slashed at the creepers and bushes that impeded his progress. His keen eyesight prevented trouble time after time. Whenever they came to ponds or streams he immediately searched out the alligators and avoided them. Similarly, he had an instinct for discovering the nearby presence of snakes and staying clear of them. He took care to point out scorpions and other harmful insects, including a large, furry, black spider that caused Venya to cry out aloud when she first saw it.

Renno led them unerringly through the forest, noting places where grass had been trampled and growth cut back to allow unknown people passage. Quite often they encountered large bodies of water or of boggy and impenetrable terrain. Renno's instincts served him well, for he promptly found a winding route along dry paths. Only once did he and Tobiko have to fashion a makeshift raft to see them across an otherwise impassable body of water. Occasionally he started off in a wrong direction but soon corrected himself, and they moved steadily closer to the Seminole town.

The unseen eyes of the Seminole took note of every move they made. The town was notified by drummers who communicated with the deep, bass-voiced drums of Africa rather than the high-pitched drums of the New World. Sometimes these drums sounded very close to Renno and his companions, but they were unable to decipher the meaning. They only knew they were being watched.

Behind Renno was Venya, carrying a tomahawk Tobiko had given her. She gripped it in one hand, ready to use it.

Bringing up the rear was Tobiko, whose natural caution made him ideal in that position. Characteristically suspicious and jumpy, he looked on either side and behind constantly, to make sure that no strange creatures or hostile humans could sneak up on them.

At last they came to signs that the wilderness was ending and that civilization of a sort lay ahead. The wilderness had been tamed and reduced to underbrush almost everywhere. Rudimentary crops were growing in the rich soil. Their quest was coming to an end. Still taking no risks, Renno moved cautiously. Tall, silent, dark men began to appear behind trees, watching every move. Finally they were confronted by a formidable man wearing alligator skins sewn together to form a stiff jacket. Clearly a sentry guarding the approach to a town ahead, he watched them with glittering eyes, his expression revealing no hint of welcome.

Renno, his face set, approached him and raised his left hand in salute.

Don Luis was short and fat, a lover of good food and wine, of pleasant company and easy living. If he had belonged to any other nation he might have been pleasant and easy to get along with. As a member of the Spanish aristocracy, however, he was a product of inbreeding, which made him arrogant and suspicious and intolerant of back talk.

Strutting self-importantly, he walked down the long corridor of the governor's palace in St. Augustine, inclining his head a fraction of an inch as he passed acquaintances. He wore the sash of the imperial assistant to the Lord High Governor-in-Chief of Flor-

ida. No one could be as aware as he of this exalted
position.

His manner did not change until he prepared to
enter the throne room at the end of the corridor.
Guards stood on duty as long as the governor, Don
Sebastian, sat on his throne. Only as he entered did
Don Luis's manner become more conciliatory. His
lips parted in the customary half smile of the cour-
tier, and he bowed low. "I await instructions from
Your Excellency," he announced.

Don Sebastian was in a foul frame of mind. He had
argued interminably at breakfast with his mistress,
whom he accused of spending far too much on clothes
for which she had no need. She had paid no attention to his threats, retaliating by declaring that unless he supported her in the style to which she was
accustomed, she would go to the bigger court in
Havana, or perhaps she would return to Madrid.
Now he looked sourly at his cherubic assistant. "It's
about time," he snarled. "Don Felipe delivered the
latest load of prisoners—twenty-eight strong—about
two hours ago. They are waiting in the cellar dun-
geons for the usual distribution."

Don Luis refused to be cowed. "Don Felipe was
late—as usual," he said. "Admiral Riley is no longer
in the city. He is marching with his entire company
to some inland point. They left just this morning."

The governor raised a plucked eyebrow and sniffed
a scented handkerchief. "Really!" he exclaimed. "This
is too much. Where does Riley think he's going?"

"It did not cross my mind to inquire. You know
how Riley resents personal questions. It was enough

for me to learn that he was leaving on an overland tour."

Don Sebastian made no attempt to hide his irritation. "I have no intention of keeping the prisoners here and feeding them when we have an agreement with Admiral Riley to take all our prisoners, train them, and use them as he will. I order you to find him at once, no matter where he may be, and hand the prisoners over to him—as per our agreement."

Only one reply was possible to such an order. Don Luis bowed stiffly from the waist and muttered, "Very good, sir."

The sun baked down suffocatingly on the hot, flat Florida plain, reminding Don Luis of summer in Andalusia. It was an unusual contrast to the heavily forested areas that dominated much of the territory.

No sound could be heard but the cracking of overseers' whips as the twenty-eight prisoners were urged forward.

Riding at the head of the column of guards and prisoners, Don Luis was in a state of near exhaustion. Annoyed with Admiral Riley for causing him to have to give up the comforts of St. Augustine for this chase across the barren interior of Florida, he was equally irked by Don Sebastian's orders to do the impossible.

Even the horses drooped, and the prisoners staggered forward, each step closer to the last. It would be typical, Don Luis thought grimly, for a large number of the captives to die before he could deliver them to Admiral Riley. The thought failed to cheer him.

At last, after an agony of marching, Don Luis saw in the distance a scene that he could have sworn was a mirage. Surrounded by a white fence was a farmhouse of clay and wood painted a pale blue. Best of all, nearby were cool citrus fruit trees. It could have been transplanted intact from the interior of southern Spain. Certain that the property must belong to a loyal subject of the king of Castile, Don Luis spurred his tired horse forward.

His guess soon was confirmed. The property belonged to a couple from Andalusia who had settled in the New World two decades earlier. Here they had prospered, and their farm covered many acres, mostly under the supervision of their two sons and four daughters.

Ordering his captives watered and fed, Don Luis was able to relax at last in the cool comfort of the farmhouse parlor. There he was attended personally by the youngest of the daughters, Juanita, a raven-haired beauty who had the natural dignity and poise of most women of the Old World. As he watched her, he was increasingly taken by her, and after a time, the generous quantities of brandy that the farmer urged on him had their natural effect, and he reached for Juanita. Instantly, she pulled away.

"If you please, Don Luis," she said, "I swore years ago that whenever I wed, I intend to be as virginal as on the day I was born. And so it shall be."

Paying no attention to her protestations, Don Luis covered her hand with one large paw and, putting the other around her waist, tried to draw her closer. "You forget that I am the lord lieutenant of the imperial viceroy," he murmured.

"I forget nothing," Juanita replied, "but I know that I must keep my vow, which I made with the Lord long before I ever knew of your existence." Sliding away from him, she curtsied respectfully and then fled from the room.

Disappointed and angry, he sat and stewed for several hours, finishing a pitcher of homemade brandy. By the time he staggered off to bed, he had made up his mind how to handle the situation.

The next morning, after an early breakfast, he summoned the captain of the guard. "Captain," he said, "perhaps you have noticed a young woman who is a member of this household. She wears her hair falling low behind her back, and it hangs almost to her knees. She is in a black dress today and wears a red apron over it. Do you know the one I mean?"

"Yes, sir!" the officer replied enthusiastically. "I know exactly who you mean."

"Good," Don Luis said casually. "Place her under arrest and throw her into irons and then march her with the prisoners. Effective as of this moment, she becomes a prisoner of the Crown."

Even the captain of the guard was astonished, and Don Luis turned away in order to avoid a further discussion.

He knew precisely what he was doing. He was sure Riley would lose his renowned temper when a large number of prisoners were thrust on him while he was en route somewhere on private business.

Don Luis intended to bring him a gift that should
soothe his anger somewhat.

Don Luis was a far better prophet than he had
realized. He caught up with the admiral about twenty-
four hours after entering the Everglades, and there
the young nobleman presented him with the twenty-
eight exhausted, almost useless prisoners.

Not even Admiral Riley dared to contradict the
orders of the imperial governor. As Don Luis had
expected, however, his anger was assuaged somewhat by the gift of the young spitfire, Juanita, who
had breathed defiance at Don Luis and the members
of the army ever since they kidnapped her.

Making the best of an unpleasant situation, the
admiral turned the prisoners over to Felix, a boat-
swain's mate who had spent twenty years before the
mast with the admiral's fleet.

Felix was said to have two personalities. On board
ship he was a tyrant to be crossed at one's peril. But
on land he was rather easygoing and tolerant, noted
among his comrades for an earthy sense of humor.

Felix lost no time in displaying his humor to his
new charges. Ordering their shackles removed, he
sat them in a circle around him. "You lads will get
along just fine," he said, "if you remember that you
have only one boss in all the world—Admiral Riley.
Whatever he orders, you will do. When he speaks,
you will obey. You may have heard about how cruel
he is, but he's only a human being, just like you and
me. For instance, you will notice that he often
scratches that bald head of his with his good hand."

The unfortunate captives snickered.

"I mean exactly what I say," Felix repeated. "He likes to rub the bald spot, and I'm waiting for the time that he's rubbing his head and patting his belly at the same time—just like a monkey would do."

After a pause, several of the men seated nearest to Felix were staring in openmouthed horror behind him. He turned and went pale.

Not six feet from him was the admiral, who had been listening to every word of his exhortation.

Felix began to stammer. "I—I—I—I was just having a little informal chat with the recruits, Admiral. I was telling 'em how you're a human being who can have all the faults that all of us have—and still be the boss." He began to edge away.

"Halt!" the admiral thundered, and Felix reluctantly came to a stop.

The arm with the razor-sharp blade flashed in the sunlight, and Felix screamed.

He stood looking down at his hands, from which the fingers had been removed by two rapid swipes of the blade. Blood was pouring profusely from the stumps.

"You're a fine one to talk about being human and rubbing my belly," Admiral Riley said, his voice taunting. "Let's see you rub your belly now!" He laughed uproariously at his joke, and then his voice became icy, impersonal again. "The scum is no use to us in his present condition," he said. "Get rid of him! Throw him into the water yonder as feed for the alligators." He turned away, not bothering to wait and watch the terrified recruits carry out his cruel orders.

Returning to his tent, Riley was in a far happier frame of mind. He had started the education of the recruits on the right note, and that pleased him, as it always did. Ordering two glasses of rum and water, he told himself that the day would not be wasted after all, and he moistened his lips as he sent for Juanita.

A few moments later the flap in the tent entrance was pushed aside, and Juanita was shoved inside. She looked much as she had at home, but she was tense now and there was a wild look of determination in her eyes. She had heard of people being mishandled by the Crown authorities, but now she had been subjected to such injustice, and her mood was dangerous. She was determined to break the chain of events that were claiming her as a victim.

"Sit down," Admiral Riley said and beamed, waving her toward his camp bed, the only place in the tent where she could be seated.

She stepped to the bed, her eyes wary, her movements guarded like an animal about to spring to defend itself.

The admiral recognized her tension and immediately sought a way of alleviating it. "Here," he said, thrusting a strong drink of rum and water into one hand, "drink this."

She raised the glass to her lips. To his surprise, she drank almost all of it in a series of long, gulping swallows. Pleased with his progress in his seduction plans, he promptly picked up a bell and, summoning

a servant, ordered another drink brought to her.
"How did you happen to land in your present predicament?" the admiral inquired, a note of sympathy
creeping into his voice.

Juanita returned his gaze stonily, revealing no inner feelings. "I was saving myself for the man I
intend to marry," she said, "so I declined to go along
with Don Luis's rotten ideas. He had other views
and took me prisoner. It seems that to be a de-
fenseless woman in New Spain today is to have no
freedom whatsoever!"

"What you need," he replied, "is a protector, someone who will stand up for you against all odds and
force your will to prevail."

She returned his steady gaze and sneered. "I suppose that you offer yourself as a protector," she said,
"and that you demand the usual price for your
services."

Unaccustomed to such candor, he laughed a trifle
uncomfortably. "You have a knack for speaking in a
way that needlessly places me in the wrong," he
said, relieved when a servant arrived with another
drink, which he gave her.

Again she consumed the drink quickly. "I gather,"
she repeated, "you are going to suggest that you take
over the role of my protector." Irony entered her
voice and a gleam of harsh amusement came into her
eyes. "I was born here in the New World, under
British rule, in fact, and the freedom that I have
learned here goes far beyond what any protector
could do for me. I search only for the real freedom,"
she said, "for the freedom of making the ultimate

choices of life, between liberty and imprisonment, between freedom of choice and no freedom of movement at all."

The admiral was surprised by the intensity of her declaration, and even more astonished by the actions that accompanied her words. She caught his right wrist with both hands, and then with the blade pointing straight at her, she threw herself on it. The sharp blade penetrated deep into her body. She was determined to give up her life with as much dignity as she had lived.

The admiral hastily drew back his arm, but it was too late. Juanita was already dying, her blood spilling out on the ground beneath her fallen body.

He looked down at her with pity. If only he had known that she would be this courageous, he could have used her to good advantage. She would have gone far as his permanent mistress, as the number two person in his far-flung organization.

With great regret, he called in the servants to clean and empty the tent. Then he deliberately washed the bloodstains from the blade.

Chapter VII

As Durati, the leader of the Seminole, and Renno of the Seneca faced each other in the center of the town of the Seminole, the prolonged silence became increasingly tense. The warriors gathered there expected an outburst by either man momentarily, with the prospect of stirring, hand-to-hand combat. The squaws, too, were on the alert, ready to snatch their children out of harm's way.

Suddenly, however, the exuberant voice of a new member of the tribe was raised in an exultant shout. "Venya!" Quanto cried in shocked disbelief as he stared at the young black woman who stood trans- fixed between Renno and Tobiko. She flew to him, her arms curling around his neck as he grasped her, and they hugged in wordless joy.

The young woman quickly found her voice. "Let no harm come to Renno, I beg you!" she cried out. "He saved my life when I thought I would surely die, and since then he has protected me as though I were his sister. He possesses rare magical powers, and among all Indians, he must be foremost in the wonders he is able to perform."

Durati, who understood the significance of her words, held up his hand. Like tribesmen everywhere, he knew of Renno's ancestors and was greatly im- pressed. He had no desire to engage in personal combat with Renno of the Seneca. The stories of Renno's prowess may have been exaggerated, but he gave credit to them sufficiently to make even him, the tribal leader, cautious.

Durati turned back to Renno, a half question in his eyes as he sought now to avoid an open conflict in an honorable fashion.

To his relief, he saw Renno smile and raise his left arm, palm outward, in the universal Indian symbol of a friendly greeting. He hastily replied with the same gesture.

As the host, Durati had the responsibility to make

his guest welcome, and this he did in a flowery speech, using the Cherokee language that was understood by Renno as well as the Seminole present. Renno was pleased to hear his words of welcome and warm intentions.

When at last it was Renno's turn to reply, he spoke slowly and distinctly in his usual terse manner. He related that he had traveled a long distance for a reason he did not describe. He assured his listeners that he was glad to be among people who prized freedom so greatly.

Durati ordered that a banquet be held that day in the honor of the newcomer from the Iroquois League. Quanto, the young warrior engaged to marry Venya, showed his gratitude by accepting an appointment as chief of a squad of warriors assigned to protect the newcomers.

Renno and Tobiko, having been assigned to a dwelling, withdrew in order to enjoy a brief midday rest. Afterward they shaved their heads on either side of their scalp locks, making ready for the afternoon's festivities.

Renno had told no one his purpose in coming to the land of the Seminole. When he and Tobiko were alone, he confided in his friend, explaining, "I will wait until after the banquet is ended. Then I will arrange for a private meeting with Durati and will tell him why I am here. Perhaps he can help locate the woman who means so much to me but who has disappeared from my life."

He had no way of knowing that Emily was in the

same community, any more than she could know he
had arrived.

When the hour came for the banquet, Renno and
Tobiko proceeded with their honor guard to the scene
where the meal would be served. They learned that
they would be seated with Durati, his sister, and
other leaders of the tribe.

As the meal progressed, Renno, who had put on
his white buffalo cape, found the food far different
from what he had been accustomed to eat in the
home land of the Seneca, or even in Tennessee,
among the Cherokee. First, he ate a citrus fruit,
which the Spaniards had introduced from their own
countryside into Florida, where it flourished under
the hot sun. The Spaniards also had introduced olive
trees, and these provided a tasty base for a minced
appetizer that appealed to Renno.

The principal dish consisted of chopped venison
and crabmeat baked inside large crab shells over hot
stones. It also seemed delicious to Renno and was
unlike anything he had ever tasted. When he finished his portion, Durati insisted that he eat more,
ignoring Renno's effort to decline politely.

As they talked, Durati grew even more informal,
and finally announced that though he was not married, his intended bride was in the town and he
wished to allow his distinguished visitor to view her.
He clapped his hands and called out to his sister.
Within moments, Ladira brought forward a light-
skinned woman who was almost cowering behind
her, expecting the worst.

At that instant, Renno recognized Emily and jumped

up in amazement. He waved away Ladira, who realized that something was amiss and wheeled angrily toward Emily as if to make her suffer for some error.

Gathering Emily in both arms, Renno protected her from Ladira's threats, and in the same motion, he removed the white buffalo cape from his shoulders and placed it around hers. It was a symbol no one except Tobiko could recognize. He was giving to the helpless woman he loved the protection offered by the manitous.

He could feel her trembling beneath his touch, and recognizing that she had suffered abuse, he announced loudly, "Emily is my woman! Where she goes, I will go. What she does, I also will do."

A moment of silence followed, as everyone absorbed his words. None welcomed Renno more than Emily, for whom his miraculous appearance resolved all her immediate troubles.

Ladira's outrage now turned to joy. When this pale skinned warrior from the north claimed Emily, her own problem was solved, and she exchanged a triumphant smile with Nalata.

Durati, of course, could not fail to oppose Renno in this matter. He had taken it for granted that Emily was being prepared to be his squaw, and the prospect that she might belong to another man confounded him. His manhood was threatened. He had to find some way to react to the occasion appropriately.

Rising to his feet, he announced clearly, "I cannot accept the statement that Renno of the Seneca has dared to make. Emily is not his woman. She is my woman. And I am willing to fight and, if necessary, to die for the right to establish that she is mine alone."

In shocked silence, the assemblage stared at the two leaders. Everyone assumed that Renno must accept the challenge.

He did so without a second's hesitation. "Durati is my friend," he said. "I am appreciative of his valor in saving the life of Emily, and I am certain he has proved himself with other fine deeds. Nevertheless, Emily is mine, and I can permit no other man—not even my friend Durati—to interfere. He or any other man who wants to try to wrest her from me must endeavor to best me in open combat."

Emily instinctively moved a step closer to Renno. He put his arm around her shoulders, drawing her close and holding her there protectively. Both recognized intuitively that the gesture on her part, as well as on his, clearly made a lie of Durati's claim.

Ladira and Nalata promptly joined forces with the unexpected ally from the north. Having had no idea of another man in Emily's past, they were delighted by the prospect of being rid of her. But among the Seminole tribe, they stood alone. It was widely understood that the chief expected to make Emily his wife when she became thoroughly accepting of the ways of the tribe. Now his authority was threatened, and he had only one way to respond.

Durati, in fact, had admired all he had ever heard about Renno, and he was impressed by the legends passed on to him. Nevertheless, to retreat now would be catastrophic, costing him the respect of his people and their willingness to follow him as the head of the nation. He had no choice but to assume a hostile stance. Drawing his tomahawk from his belt, he twirled it overhead and then flung it into the ground inches from Renno's feet.

Renno responded by picking up the tomahawk and brandishing it under Durati's nose. He was accepting the challenge. He was also reluctant to engage in the combat. Durati was apparently responsible for having saved Emily's life, though he felt that ultimately he would have to hold Durati responsible for Emily's deplorable state. For the present, his honor had been questioned, and he could see no way to avoid a deadly personal combat. A thin smile crossed Durati's face as his challenge was answered.

The fight, Emily saw, was inevitable, and she accepted it in the calm spirit of an Indian wife. Her attitude was sincere because she did not, in any way, doubt the skill that Renno would demonstrate in battle. Because he was superior he would triumph; the only question in her mind was how he would win.

A murmur of excitement arose from the warriors, their wives, and the young people as they anticipated the coming contest. It swelled in volume, only to be cut off sharply when the deep bass drums of the sentries sounded in the distance. The gathering grew quiet and everyone listened intently while the full message was received, but when it ended, everyone began to talk.

Unable to interpret the message, Renno looked questioningly at Emily.

"It appears that a large party of white foreigners,"

she told him in a low voice, "is coming in boats in this direction. They are all heavily armed, and it is assumed they mean no good to the Seminole."

In that instant, Renno made up his mind. "Our personal feud must wait," he called out in Cherokee to Durati. "I offer you my help in the battle that I understand is to come."

Accepting in the spirit in which the offer was meant, Durati instantly held out his left hand.

Renno clasped it, and as his fingers met Durati's, they agreed to postpone their personal feud until the crisis passed.

Wanting to see for himself what his scouts had reported, Durati went off to spy on the approaching forces. He was accompanied by Renno and Tobiko, who joined him without asking permission.

They crossed a wide river in a shallow-draft native boat, ignoring the alligators sunning themselves. Durati paddled the boat into an area that was free of the creatures and leaped out onto the bank to pull it up on shore. He motioned to Renno and Tobiko to follow him, and they sped through the dense foliage of the Everglades. Renno was glad Durati took the lead, because he could not have managed that pace with the chief's efficiency. Only a man born and raised in this interior swampland could have traveled as swiftly and confidently as Durati did, guiding his companions safely through the treacherous terrain.

After marching for nearly an hour, they could finally hear the enemy party, which was making no attempt to conceal itself, as they boldly paddled upstream toward the Seminole village. The men were shouting from boat to boat, open and confident about what they were doing.

Following the lead of Durati, Renno and Tobiko concealed themselves in the underbrush and watched the approaching enemy.

Renno nudged Durati and whispered a question. "Where could they have obtained those native boats?"

"I believe they must have bargained for them from another tribe," Durati answered. "They needed the boats, because they could never find their way by land to our village through the swamps and quicksand. They must have made their way by land to this river and bought the boats from a tribe—or even stolen them."

It was the leader of the column of boats that attracted Renno's closest attention. He wore the faded epaulets of an admiral and was heavily armed with two pistols in his belt. The men who were serving under him clearly were doing everything possible to avoid coming near his right arm, with its short, gleaming blade. He sat alone up front in his craft, silent and forbidding, letting others do the paddling.

Of even greater interest to Renno was the leader of one of the other craft. He recognized Ben Whipple instantly. Whipple had largely regained his strength after the hardships and cruelties he had suffered on the journey south, and he seemed to be in good physical condition. An ammunition belt hung over his shoulder, and he carried a pistol and a long-handled knife. But his attitude did not match the easygoing, almost indolent air of his companions, who seemed to be in no hurry to reach their goal.

Whipple seemed to be pushing and straining every nerve. He was eager for a physical showdown. His eyes burned brightly and color flamed in both cheeks. He had a personal score to settle.

Giving the signal that they had observed enough, Durati led them back to his town at a pace that left Tobiko gasping.

"I saw from your expression," Durati said to Renno after they arrived, "that you recognized the man called Whipple."

Renno was surprised. "How do you know him?"

"I made him prisoner when I took Emily as a captive," the Seminole said. "He had previously captured her and was intending to take her to his hideout when I interfered with his plans."

Having had no opportunity to hear Emily's full story, Renno now understood what had happened. But he still could not account for the abuse she evidently had suffered while in the Seminole camp. Now he knew the villain who was responsible for her presence here.

"Who are the men with him?" Renno asked.

"They are called freebooters by the Spaniards," Durati said. "They work closely with the men of Spain, and they capture the ships of England and France and the United States. They make prisoners of any men they do not kill. They are very evil. We regard them as potentially the worst enemies that the Seminole could have. They are under the control of that man with the short blade for a hand."

"Have you figured the best way to fight these freebooters?"

Durati sighed. "We must rely," he said, "on the skill of our warriors. That is all we can hope for when we face a company that has superior arms."

"I have thought of little else since we glimpsed them through the forest," Renno said. "I have worked out a plan that may be able to stop their advance and perhaps gain us a victory."

"Listen now with care, O Durati," Tobiko exclaimed fervently while his words were translated by Renno into Cherokee. "This is no ordinary warrior. As the descendant of the great white Indian, he has proved himself in thought and deed to be capable of upholding the noble tradition of his line."

Durati had no need to be persuaded. Having no defense plan ready, he was eager to accept an idea offered by a warrior as prominent as Renno. He raised two fingers to his lips. Immediately, the song of the tree myrtle, among the most melodious of birds in the Everglades, sounded loud and distinct.

One by one, the warriors of his tribe responded to the summons. Coming silently from every direction, they crept up until they were on them before even Renno's acute hearing could make him aware of their presence. Impressed by their stealth, he decided to make good use of it whenever he could in the battle ahead.

Durati spoke to his men. "We will be attacked by a superior force of fighting men, all armed with strong firesticks. I beg you to listen now to the voice of Renno." Aware of the enmity between the two men, the braves were respectfully silent as they turned to look more closely at Renno.

"Hear me, O warriors of the Seminole," Renno said earnestly, gesturing effectively to convey his meaning. "I ask you to join forces with me, whether you have long fought under your nation's banner or are new to such combat. We need every warrior's strength in overcoming a foe who is strong and shows every confidence of defeating any opponent. We cannot use tactics employed for many years by the warriors who were your forebears. Instead, we must adopt techniques used in Rome many uncounted moons ago by a great general who had the motto 'Divide and conquer.' I propose that we create as much confusion as possible and divide and conquer this foe. Let every man do his duty today, and we shall vanquish the invaders of your land.

"Durati, you must send a few of your best hunters and have them bring back one deer, shot in the head so that it does not bleed too much. Have them bring it back to camp, where they will butcher it over a skin, trying to save as much of the entrails and blood as they can. Quickly—before our enemies arrive!"

Durati motioned toward four of his best men, saying, "You heard Renno. Move fast!"

Renno continued speaking to the rest of the Seminole for several minutes after the hunters left, and his listeners gave him their full attention. The tactics he outlined were bold and imaginative, and he strongly made the point that if every man did what was expected of him, the defenders had an excellent chance of destroying the freebooters.

When Renno finished speaking, an elderly warrior with white hair at the temples spoke up softly. "I have taken part in many councils of war over many years," he said, "but I have seldom heard such words of wisdom as those of Renno. Let us adhere to the rules he has laid down, strive together to accomplish the goals that he describes." A murmur of assent showed the men's agreement before they scattered, each with a specific function in mind.

Since the freebooters would be making their approach in boats, it was essential for the defenders to concentrate their efforts on the waters that lay between the village and the enemy's line of advance. Renno himself commanded a small cadre of sharpshooters with bows. They concealed themselves in the dense vegetation away from the water's edge and the alligators, while other groups took up positions elsewhere along the shore, in accordance with Renno's plan. Still others were held in reserve, ready to move into action on orders from either Renno or Durati.

Included in Renno's group was Quanto, the blacksmith who had been reunited with Venya, who had with him a number of spears reminiscent of weapons he had used in Africa in his youth. He was even more skillful with their use than with a bow.

When all of the Seminole were ready for the coming attack, a stillness settled over them, and the only sounds that could be heard were the occasional piercing cries of the birds that dwelt in the lush vegetation of the swamp.

Finally, after a long wait, Renno's men spotted the first of the freebooters' boats as it came into view, followed slowly by the remainder of the tiny fleet.

Though one of the most difficult feats in battle is patiently holding back an attack until the right moment, the Seminole, hardly neophytes in war, responded to Renno's orders and held their fire. They had been struggling against enemies all their lives, and they understood the necessity of fighting to maintain their independence.

Although tempted to attack as the frail fleet of freebooters' boats inched closer, not one man disobeyed Renno's rule that he personally would begin the attack, and that until then they were to allow the enemy to keep moving closer.

Finally, when the lead boat in the approaching armada was no more than forty feet away, Renno cried out, "Now!" He fired an arrow at the waterline of the leading craft rather than at the occupants. His shot landed only an inch above the surface of the muddy water.

That signal to open fire brought a flight of arrows all aimed at the waterline. Quanto threw a heavy spear that cracked through the thin shell of the boat's exterior and left a gaping hole. A second heavy spear followed, and water poured into the craft.

Concentrating successively on one boat at a time, Renno aimed at points directly above the water line. The Seminole followed his lead expertly, and one by one the craft were disabled.

The hunters, who had returned with the deer and butchered it as Renno had instructed, placed the entrails and blood-soaked skins in a small, leaky boat. At Renno's cry of "Now!" they launched the boat down the river toward the attackers. When it passed the alligators, Renno pierced it with three arrows just above the water line. Quanto also threw a heavy spear that went through one side of the boat and came out the other. The boat, still heading downstream toward the freebooters, slowly started to sink.

As the deer blood and entrails mixed with the water, the alligators along the banks came alive, crawling as fast as they could toward the sinking boat. The entrails and blood were quickly consumed, and the alligators—now thoroughly aroused—swam frenziedly toward the noise created by the freebooters as their craft were slowly sinking.

So far, Renno's strategy was working admirably. The boats were in water four to six feet deep. Rather than let themselves sink and become easy victims for the oncoming alligators, the freebooters were so busy trying to bail their craft that they could not fire at the Seminole. This pleased Renno greatly, for if the enemy had been able to fire, their high-powered muskets would have rendered the defenses of the Indians useless.

Admiral Riley's voice rose to a roar as he instructed his men to save their boats and paddle toward the far side of the river.

The freebooters, seeing the oncoming alligators, desperately sought to carry out the admiral's orders.

The alligators now reached the first sinking boat and began to devour their victims, whose agonized cries could be heard by everyone.

At last, Renno decided the time had come to attack their enemies individually, and he signaled his intention by putting an arrow through one of the paddlers in Admiral Riley's boat.

The defenders joined in Renno's new onslaught, and the freebooters, now paddling for the far shore, were hit hard.

Most of the struggling men made for the far shore. That was exactly what Renno had anticipated. Beckoning to Durati, he spoke to him urgently as a smile broadened on the Seminole's face.

Then Durati disappeared, and soon the men under his command were moving in small units to the rear, from where they could approach the far shore by a less obvious route and surprise their enemies. Their boats of alligator skins were extremely lightweight, each big enough to carry four men. In these, the Seminole put out from several points on shore and made for a point farther upstream. After landing, they launched a furious attack, prepared to fight until they had annihilated the isolated enemy. The attack by the freebooters seemed to have been contained, and for the first time, the Seminole community was no longer in danger. Even Renno was able to relax somewhat. Suddenly, however, he saw movement on a peninsula to his left. As he peered though the screen of bushes, he involuntarily stiffened.

There, standing alone, was Ben Whipple, who was studying his surroundings intently.

All else faded from Renno's mind, and he thanked the manitous for their intervention, saving Whipple to become his personal opponent in a face-to-face combat. Now, at last, he could obtain retribution for the evil that Whipple had done in murdering his father and abducting Emily.

"I am going after Whipple," he told Tobiko, who was still close beside him. "Be sure that no one else approaches that stretch of land, no matter what may happen there. I am summoned by the manitous to meet my destiny. Nothing must stand between me and the fulfillment of my goals."

Not waiting for a reply, he crawled off to a tiny, one-man craft. Paddling it silently, he brought it to the tip of the same peninsula where Whipple had been standing. But as Renno came ashore, the man was now nowhere to be seen.

As Renno walked slowly along the peninsula, Whipple dropped on him from the upper limbs of a tree. Too late, Renno realized that he had fallen victim to one of the oldest of tricks.

Even though surprised, his reflexes automatically responded. As he felt the crushing weight of Whipple's body on his shoulders, he hunched forward and thrust his torso up. This caused Whipple to slide to the ground with a crash, dropping the long-handled knife he had been holding.

He fell in front of Renno, who attacked, only to find that Whipple had a pistol pointed at his head. In Whipple's eyes was a look of venomous triumph.

Without time to think, Renno had only a moment before Whipple would shoot.

With a terrifying scream—the renowned battle cry of the Seneca that caused even the hardiest of men to shudder—he threw himself at the pistol, using all his force and agility, and employing both hands to grasp his foe's wrists he tried to deflect the weapon.

As Renno grabbed for the gun, Whipple grimly squeezed the trigger. The bullet whistled off into the underbrush.

Now, with his weapon unloaded, Whipple attempted to grapple with Renno but was no match for him. Expert all his life at a sport in which every young Seneca competed, Renno had no difficulty in overcoming him and snapping a blow to his head, causing Whipple to lie sprawled dazedly.

At the same moment, Renno became aware of a large bird circling above the treetops nearby. His heart pounded when he recognized the beaked outline of a hawk. Its circles seemed to focus the rays of the sun directly on Whipple, penetrating the Everglades' haze.

Renno was instantly reminded that in his belt he carried the stake from his father's funeral pyre. Drawing it and holding it with both hands, he drove it with all his force into Whipple's heart.

The hawk circled gradually higher and higher until it disappeared from sight.

Admiral Riley's commanding voice caused his men to rally to his side. Meanwhile, Tobiko and Durati led the Seminole braves toward the scene.

Long before the help could arrive, however, the issue was to be settled by Renno, who had quickly made his way to the spot. As both he and the admiral sought the advantage, Riley bore steadily down on his foe, his lips parted in his customary half laugh and half sneer. Already he had suffered an unexpected defeat, and he was determined to put an end to this savage.

Renno, awaiting Riley's moves, was under no illusions. In Riley, he was facing a dangerous opponent, a man schooled in murder, a man who made Ben Whipple seem an amateur in comparison.

Renno was aware of the power of the blade attached to the admiral's arm, and he had respect for its ability to inflict lethal damage. Instinct warned him to keep ample distance from the blade, which could kill with a single swipe.

What Riley could not realize was that Renno carried one invisible weapon that he had not found necessary to employ in his brief, convulsive fight with Whipple. Ordinarily, he carried in the small of his back a sheathed, lightweight, deadly hunting knife that General George Washington had given him after one of his scouting missions for the Continental Army. That weapon, a favorite possession, had been used only in times of great emergency. This was such a time. He reached around and suddenly produced the knife, which glittered in front of him.

Riley halted and looked at his opponent. "Put down the blade!" he ordered. "We fight on equal terms."

"Equal, do you say?" Renno laughed aloud. "I'll throw aside my knife when you discard your vicious blade."

"The blade goes where I go," the admiral said with even a tinge of regret in his voice.

"In that case," Renno answered, "I'll continue to use my knife."

Stealthily, with the grace and lightness of foot of a dancer, Riley began to advance, step by step.

Delicately but firmly, Renno retreated. Each backward step was solidly placed, and he took no chances that he would stumble or lose his balance, because he knew that if he was caught off guard his opponent would leap forward and sever his head with a single stroke of the deadly blade.

Riley kept trying to inch closer, but Renno kept his distance successfully.

If he moved close enough to use his own blade, he would be placing himself in extreme jeopardy. Somehow, he had to strike from a distance while holding the enemy at bay—namely, by throwing the knife, a feat far easier said than done.

Renno knew he would have only one opportunity to throw the knife. He retreated with exaggerated slowness, one step at a time, watching for any possible opening. He kept testing the weight of the knife, and he assumed that he could throw it with accuracy. Beyond that, the issue was in the hands of the gods.

Riley, conscious of the knife gleaming in his foe's hand, kept looking for an opening that would enable him to suddenly rush forward, taking the initiative to end the struggle with a single swipe. He concentrated so completely on the knife that he failed to watch his footing, and inadvertently he stumbled over a hidden root.

Afraid of losing his balance, he raised both arms instinctively. As he did so, his arm with the curved blade banged into a scrub pine directly behind him. In a mishap that would have been impossible to forecast, he banged his elbow into the tree with such force that tears came to his eyes. He stumbled, and as he fell to one knee, the blade cut deeply into his other arm. Angry and disgusted, he tried to pull away, but the elbow was still painful and did not respond properly. Blood began to flow freely, and to his horror Riley realized he had wounded himself severely.

Rather than fall captive to this pale-skinned Indian, he resolved to do away with himself instantly, and without hesitation deliberately slashed the artery in his neck.

Renno watched in openmouthed amazement at the strange ways the gods had acted in inflicting punishment on those lacking in righteousness. Soon Riley lay in a pool of blood at his feet.

The fight to the finish was ended.

However, the battle was not yet finished. Renno could see activity in the distance, where twenty or more warriors were locked in combat with at least as many freebooters. The advantage, he saw, was all in favor of the white men, whose firearms were far more lethal than the arrows the Indians possessed. What made the battle critical was that the fighting had shifted to a spot near a large number of women. They had been watching the battle. Renno saw the women there, and he was galvanized into immediate action when he spotted Emily, who was protected by the magical white cloak that he had given her.

In spite of the relative safety offered her by the

cloak, however, Renno wanted to take no needless risks. Bullets and arrows were flying, and he knew that even the gods could not offer absolute shelter in the confusion and heat of battle.

Wasting no time, he paddled his little craft toward her, almost overcome by a feeling of desperate helplessness.

Rallying steadily under Durati, the Seminole were holding their own and refusing to retreat despite the concentrated enemy fire. However, within an instant the odds changed.

An enemy bullet smashed into Durati's chest, sending him sprawling to the ground. The Seminole, without a leader, quickly started to fall back.

Emily crept forward, keeping low to avoid the enemy's fire. When she reached Durati, she stopped and took his head into her arms. Durati, who had been trying to crawl, was now effectively halted. Now none of his followers dared leave the field while he and Emily were exposed in the front ranks.

Renno's worry over the fate of his comrades was mixed with astonishment at Emily's courage. He paddled harder, throwing all his energy into each stroke. His little craft shot forward, and when it pulled up onto the beach, he tumbled out and raced forward. Crawling, running, and dodging, he reached the front ranks a few feet from Emily. She sat in an exposed position, holding Durati's head in her lap, seemingly oblivious to the bullets and arrows singing through the air. She was as poised as a queen, straight-backed and secure. As she saw Renno approach, she motioned him to keep quiet and not to let the Seminole chief know that he was there.

He responded by urging the Seminole braves to hold their ground and to move forward again. Having retrieved his bow and arrows, he quickly took aim and shot arrows continuously at the foes who were hiding in the thick underbrush.

His example had a steadying effect, and the Indians started to advance again. One by one, the warriors joined in his counterattack, and as they began to give as good as they were receiving, their own panic subsided, and the worst of the crisis was ended.

Once again able to devote attention to Emily, Renno saw her clasping the inert body of Durati close as she spoke to him.

In the din of battle, amid the shots, the screams of the wounded, and the Seminole's shrill war cries in defiance of their foes, he could just make out the sense of what was being said.

In a harsh, hoarse voice, Durati seemed to be assuring Emily of his love for her. Emily was responding that she loved him alone.

Hearing those words was a shock to Renno, who had no conception of what might have occurred between them during their weeks together after Durati had rescued Emily from Whipple. For all he knew, they had been lovers, and this scene might confirm such a relationship.

But Renno was more sensible than to worry about what might have been between Emily and another man. It truly was enough to know that he loved her and that she loved him. That meant he must trust her beyond all reasonable doubt, having complete faith in her loyalty to him, regardless of the circumstances. If he failed to show his trust, he did not love her. This was his creed—and now was the time to prove it.

He looked at her tenderly, love gleaming in his eyes as he heard her speak soothingly to the dying Durati.

Emily met Renno's gaze, and in that moment, he knew he had never seen such love, such tenderness expressed by one person toward another. With all her heart and all her soul she was telling him to trust her, to make no fuss, and to let her give comfort to Durati during his last moments on earth.

He answered her in the only way he knew, by responding with complete, trusting love expressed without qualification.

A single look at Durati was enough to convince Renno that the Seminole leader was not long for this world. His eyes were glazed, and he had great difficulty in sucking in enough air to remain alive. And in these final moments he was dependent upon Emily to offer the solace and love that he craved. It was equally plain to Renno that he was entitled to all the comfort that could be given by the woman he loved in his own way, who quite evidently could forgive him for the mistreatment he had allowed her to undergo.

Emily and Renno continued to gaze steadily at each other, and in this moment of supreme crisis, they were united as never before. Their love was firm and sure, Renno knew, meeting the test, and neither of them faltered as Durati breathed his last.

Emily laid his head gently on the ground and gestured to Renno that the end had come. Only in that moment did Renno realize the extent to which the gods had taken charge while he and Emily were feeling their way toward their own future.

With the admiral missing, the freebooters were without a leader, and their pace slackened. Meanwhile, Quanto had unexpectedly stepped into the breach for the Indian defenders.

Unaccustomed to the methods of fighting practiced by white settlers, Quanto reverted to the tribal practices of Africa, where a warrior proved himself in battle by working himself into a fever pitch and maintaining a level of combat in which he surpassed normal levels of conscious effort.

Beginning slowly and exercising no care for his own welfare, the warrior hurled spear after spear at the foe, concealing himself as best he could behind the thick tropical foliage and letting fly whenever he saw an enemy crouching in the brush.

Quanto's comrades followed his example, sending countless arrows in the direction of their foes.

Gradually the pace of battle increased, and the Indians' success impelled them to make still greater efforts. They called on their gods for help, and as they raised their voices, they increased the pace of their shooting and spear-throwing. They were beginning to enjoy the experience. For every warrior they lost, they managed to incapacitate at least three of the enemy.

The freebooters, without the admiral, now were foundering. Instead of maintaining their own drive in order to counter the Indians' attack, they continued to falter. As they did, they lost the sense of cohesion, so essential in battle.

Though hardly more than a savage, Quanto was endowed with an instinct for battle that helped him now in this moment of crisis. He knew that he and his comrades must strike hard and split the buccaneers' forces apart before they could rally and hit back.

Summoning his full strength, he stood erect and shouted in his native dialect, calling on the gods of his ancestors to assist in ridding the earth of the enemies who would rob the Seminole of their homes and drive them into the inhospitable wilderness.

Quanto's enemies, like the Seminole, could not understand one word he was shouting, but the Indians were encouraged, while the freebooters were dismayed by the loud curses he was directing at them.

Acting like a man in a dream, a leader convinced of his immortality, Quanto moved into the open, and completely ignoring his safety, he advanced toward the enemy as he called curses down on their heads. Only the iron resistance of the admiral could have withstood the Indians' advance.

The battle ended abruptly. The ranks of the defenders broke, and the Indians swarmed forward, using their hatchets now instead of their arrows in a final burst of energy that ended the struggle on a bloody but triumphant note. Incredibly, the Indians, using strange and unusual tactics, had defeated a large party of armed white men who could employ modern means of war.

The last remnants of the freebooter force had been compelled to flee, leaving their dead and wounded. Making their way with great difficulty through the swampy forests, they started on their long, difficult journey back to the coast. With their power destroyed for all time by the courage of the Seminole, assisted by Renno and his comrades, they never again would be a major force in America.

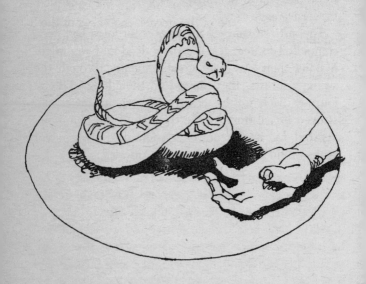

Chapter VIII

The bodies of the freebooters were burned in a common pyre with the Seminole warriors who had died in the battle.

That night, the women of the tribe prepared a simple though substantial banquet, after which the tribe went into solemn session. Each individual, male and female alike, was allowed to vote on the selection of a new tribal chief to succeed Durati. According to the custom of the tribe, valor was the principal criterion. As a consequence of his extreme gallantry in battle, Quanto, one of the newest members of the Seminole, was unanimously elected. Two elders were elected as his deputies; their function was to remind him of the nation's customs in his various duties.

And so it happened that Venya, who only days earlier had been a slave and a fugitive, became the first lady of the Seminole. Her lack of familiarity with their language was overcome by having several maidens assigned to her as translators. They easily were able to convey to her the meaning of Seminole words and expressions, and she responded with a quick perception of the significance in each case.

Venya, who had listened intently to stories related by other women, founded a new custom almost as soon as her husband was chosen. She announced that henceforth two women would be assigned to serve as her housemaids, and she selected none other than Ladira and Nalata. With their own plans in ruins after the death of Durati, they were reduced to servitude with nothing to which to look forward but days of bleak despair.

Loyal to Renno, Venya merely smiled when she heard of the two women's reaction to their plight but made no reply. In months to come, she would give them ample reason to regret their harsh treatment of Emily.

That night, Emily was safely ensconced in an inner room of the guest cottage that Renno occupied. The building was known as a chickee, consisting of a series of rooms thatched with large cabbage palms. Mostly of pole construction, their roofs hung down to within four feet of the ground. Breezes thus kept the dwellings well ventilated, since in the absence of walls only the poles holding up the roofs could interfere with the movement of air.

Taking no chances, Renno had assigned Tobiko to guard the house. He was making certain that nothing further threatened Emily again until they left the land of the Seminole.

He gathered an armful of fresh young boughs and arranged them into a bed. Exhausted after the battle and the celebratory banquet, he soon fell asleep. In a dream, he heard someone calling his name from a great distance, and he found himself deep in an endless grove of trees. They were not, however, like the foliage he had found in the Everglades. These were the trees of the North, sturdy oaks and elms, cedars, maples, and pines. Hearing a voice calling to him, he began to follow it, beating his way silently through the thick undergrowth. At last he came to the near bank of a river, and he knew at once that this was the Great River he had heard about from his childhood. The current was gentle, but he realized that he would be unable to swim to the far bank, because it was not yet time for him to join his ancestors. He looked up and down both banks, seeing nobody, but again he heard his name being called, and at last he made out his father.

Ghonkaba was changed for the better. The front of his shirt was no longer smeared with blood, and his

wet scalp lock suggested that he had been swimming. He looked fresh and alert as he stood on the
far bank, his arms folded, a happy smile on his face.

"Greetings, my son!" he called. "I summoned you
here even before I went on to meet those who await
me. I have crossed the river at last, thanks to your
great skill. You have killed the man responsible for
my death. And you have freed me to enjoy eternity
in this land where I shall reside for all time."

Renno felt as though a great weight had been
lifted from him. At last he could go on with his life.

"At an appropriate time in the years ahead, I shall
welcome you to this land of your ancestors, as you
deserve to be welcomed," Ghonkaba said. "I am
proud to stand here as your father, and I shall take
pride for all time that you are my son."

Renno replied quietly, "I did my duty as I saw it,
my father. I do not deserve special praise or rewards."

"I must tell you something in the greatest of confidence, my son. Now that you and Emily have been
reunited, you will begin to travel north to your home
in the land of the Cherokee. You will have many
temptations, many reasons to tarry on the journey.
Do not tarry!"

Renno was puzzled. "What do you mean?" he
asked.

"You will find many reasons for taking your time
on your northward journey," Ghonkaba told him.
"You will believe you have cause, as will Emily, for
delaying, for staying here or staying there, and letting time ease past. I beg you, do not do it! Use all

possible dispatch and return as rapidly as you can to your home in the land of the Cherokee."

Renno was disturbed by the feeling of urgency that his father conveyed. "Why must we rush?" he demanded. "What is wrong?"

Even as he spoke, the figure of his father began to fade, and the landscape on the far side of the Great River began to grow indistinct.

Renno was frantic; he was being cut off before his questions were properly answered. "Wait!" he cried. "Don't go yet! Answer me first. Why is it necessary that we hurry back to the land of the Cherokee?"

But the figure continued to fade, and soon the entire land on the far side of the river became an indistinct blur.

Renno was sadly aware that the conversation was at an end and that no matter how he tried, his questions would not be answered. A veil was drawn deliberately between his world and the world in which Ghonkaba now lived. His father had hinted at the urgency, and that had to be enough to impel him to move with rapidity. He could ask no more and find out no more.

Soon Renno awoke with a jolt. He was alone in his house, and he was suddenly very cold. He was gratified that his father finally had been admitted to the land of his ancestors where he belonged, but at the same time, the warning remained with him. For reasons that he could not understand and that might just now be developing, he was needed at home, hundreds of miles away. All he knew was that he would be wise to heed the words of his father and do what had been recommended. He looked at the sky, impatient for the morning to come so that he could begin his journey.

Anxious to keep faith with his father, Renno made ready to leave with Emily and Tobiko soon after dawn. They carried supplies provided by the Seminole, and Renno again had folded his cape so he could wear it at his waist, the weather being so hot that he could not wear it around his shoulders. A large party of Seminole, led by Quanto and Venya, accompanied them to the relative safety of dry land several miles from the town, and there they parted company.

Emily was dressed in Indian attire, Renno having explained that the journey would be easier for her if it appeared that she, too, was an Indian. She carried a rifle, which she assured him she was fully prepared to use.

Tobiko led them north by an inland route not far west of the Atlantic. This way they avoided Spanish communities directly on the coast. They could travel far more rapidly and without fear of being halted unnecessarily. Emily, hardened by her many weeks of living as a Seminole, kept up the pace set by Tobiko; at no time did she falter or slow their progress.

Averaging almost twenty-five miles a day as they were, after ten days Renno began to wonder how soon they would leave Florida and reach the southern border of the United States.

Late one afternoon, Tobiko called to Renno and

pointed. There, directly in their path, the wilderness
thinned out to a vast plain bordering a large river
that flowed into the Atlantic. On the riverbank were
several score of buffalo. The animals were in a traveling formation; that is, they were surrounded by young
bulls who acted as sentries. Cows were shepherding
their calves to the bank, escorting them past silent
rows of warrior bulls. Meantime, the older animals,
bulls and cows alike, rested on the grass, stretching
out during this hour of respite. Renno and Tobiko
exchanged a glance, and in that moment made a
decision that greatly affected their immediate future.
They were in a great hurry, it was true, but neither
could resist the temptation of fresh meat.

Instructing Emily to remain where she stood, Renno
then started forward with Tobiko, after they had
made certain that their weapons were loaded and
ready for immediate use. They took care to stay
upwind at all times, so no human smells would be
carried on the wind toward the herd and warn the
buffalo to scatter.

Never before had Emily hunted buffalo in the
Indian manner, and she found the occasion exciting
in the extreme. The settlers' way was to attack from a
distance, shooting at the targets from as far away as a
rifle could be fired accurately. The Indian method
was much more direct: warriors crept up on the
unsuspecting animals, and selecting a target, fired at
it from very close range.

Communicating with sign language, Renno told
Tobiko that he would like to be the one to kill the
buffalo, but he yielded to his friend the honor of

selecting the right animal. Tobiko chose a sturdy and
heavy young bull not yet of age. It appeared to be
about a year and a half old, so the meat would not be
too tough for eating. When they reached a point
some thirty feet from the rear of the animal, Renno
stepped forward boldly, and after taking several strides,
he raised his rifle to his shoulder, peered down the
barrel, and squeezed the trigger.

The shot was good, and the animal dropped to the
ground almost immediately. A single bullet to the
head had killed it instantly. As it collapsed, first
falling to its knees and then to the ground, the entire
herd sprang to life. An old cow gave the signal,
trumpeting loudly, and soon the herd was in flight.

How the animals managed to arrange themselves
in a warlike formation was something that no human
being had ever been able to figure out. The active
young bulls—the warriors of the tribe—gathered on
the outside rims, and directly inside them came the
equally vigorous and active young cows. The elders
of the tribe and the younger ones all crowded into
the center, protected by two layers of guardians.
They began to pick up speed instantly and soon were
thundering away from the river. To Emily, it was a
frightening sight: tens of thousands of pounds of buffalo on the move.

As the herd thundered toward where Emily was
standing alone, she was frozen with fear, expecting
that she might be trampled. She thus remained im-
mobile, unable to move as the huge animals, their
nostrils flaring, their tiny eyes wild, raced in her
direction, veering away only at the last moment. A

collision appeared inevitable again and again, but it always was averted.

The stench was overpowering. The dust kicked up by the frightened beasts caused Emily to cough repeatedly. Breathing became extremely difficult.

Suddenly the ordeal ended. The guards at the rear of the thundering herd were disappearing from sight, and quiet descended. Only then was she able to run to Renno's side. He clasped her reassuringly in his arms.

Tobiko, who had put his rifle on the ground, reached for it hastily as he heard the hoot of an owl. All three turned toward the sand dune where the sound seemed to be coming from. On the dune were the three trees Renno had described to Rusog when they had parted.

Renno shook his head and held up a hand to prevent Tobiko from shooting. He imitated the cry of an owl, then grinned broadly.

To the astonishment of Emily, Rusog immediately appeared at the crest of the dune and came toward them at a loping walk. He and Renno embraced like brothers, and then, after turning to Emily, he also embraced her.

"I have used those palm trees well for food and water," Rusog said, "and I had intended to wait until tomorrow. If you had not appeared by then I would have started my homeward journey alone."

"My mission required longer than I hoped," Renno replied, "but I succeeded, as you can see from Emily's presence, so all is well."

He explained to an amazed Rusog how he had

found the white buffalo that he had been directed to slay, and how the cape made from its hide had served him well in combat.

Together they butchered the slain buffalo and put the meat over a large fire to smoke. Then, while they ate their fill of buffalo steak, they informed each other of their respective developments. The conversation then turned to Rusog's problems in the State of Franklin.

"I am certain in my own mind," Emily said, "that Ben Whipple was responsible in some way for the attack on my father. When he was a captive of the Seminole, they took away all his belongings, and they gave me these."

Quickly she unbraided her hair and took from it two gold coins, which she handed to Renno.

Turning the coins over in his hand, Renno said, "We must keep these under close watch until we get to Knoxville. I do not know for certain, but I think they should be valuable evidence to prove that Whipple was guilty and that Rusog is innocent."

"I have guarded them as I have guarded my own life during the entire time I was with the Seminole," Emily assured him, "and I shall keep them until I hand them to my father."

Their journey was delayed while they continued to smoke the buffalo meat. Not until the following morning did Renno declare that the time had come to resume their walk. Their speed in the wilderness was now much enhanced by the fact that they no longer needed to stop and hunt for meat.

After they had crossed a large river on a makeshift

raft that Rusog and Tobiko hastily made, they were
safely within territory that was very familiar to Tobiko.
With him in the lead, they made steady, rapid progress as they worked their way through the thick
wilderness of pine trees. Tobiko used many shortcuts
as he guided them toward the main town of the Ais.
Almost immediately the drums of the Ais began to
speak, announcing their presence in the neighborhood. Tobiko, listening closely, became increasingly
worried but kept his concerns to himself.

Renno, who became conscious of his disturbance,
finally spoke that evening after their customary supper of smoked buffalo meat. "What is wrong, my
brother?" he asked.

Tobiko frowned, his normally impassive face lined
with worry. "I am not sure," he said. "The messages
have identified me as a member of this party, and
they talked back and forth about my being just in
time for the sad ending. What it is that is sad and
what it is that is ending, I do not know, but I do not
like the sound of the message."

Not until the following noon hour was the situation
clarified. Then a group arrived from the town, including the elderly sachem, the chief medicine man,
and a slender, worried-looking young woman named
Gilela. After Tobiko proudly presented her as his
wife, he and she retreated to hold a private conversation. Later, Tobiko went to Renno, his face long. "I
have news that is bad—very bad," he said. "My
young son, Bentho, has been attacked by evil spirits.
It seems they may kill him before a way is found to
drive the spirits elsewhere. It appears that I have

returned home after many months just in time to watch my son die."

Renno exchanged a quick glance with Emily and knew they were of one mind. Both of them believed that the Indian idea of evil spirits was rooted in superstition. Although the gods indeed existed and performed many feats of valor for the good of man, no one had ever been able to prove that the gods caused evil or that they were deliberately trying to punish individuals, particularly the innocent who had no part in actions contrary to the will of the gods. A small boy therefore could not be held responsible for himself, much less for what his parents had done.

"Let us withhold judgment," Renno advised, "until we have seen the child with our own eyes and have determined his condition with our own senses."

Remembering the many miracles that he had performed in the past, Tobiko was satisfied, though Gilela remained disconsolate.

When they arrived in the town, they went straight to the house of Tobiko, a large dwelling, suitable for the subchief of the tribe. In one room a half-dozen medicine men were filling the air with burning herbs that gave off a foul smell. In the middle of the room on a bed of pine boughs was little Bentho, a boy of about ten years who looked like a miniature version of his father. He was pale and evidently suffering great pain.

As Renno, Tobiko, and Rusog watched, Emily took charge at once, clearing out the noxious fumes. She directed the medicine men to leave the hut, and when they hesitated, she turned to Tobiko, who

ordered them to withdraw. Then she went to the
child, and removing the blankets, she bent close to
him, beckoning to Renno to join her.

"Look there," she said, pointing. On the shin of
his left leg a bruise had become badly infected. It
was filled with pus. The entire leg was swollen to
nearly three times its normal size. The pain was
dreadful, and the child suffered in silence, his face
pale, his teeth clenched together to prevent crying
out aloud. He was doing his best to maintain a phleg-
matic Indian attitude, but the effort was almost too
great for him.

Emily knew what had to be done, and using the
common language that Renno had found useful in
communicating with Tobiko, she spoke loudly in the
accents of one familiar enough with Indians to know
how to handle them.

"Bad medicine has been at work here," she declared firmly. "But we can control it with stronger,
good medicine that will cure the child. First, let a
fire be lighted in the nearest pit, and let cooking
stones be added to it, so that they may gather warmth.
Let it be done quickly."

Under her direction, and with Renno and Rusog
assisting, a large fire was lighted, and stone cooking
blocks were added to the fire. As soon as they became hot, she ordered them removed and placed a
double length of blanket on the boy's infected leg to
avoid needless blistering. Then, using tongs, she
took the cooking blocks and put them around the
infection. The heat was so great that the child cried
and squirmed in an attempt to get away. Emily

urged Tobiko to hold his son firmly and prevent him from dislodging the blocks. While the blocks heated the leg, drawing the infection, she took Renno's hunting knife and plunged it into the fire, holding it there until the blade became red hot. She removed it, let it cool, and then murmured to Tobiko, "Hold him firmly. And no matter what happens, do not allow him to pull away!"

To the horror of those who watched, she plunged the knife into the infection. From a single slash, blood and pus began to spurt. Bentho screamed. Then, where the pus seemed thickest, she cut a cross mark in the opposite direction. When the operation was finished, she added more hot cooking blocks.

Now Bentho grew quieter and lay very still. Emily spoke soothingly to the frightened child, and Tobiko, faithful to his trust and believing in the powers she exerted, translated for Bentho and for the wide-eyed Gilela. Renno and Rusog also did their best to offer encouragement.

Emily handed the knife to Renno. "Here," she said, "heat the blade and scrub it well before you put this knife back into your belt. Make sure that nothing remains on it."

Eventually, the stones were removed and the cloth was lifted. The leg had been reduced in size until it was only slightly larger than normal, and the puffiness was largely dissipated.

Emily insisted on washing off the wound, and then, after putting on a poultice of wet herbs, she covered it with wet moss and she again added hot stones.

By now, Bentho was becoming sleepy, and as the pain subsided, he was ready to doze. Emily made him as comfortable as she could. Then, immobilizing the leg so that he could not move it, she left him to drift off to sleep. She smiled at Gilela and said to Tobiko, "You may tell your wife that her worries are at an end. The infection is gradually leaving your son. When he awakens, he will be recovered."

Gilela, her eyes filled with tears, nodded dumbly, aware that this white woman possessed magic far more potent than that of their own medicine men.

Later than night, when Emily and Renno were alone, she unburdened herself. "I sometimes wonder," she said, "how Indians have managed to live in an atmosphere in which superstition plays such a large role. They seem to be helpless in the face of such problems."

"They do what they can," Renno replied. "Only the strongest and the bravest survive. The others die out, and as one generation succeeds another, only those who have the stamina to overcome the various ailments live to see the next day."

She nodded, deeply impressed by his argument. Now, for the first time, she knew how it happened that the Indians grew stronger generation by generation, instead of succumbing.

The following morning Bentho was much stronger. His leg was almost normal as the infection continued to drain. He was well on the road to recovery.

Gilela, almost overcome by emotion, was ready to prostrate herself before Emily. Even the medicine

men bowed from the waist when they were admitted
to Emily's presence.

Tobiko had his own interpretation of what had
happened. "I was faithful to Renno in all things," he
said, "and the gods who watch over him have rewarded me in their own way. They have saved the
life of my son, and I am free of the curse of evil."

Renno saw no need to linger any longer in the
land of the Ais. They had performed a great deed for
Tobiko and his family, and the time had now come to
push onward to the land of the Cherokee. Foremost
in Renno's mind was the warning he had received
from his father. He had no idea why time was important, but he was anxious to fulfill his instructions as
best he could.

His farewell with Tobiko was far more difficult
than either of them had expected. They had been
through many harrowing experiences together, and
the bonds they had formed were deep and firm.
Both had to rely on their stern Indian heritage so
that neither showed emotion when the moment came
to go their separate ways.

Their faces drained of all expression, they raised
their left arms in formal salute. Their eyes met, and
for an instant both of them wavered, but they recovered their poise at the same moment, and no expression flickered on either face.

At last Tobiko broke the spell. He reached down
and removed from his right wrist a leather band
made of the outer skin of a buffalo. It was firm and
hard, made of the toughest outer skin, and it served
as a perfect wrist-guard. Renno slipped it on grate-

fully, aware that it was one possession that meant
more to Tobiko than almost any other. He was giving
up an article of great value to him out of friendship
for the Seneca, who could ask no more of any man.

Shortly thereafter the party started out again north
through the wilderness, with Renno in the lead and
Rusog bringing up the rear. They made excellent
time, never stopping and never, so it seemed, defer-
ring in any way to Emily. She was expected to keep
up the pace, without complaint, and this she did
after the manner of one born and bred an Indian.
Renno was very proud of her, but Indian style, he
said nothing, letting his praise be taken for granted.

At noon they stopped for a light meal of smoked
buffalo meat and water from a pond. They ate rapidly, intending to take to the road again as quickly as
possible.

Content with her lot in life and glad of the opportunity to sit for a short time, Emily was looking down
at the water when suddenly she froze. A brown
snake about eighteen inches in length had emerged
from the water and headed straight for Renno, who
was seated nearer the pond. It was drawing back its
head to strike, two deadly fangs protruding from its
narrow mouth.

The action that followed was so swift that even
later, when they tried to reconstruct the events of
the moment, it was not easy to follow. When Renno
belatedly became aware of the existence of the snake,
he drew his knife in a single, swift motion, and
slashed at it, removing the head from the rest of the
body.

He acted too late, however, to save himself from being struck. Emily, lacking the poise of the native Indian, raised a hand to her mouth to prevent herself from gasping aloud in dismay when she saw the head of the snake with its fangs still embedded in Renno's wrist.

Renno was smiling, however, as was Rusog, and when the truth dawned on Emily, she was so relieved that she felt weak. The fangs of the deadly water moccasin had just partly penetrated Tobiko's leather wristlet that Renno was wearing for the first time. The band had saved his life.

Thinking about the incident later that afternoon, Emily had good cause to ponder on the means the gods used to protect those who believed in them. Tobiko had offered Renno one of the few objects of value that he possessed as a means of expressing thanks for all that had been done for him, and that object in turn had saved Renno's life.

In midafternoon the steady beat of the drums of the Ais stopped following the travelers, and it was not long before they had reached the wilderness of Georgia, where they heard deeper, more ominous drums. These were the drums of the Yamasee, by far the largest and most powerful of the tribes that dominated the unsettled part of southern Georgia. Renno and Rusog knew they were being described in detail, with particular attention being paid to their war paint, but they paid no attention. Without hesitating, they continued stolidly on, but Emily, sensitive to their moods, noticed a new caution or sense of urgency awakened in them.

The two warriors did not speak, but Emily realized that something unusual was in the wind when they appeared satisfied as they stopped for the night at the crest of a hill that rose beside a brook they were about to cross. There they both attended to their weapons before they ate, lit no fires, and seemed to be listening intently for alien sounds even as they consumed their dried buffalo meat.

Finally she could tolerate the suspense no longer. "What is wrong?" she asked.

"The Yamasee," Renno replied calmly, "are curious about us. They are wondering why—according to the best of our ability to read their signals—a warrior of the Seneca and a brave of the Cherokee are passing through their territory with a comely woman who could be a member of either nation. I congratulate you on the excellence of your disguise."

A trifle impatiently, she waved aside the intended compliment. "What are they doing to relieve their curiosity?" she demanded.

Renno and his brother-in-law exchanged a glance, and Rusog actually giggled.

"They will do what virtually any tribe in America would do under the circumstances," Renno said lightly. "They will attack when night comes. If there are survivors among us, we will be questioned. If there are no survivors, the attack will have taken care of the matter. Finish your supper. We have plenty of time left before we will be called on to entertain visitors." He glanced up at the sky, which was just beginning to grow dark.

"I had enough difficulty when I was a prisoner of the Seminole," she replied tartly. "I know nothing about the Yamasee, but I have no intention of becoming their prisoner too."

Rusog looked stunned and shook his head violently.

Renno, however, remained calm. "I give you my word," he said, "we have no intention of losing you, even for a short period of time, to the Yamasee or to anyone else. Never fear, we will have some surprises in store for them when they arrive here." He helped himself to more buffalo meat.

He seemed unconcerned, as did Rusog.

Finally, as it grew dark, the two warriors roused themselves to action. They took arrows from their sheaths and tested them, though they paid virtually no attention to their rifles. At last Renno seemed to remember Emily's presence. "No matter what may happen," he instructed her, "do not fire your rifle unless I have fired mine."

After a few minutes had passed, Renno placed one ear to the ground and listened intently. He sat up and chuckled aloud. "Now!" he said, and notched an arrow into his long bow.

Rusog did the same.

"Hide yourself in the tall grass," Renno told Emily. "Make no move and say nothing that will let the enemy know you are even present."

Emily stretched out in the knee-high grass, her rifle within easy reach.

Renno inspected her critically. "Pull your left leg

in a few inches closer to your body," he directed. "That's right; now you cannot be seen. Just remember, do not fire unless I give the word. And no matter what happens, do not give away your presence."

To give her additional protection, he placed the white buffalo cape over her.

In essence, Renno's plan was very simple. He intended to allow the Yamasee to walk into their own trap.

One of the Yamasee appeared, tall and dark, with a deep scowl creasing his face. He advanced cautiously into the open, clutching a British flintlock that had been used by the redcoats during the earlier phases of the American Revolution. The Yamasee apparently were using such weapons in preference to the bows of their ancestors. This Yamasee rapidly learned the difference between the two types of weapons.

In the tall grass, Renno, invisible to the man, nocked an arrow into his bow and, pulling it taut, released it with a sudden twang. The weapon was true to its mark and found its target instantly. The Yamasee brave raised his hands in protest and in sudden realization that he had been trapped. He dropped to the grass and died without a sound.

That was only the beginning.

In the moments that followed, three other Yamasee warriors appeared from the same direction. One was looking for his fallen comrade, while the others searched for some sign of the hidden enemy.

Rusog was waiting for them and greeted them with a well-placed shot, splitting the air with an arrow that found its mark in the upper chest of one of the attackers.

By this time, Renno was ready to shoot again and brought down yet another warrior with an arrow that landed in the right shoulder of the Yamasee and incapacitated him for further combat.

It was Rusog's turn to fire again, and Emily watched in wonder as he, too, hit the last remaining Yamasee with an arrow that drew a howl of pain from its victim.

Even now, however, the battle was not yet ended. Renno raised a hand in warning, then held firm as two more Yamasee appeared on the scene. He and Rusog, abandoning concealment, shot simultaneously, killing one and wounding the other.

On their feet now, Renno and Rusog were moving forward with impunity, their long knives glistening in their hands. Emily had to shut her eyes and avert her face as they went about the last, grisly ritual of having won a battle. They were busy scalping their dead foes, while the surviving Yamasee fled as best they could from the field. Not yet enough of an Indian to be able to watch this grim process, she realized a distance still separated her from the Seneca she intended to marry.

Chapter IX

Knoxville, capital of the State of Franklin, had long since settled down for the night, and it was very quiet in the small frontier community surrounded by endless acres of wilderness. At the fort, the militiamen who had come on duty at midnight yawned and sipped hot coffee as they peered out from the

town, across the bend in the nearby river. Instinctively they spoke in low tones.

Only in the private dining room at the rear of the
Mermaid Tavern was any sign of life to be found.
There, three sergeants and two corporals, all just
relieved after eight hours on duty at the fort, had
gathered by prearrangement for a glass of beer. They
were served by Ted Thomas, the burly young propri-
etor, who confined himself to a single remark. "Be
patient," he said, "Al will be along any minute."

The militiamen nodded, but no one spoke. They
and young Thomas shared a common background: all
had been born on the western frontier, and all had
grown up in the Tennessee country, where the State
of Franklin recently had been founded. They had
attended school together for a few years, and since
that time they had grown up in a rougher school,
where they suffered hardships, fought innumerable
Indians, and learned the primary law of subsistence
here—that every man had to stand on his own feet if
he hoped to survive.

A few minutes later, Lieutenant Al Thomas came
into the room holding a full schooner of beer in one
hand. He looked remarkably like his brother, Ted,
except that he was a shade thinner and was better-
muscled. He had the same quick energy, the same
insolent stare, the same air of independence that
marked almost everyone who had been born in this
free frontier world.

The enlisted men started to rise, but the lieutenant hastily waved them back to their seats. "As you
were, fellas," he said. "Hellfire! I was just promoted

to my new rank about a month ago. Give me time to get used to it before you start paying me military honors." He laughed heartily at his joke, then drained his glass of beer and wiped his mouth on the back of his woolen sleeve. "Alley-oop, Ted," he called, and threw the empty mug. His brother caught it, grinned, and went off to refill it.

Lieutenant Thomas crashed into a vacant chair at the table. "I asked you lads to meet me here to-night," he said, leaning forward, his elbows on the table, "because we have so much in common. Like me, you're junior leaders of the militia. You were born in this country, and you know the real story of the region, as nobody else on earth knows it. We all have the same point of view, and we all exert the same influence."

The others nodded as they listened. Al Thomas had been accepted as a natural leader by the group, and the younger men in Knoxville had grown accustomed to following his orders.

"Governor Sevier and Colonel Johnson," he said, "have won themselves a national name by the way they've fought Indians over the years, and we can't take that away from them. But I called this meeting tonight because they're going soft. As they've grown older and have acquired new positions with greater prestige, they've taken it easy. They don't have the same attitude that they used to display when they were younger. Once upon a time, they both seemed to believe in the motto that we believe in—that the only good Indian is a dead Indian. Now they've made deals with everybody from the Seneca of New

York to the Cherokee of western Tennessee. In fact, Colonel Johnson's daughter is actually engaged to an Indian. That's something they wouldn't have tolerated for a minute when they were young. The time has come for us to assert ourselves as the future leaders of this state and to return Franklin to the purity this land had when our fathers arrived here, all of them standing together to fight for the values of civilization."

The others stirred in their chairs and cheered. "It's about time that you took this attitude, Al," one muttered. "Somebody has to stop this damned collaboration with the uncivilized, no-good louts!"

Ted Thomas, who had been listening in the background, came forward and crashed a thick fist on the table. "What we're proposing is a simple return to basics. It should go something like this: Judge Hill postponed the trial of the Cherokee, Rusog, but months have passed and no trial has been held. We should make our first demand that the trial be held at once, and that the guilty be punished. Even though Johnson's daughter is going to marry Renno of the Seneca, the colonel can't very well object when he himself was attacked and robbed."

"As a symbol, the trial is vitally important," Al Thomas put in. "And we've got to demand that justice be done. Remember, we fought for justice," he added forcibly, ignoring the irony that he and the other men were all too young to have taken part in the American War of Independence. "We won, and now that we're a free country, we can't stand aside and let ourselves be robbed of what's rightfully ours."

"Just look at the thousands of acres to the west of us that the Cherokee claim is their land," Ted agreed. "Who gave them the right to demand such land as their very own? Who said that some of the finest hunting and fishing land in all of America is exclusively theirs or that the soil that's so rich anything will grow on it belongs only to them? Show me one agreement on paper that cedes them that land. I tell you, lads, we've got to stand up for our own, or the Indian lovers will destroy us and will turn every inch of property back to the scalp-takers!"

The scene at the tavern was far from unique. While soldiers in Knoxville were fretting over the delays in bringing Rusog to justice, the passage of time was having an identical effect on young warriors of the Indian nations that lay to the west. In the land of the Cherokee unrest prevailed, caused likewise by the postponement of the trial. Once again, young fighting men were responsible for the unrest. They had not taken part in any joint enterprises against the British or their Indian allies during the war, and they had never fought side by side with the American colonists. All they knew was that Rusog, the grandson of the sachem of all the Cherokee, was unfairly persecuted, and they were convinced that anti-Indian elements were responsible.

No one held these opinions more firmly than did Ruddik, a young war chief who was the youngest of the rank in the hierarchies of the Seneca and the Cherokee. Having taken part in battles with the other major tribes of the area, including the Choctaw and the Creek, he had served with sufficient distinction that he had won a considerable measure of respect from warriors of his own age.

A dozen of them were in the field together, engaged in training exercises. After spending the entire day practicing tracking, they sat down together for their evening meal, and after they had eaten, they relaxed, passing a long pipe from hand to hand as they stared into the flames. The talk veered to their favorite subject.

"We have been taught," Ruddik said, "to obey the voices of our leaders at all times, so what I have to say causes me both hesitation and grief. I feel that Loramas and Ah-wen-ga are too old to be the joint sachems of our people. Casno, who acts as regent for the Seneca in our midst, is closer to our own age, but he is basically a medicine man and hence is far more cautious than Renno would have been if Renno were guiding the destinies of his nation. I say that we must put a stop to the greed of the Americans before it overwhelms us. Before we know it, we may be forced out of our homes, as so many tribes have been forced to give up their lands and move to new places in order to live."

The doctrine he preached was heretical, but his words seemed to make sense. Passing the pipe slowly, the young braves listened, and one by one they nodded their approval. The time was ripe for a rebellion against the authority of those who guided the tribes.

"Remember that the people of the Choctaw and of the Creek and of the many nations of the Iroquois

League north of us all waged war against the Americans," Ruddik said forcefully. "These tribes sided with the British in the war that has only recently come to an end.

"The Cherokee and the Seneca," Ruddik went on, "alone, of all the tribes in this world, have stood beside the Americans and have been their allies in their struggle for freedom. But the Americans turn out to be perfidious and filled with treachery. Look at what has happened. They arrested Rusog, the son of Wegowa, the son of Loramas. They have invented false charges against him, and they intend to put him on trial for his life. What gives them the right to try him? What gives them any authority over him? By what right do they take the mantle of responsibility on their own shoulders and dare to say that he is innocent or guilty?"

The others were influenced by his words and several stirred as he spoke. One, a very young warrior, bit so hard on the stem of the pipe that he split it in two.

"You are right, Ruddik!" he cried out.

"The arrest of Rusog was nothing but trickery. Next they will find him guilty, and before we know it, they will fine our nation and we shall be forced to evacuate and move farther to the west. They keep inventing new tricks and new ways to cheat us of our property and of the precious soil of our ancestors that have been ours for generations."

The entire assemblage was aroused now, and the young warriors began to mutter to each other as they glowered and shook their fists.

"Let me make a prediction," Ruddik said loudly. "If the Americans hold Rusog in prison again on their false charges, we will break our treaty with them—no matter what our elders say. And we shall fight them to the end!"

Crickets chirped, a bird burst into wordless song, and the soft rustle in the underbrush indicated only that a small animal was making its way through the foliage. Peace reigned in the wilderness.

Renno had caught several large fish for supper, which Rusog had cleaned and which Emily had then cooked. For the second time since they had taken to the road in the land of the Seminole, the travelers had a hot supper to eat. Relishing every bite, they talked about the past and the future, and their thoughts inevitably strayed toward the coming trial that Rusog would face when they returned.

Taking turns, Emily and Rusog once more gave Renno their versions of what had happened on their journey to the State of Franklin.

Renno listened, nodding and occasionally interrupting to ask a quiet question. Finally, when they were finished speaking, he nodded sagely. "It seems to me," he said, "that when these stories are pieced together, the evidence is very clear. Ben Whipple was the villain who was responsible for all the villainy."

"I am certain," Emily added confidently, "that you will be cleared of all charges and be free to come and go as you please, Rusog."

Rusog plucked a blade of grass and nibbled on the white portion near the root. "I am totally innocent of all wrongdoing," he said. "I would never attack your father, Emily, nor would I steal his property. This should become evident for all to see eventually, and I hope that I will be judged innocent. What I fail to understand is why they chose to arrest me for a wrongdoing when I did no wrong. And why they treat me as though I am a criminal."

Emily was unsure of the answer and looked uncertainly at Renno.

He replied positively. "The white man and the Indians," he said, "have different ideas of justice. We who grew to manhood as Indians understand fully what our rules are, what we are allowed, and what is forbidden. The white man has relatively few rules, but he is much stricter in their application. It is difficult for those of us who are foreign to their ways to understand what they do and why they do it."

Returning Emily's intent gaze, he continued, "The Indians rely on the manitous to guide them to justice. With the aid of the manitous, we know who is guilty and who is innocent. Through this system of aid from the gods, we never make a mistake in our determinations. The white men, however, have no such aids and they flounder on the way. Therefore they must hold trials. We have no need for trials, but they reason that such acts are important to their concept of right and wrong. I must warn you of one thing, Rusog. When dealing with the white man, we must abide by his rules. The crime against Colonel Johnson took place in territory that the State of Franklin claims. Their rules must apply, and we are obliged to abide by them, just as when they come to the towns of the Cherokee and of the Seneca they are obligated to abide by our rules and to be judged by our own system of justice. Your innocence speaks for itself, and as they are just men, as we are, they will reach this same conclusion and you will be set free. If you exercise patience and goodwill, all will be well with you. I am sure of it, and I am certain the manitous guarantee it."

Rusog plucked another blade of grass and chewed on the white part. "You have relieved my mind," he said. "I trust in the manitous, and above all in your words, Renno. I have no doubt that all will be well when we reach Knoxville and I am put on trial for a crime that I did not commit."

As a young man, John Sevier was noted for the ferocity of his temper. It was said in those days that if he was aroused, no man in Tennessee or Kentucky was his equal. And, futhermore, that any Indian would be well advised to keep his distance—or risk instant extermination. As he grew older, Sevier learned to keep his temper in check. In recent times, especially since his election as the first governor of the State of Franklin, he was described as positively statesmanlike in his attitude and self-control.

On this afternoon, he paced the confines of his office as he tried in vain to curb his soaring anger. After more than an hour he sent an aide to summon Colonel Johnson, the head of his militia, and Benjamin Hill, who had replaced Johnson temporarily in the Franklin judicial system.

In response to the urgent summons, they showed up hurriedly and found him still pacing. In one hand, he carried a horsewhip. For years, he had used it as a pointer and as something of a trademark. Now he swung it recklessly over his head.

"Thanks for coming so promptly, gentlemen," he said. "We're in one hell of a fix. And the worst of the situation is I can see no solution." Judge Hill glanced at Colonel Johnson, who reputedly had the ability to calm Sevier when his temper became ungovernable.

Roy Johnson smiled genially and looked at Sevier, his face innocent. "What is your complaint, John?" he asked quietly.

"We crossed the mountains into this territory when nothing was here but wilderness," Sevier said angrily. "We built our civilization out of absolutely nothing. We did it by obeying the laws, the laws of nature, the laws of the British Empire, and ultimately, the laws of our own colonies. Never once did we fail to take into consideration the basic rule that laws had to be obeyed!"

His companions were silent, and he scowled as he continued forcefully.

"If I had my way," Sevier said. "I'd throw every last one of the young whippersnappers into jail until they learn some manners, and that would be the end of it. The trouble is, there are too many of them for us to handle in that manner. The whole state can collapse if we get overly tough with them. We've got to walk on eggs, so to speak, and that's what's bothering me most."

"I can guess who you're speaking of," Colonel Johnson interrupted.

"The Thomas brothers!" John Sevier exclaimed in annoyance. "And between them, as you know, they've managed to influence much of the younger generation, including some of the militiamen. In my day, I would have thrown them all out, but I don't believe you could do that now."

"Absolutely not," Colonel Johnson answered quietly. "If we tried anything like that, the entire militia would be disrupted, and we would be without an army. We have a choice: either we keep peace with our own men in uniform, or we give up any hope of maintaining an armed force for security purposes."

"This is one hell of a fix," Sevier repeated. "Theoretically, we could always call on the other states of the United States for assistance, but the government is almost nonexistent. We should be able to call on a national government for aid, but dammit, we have no such organization. The whole United States is ready to fall apart before it gets really started."

"I certainly agree with you that the Thomas brothers are rabble-rousers," Colonel Johnson said.

"Yes," the judge added, "and they have a bad influence on others. I see very little new in the situation."

"One thing is definitely new," the governor said. "If you had heard them carry on, as they did in a three-hour meeting with me today, you would know they're demanding their pound of flesh. They insist that we find Rusog guilty and punish him. They want to see the Cherokee put in their place."

"That's demanding the impossible," Johnson exclaimed. "In the first place, I doubt that Rusog is guilty, and I believe Ben agrees with me."

"Little question about it," the judge replied. "No telling what will come out in court, of course, but based on the evidence the case against Rusog is flimsy. I'm not yet prepared to say that he will be found innocent, but unless some strong contrary evidence is presented, any court would have little choice but to set him free."

"That won't satisfy the Thomas brothers or their followers," Sevier warned. "They are out for blood."

"Damn fools!" Colonel Johnson declared.

"No man west of the mountains has had a reputation to equal mine as an Indian-hater," Sevier put in. "I fought in more battles against more tribes than any other man who ever picked up a flintlock. They've given me a peck of trouble, and I've given it back in full measure. But dammit! I've learned, and I'm fair! I never made a claim that couldn't be substantiated. And I never was against any man just because of who he is."

"Our basic problem is simple," Colonel Johnson said quietly. "All too simple. If we give in to the Thomas brothers and their demands, we will be denying some of the very principles of justice on which this country supposedly is based. We will be turning our backs on the beliefs for which we fought and won the Revolution."

"I have to agree with you, Roy," the governor said. "Either we stand by principle, or we give in to the Thomas brothers. But what troubles me is this question: as a state are we too puny and too badly organized to have any real alternatives?"

"I think you're letting your natural pessimism get hold of you, Jack," the judge remarked. "I don't see the picture nearly as dark as you claim it is."

"The Thomas brothers and their followers," the colonel said firmly, "aren't yet in a position to lay down the laws and make the rules that everybody in the State of Franklin would have to obey. In one way or another—somehow—right will prevail, and the law of the land will be obeyed. I don't know how we'll work it out, but something will happen to defuse this crisis in a hurry and common sense will rule. Certainly, in the militia I am prepared to hold firm and steadfast!"

Never had Casno encountered anything as disgraceful as the dilemma that faced the Seneca of the South and the Cherokee. With only rare exception had the word of the elders ever been questioned, their advice ignored. Perhaps the war against the British, which had set brother against brother in strange conflicts, had been responsible. Whatever had set off this odd and sinister change of events, Casno had never known anything quite like it, apart from the decision made by Ghonkaba to defy his father, Ja-gonh, and other elders when he left the land of the Seneca to fight for the colonials under General George Washington.

Casno heard footsteps and was surprised when he saw Ghonkaba and Toshabe's younger son, El-i-chi. Properly standing at attention, he raised his left arm stiffly in salute. "I bring you greetings," he announced formally. El-i-chi always harkened to the past and invariably did things in old-fashioned ways. He wore only the single eagle feather of a junior warrior, but his manners were those of an ancient war chief with white hair and rows of scalps on his belt.

"Sit down, boy," Casno said, "and tell me what brings you here."

El-i-chi promptly lowered himself to a cross-legged, sitting position beside the fire over which some soup was cooking.

"I have the greatest of respect for you, Casno." He spoke solemnly in a low, intense voice.

Then he seemed to brace himself. "I beg your pardon a thousand times, and may the gods and those who represent them forgive me for putting this into words, but I agree with Ruddik."

Casno looked at him without changing his expression. "Tell me more of your thoughts on this matter," he urged.

"As you know," El-i-chi said, "Ruddik believes that the white man hates the Indians and lives only to take advantage of us. He believes that a great conspiracy exists to punish Rusog, and through him, to punish us all. Rather than tolerate insults to Rusog for as long as one moment, it is his firm belief that we should fight for our rights. Granted that our firesticks are not nearly as powerful as those that the men of Franklin possess. Nevertheless, we have many more men who are willing to lose their lives for the sake of our liberty, and if we go to war with the men of Franklin, we shall win!"

"Do you mean to suggest," Casno asked, "that we go to war against the people of the United States?"

"Why not?" El-i-chi replied, his tone respectful, in spite of an underlying note of bravado. "We have nothing to lose and everything to gain by standing on our own feet. If we give in and let them punish Rusog, we shall soon lose these lands and be forced to move again. We who are Seneca moved from the lakes that were our home to this place. And now that we are feeling at home here, we would be forced to move again."

Casno knew it was foolhardy to argue with someone of El-i-chi's age and disposition, but he could not resist.

"We helped the Americans to achieve their freedom," he said. "They are our firm allies and they shall be our allies for many moons to come. We cannot fight them now, and we cannot desert them now. I will grant you that there's a misunderstanding of sorts about Rusog. But with goodwill on both sides, surely the problem can be solved."

"By the time it is solved," El-i-chi argued stridently, "we shall have lost our hunting grounds and be forced to move again, as will all of our allies and neighbors. We must stand up to the Americans now and threaten them with extermination unless they bow to our will."

"I know this is difficult for you to understand, El-i-chi," Casno said, "but let me speak further. The issues are far more important than the simple answers that you have given to many complex problems. You must rely on those who are older and wiser, on those who have had much experience in dealing with the ways of the world and the powers of various nations. I believe that by following their leadership, our nation will prosper, and we shall enjoy many fruitful years of peace and prosperity and happiness together."

"I mean you no disrespect, Casno," El-i-chi said, "but the words you have just spoken are precisely the words that Ruddik has predicted you would say. We cannot bow our heads to the elders except at the cost of bowing them to the Americans. Either they affirm Rusog's innocence or we go to war."

Casno recognized that El-i-chi would not listen to words of reason and would ignore anything further. He was clearly beyond the control of his mother. The one person who could handle him was Renno, who was still away.

This left but one alternative: to allow El-i-chi to find his own way. And meanwhile to pray to the manitous that he would be spared any harm caused by his stubbornness and his shortsighted attitudes.

Casno raised his hand to show that he wished to change the subject. After a few minutes, El-i-chi left, apparently feeling better for having delivered himself of an ultimatum.

When he was alone again, Casno sat and stared up at the distant horizon for a long time, his arms folded across his chest in the classical pose of an Indian trying to overcome his own feelings. To an observer, he presented the tranquility for which his people had long been noted.

The small incident brought him closer to recognition that the situation that separated the Seneca and the Cherokee, on the one hand, from the people of the United States, on the other, was far more serious than he had been willing to admit.

As Renno, Emily, and Rusog reached North Carolina and worked their way westward to the mountains, the distance ahead began to seem insignificant. The worst of their problems appeared to be behind them. The forests were filled with game, fish, and edible plants, and they no longer had to rely on the supplies of smoked buffalo. They were far enough north now that they were in the lands of tribes that had a long history of association with both the Seneca and the Cherokee. These tribes allowed free passage to the strangers who wore war paint. For the first time in the months that had elapsed since they had started their separate journeys southward, a relaxed atmosphere prevailed. Although they maintained a rapid pace as they made their way through the forest, Renno, always aware that Emily was a member of the party, repeatedly showed his considerateness toward her in small but reassuring ways.

Renno and Emily now were able to think primarily of themselves, and gradually, as their anxieties and tensions decreased, they reawakened to the sheer joy of spending time together. They enjoyed many of the things they had taken for granted in the past: swimming in cool lakes when they were tired after a long day's walk, the smell of meat cooking over an open fire at night, walking through the wilderness, where the only sounds were the occasional rustle of small animals and the excited chirping of birds.

Inevitably, Renno and Emily turned to each other more than ever. The feeling of intimacy that bound them together became more intense, and with it, their desire for physical contact grew until it became virtually unmanageable.

Fortunately for both of them, they were not traveling alone. The presence of Rusog inhibited them somewhat and made it impossible for them to sleep together.

They shared a desire to stay apart until they were married, and for that reason they were privately glad for Rusog's presence.

Nevertheless, they were lighthearted, and they enjoyed their evening sessions together when they planned their long-range future.

One night, when the air was balmy and all three felt lazy after eating a hearty dinner of fish that Renno had caught and of a duck that Rusog had shot, Emily began to speculate about the future.

"You know," she said, "it's really wonderful, when you stop to think about it, that you two are brothers-in-law. In the years to come, when each of you is the head of his own people, it should make much easier the union of the Seneca and the Cherokee. I can see the day coming, perhaps in our own lifetime, when they will become truly one people."

Rusog, who had eaten too much, answered indolently. "Anything is possible," he said, "provided the manitous will it."

"Well," Emily said, "it doesn't take too much imagination, thanks to our future marital alliance, to see the day coming when the Americans, the Seneca, and the Cherokee will act together as one people, thanks in large part to us.

"I pray," she continued fervently, "that nothing will disturb this newfound unity that we have established. Together we can rid the world of ignorance, just as we hope to rid it of improper behavior. And together, secure in the knowledge that what we do is done in unison with our fellows, we progress toward the goals set by our respective gods. No more than that can any people want or desire."

Roy Johnson's recovery from his ordeal was slow but steady. Little by little, he regained his strength, energy, and verve. Instead of being awake at dawn, and soon thereafter handling either personal affairs or business of state, he slept until eight or nine in the morning. Then, at his wife's insistence, he ate a leisurely breakfast. In order to slow his pace, she made it her business to sit with him while he ate.

Ordinarily, he was in an easy frame of mind, but this morning he was distracted and aloof, and Nora Johnson assumed he was once again worrying about their daughter.

"What's wrong, dear?" she asked.

"It's nothing new," he said. "I'm thinking that my expedition to the Choctaw failed and I should undertake it again soon, as a suitable gesture. But I'm thinking also, and particularly, about the damned Thomas brothers."

"Oh, that," she replied, and knew she would have

her hands full curing his sense of dissatisfaction and unhappiness. For some reason, the activities of the Thomas brothers, in relation to the court case now pending, in which the colonel would be a star attraction, seemed to distress him more than anything else.

"I was too wrought up at the time to tell you about it," he explained, "but last night after the senior staff meeting, I ran into Al Thomas. He was just leaving his brother's saloon as I came by. We had an unfortunate meeting."

Nora raised an eyebrow, but said nothing.

"He asked me," Colonel Johnson said, "whether I would cooperate with him and his brother and the other young idiots who are trying to cause trouble between us and the Indians. I asked him what he meant by cooperation. He suggested—without saying it in so many words—that I go on the witness stand and intimate that I saw Rusog attacking me.

"I told him it's well known that I didn't see anyone attacking me. So he said he wasn't asking me to tell an outright lie. All he wanted me to do was intimate that it was probably Rusog who was assaulting me. If I establish that much, he said, there ought to be no problem whatsoever in finding Rusog guilty."

"But that *would* be telling an outright lie," his wife said indignantly. "You would hardly do that, especially after you have sworn to tell the truth!"

"He knows all those things," the colonel said in disgust. "He simply urges that I do it in order to make it more likely that the court finds Rusog guilty. That would clarify everything, he pointed out, and would make all the questions involved much simpler to handle."

"I fail to see where anything would be simpler," Nora objected.

"Exactly," her husband replied. "It would be a move for the sake of propaganda and would have no connection with truth. If I lied, it would be easier to influence the majority of our people who are still sitting on the fence and are waiting to hear my account of what happened."

"But that would be so unfair to Rusog!"

"That's what I told him," the colonel said, "and believe it or not, he had the nerve to laugh. He said we're in a war to control the minds and the feelings of people and that this would be a highly effective weapon in that war. He's one of those determined to see the State of Franklin move westward and incorporate practically the whole of the Tennessee country into our state. The fact that we'd be taking over a great deal of Indian land—many thousands of acres—is totally irrelevant to them. They don't care how we do it, and Al Thomas reflects that view. He thinks the attack on me is a splendid excuse, a valid reason for moving in what he feels is the right direction."

"Do the young men of today have no scruples, no decency, no standards?" his wife demanded indignantly.

Colonel Johnson shook his head. "It has been true for many hundreds of years," he replied, "for a generation that grows up during a war to be utterly without a soul in the years that follow it. Many of those who grew to manhood during the War of Independence, but took no active part in it, lack understanding and are without feeling for the essence of right and wrong. They know what they want. And they're determined to get it, regardless of the way they go about it."

"Obviously," his wife said, "you're not going to perjure yourself in order to satisfy the savage desires of the young. Just what is it you intend to do to counter them and to put them in their places, once and for all?"

"I've been giving the matter a great deal of serious thought ever since it was forcibly called to my attention." Colonel Johnson lost his appetite for oatmeal and pushed his breakfast dish away from him. "All I can do is take the stand and tell the truth and let the chips fall where they may, even though some important people feel that we will be creating a division in the state that will be impossible to heal. I say we've got to be truthful and let the facts of life build on those truths. The only way to be honest with ourselves as a state and as a nation is to be honest as individuals. Whether the young like it or not, we've got to stand for truth and decency in our personal lives. I see no other way."

"What would you do," Nora inquired, "if the young people continue to insist that you perjure yourself?"

"Let them insist all they please. I've told the truth all my life, and I'm damned if I'm going to start telling anything else now. I will be truthful, regardless of whether Franklin stands or falls. And I have sufficient faith in the Almighty to believe that by being honorable and truthful, we increase our chances more than one hundred-fold in favor of survival!"

Tebotha, the father of the inflammatory young Ruddik, war chief of the Cherokee, was a contented old man. He had spent many years as a medicine man for the entire Cherokee nation. Filled with respect, as he himself respected the Corn Mother and her son, Breath Holder, he lived in quiet contentment. He had made it his business to get along with everyone in authority, and his relations with Loramas, the sachem of the Cherokee, and with Casno, the principal medicine man and the regent of the Seneca, were excellent.

With increasing concern, he had observed the turmoil in Ruddik, whose hatred of the Americans was deep. Tebotha deeply regretted that he did not know or understand his son well. Ruddik had been born to him late in life, when he had been married to his second wife, who was many years his junior. As a result, he had felt too old to have the customary relationship with the boy. Now, as he grew older, he was making his principal goal in life establishing a warm and intimate relationship with his son.

Tebotha spent an entire afternoon with Ruddik and listened as the young war chief held forth on the injustice that the people of Franklin were inflicting on the Cherokee by having arrested Rusog and threatening him with a long imprisonment.

The older man knew virtually nothing about the Americans and cared little about them. His entire life had been spent with the Cherokee, and he had no concern for the newcomers in the rich valleys of Tennessee.

His one desire was a close relationship with Ruddik, and he listened impassively to the younger man's denunciation of Franklin and its citizens. He could not understand the hatred but nevertheless was affected by it, so great was the intensity of the discussion.

"I do not know why I burden you with all this, my father," Ruddik said. "I seem to be talking into a howling wind that drowns the sound of my voice. The older generation ignores my words, and those who are younger heed them, but lack the will to fight. They will let the white men mock and abuse Rusog, and will pay no attention to what happens thereafter to our people. I do not know how to arouse them."

Tebotha was filled with a desire to help his son and do it any way that he could. "Perhaps I can assist you," he said. "It may be that I know ways to instill a fighting spirit into those warriors who are reluctant to take up arms."

Ruddik was thunderstruck. He had grown up feeling disdain for his father's profession and for the strange ways in which a medicine man practiced. But now anything that might help him to gain his ends was worth pursuing. "I will be grateful for all you can do, my father," he said humbly.

Certain now that he held his son's attention, Tebotha hastened to explain. "For many generations," he said, "the Cherokee have been a peace-loving nation. We have followed the teachings of the Corn Mother and of her son as we have tilled our fields and caught animals in the forest and fish in the waters and streams. On rare occasions through these generations, we have needed to fight against enemies jealous of our simple ways of life who would take our freedom from us. But we are not fighting men. We are simple farmers and hunters.

"I will inform you in part," Tebotha then said, "of a sacred secret of the medicine men of the Cherokee. I have access to a magic leaf that instills in men the desire to fight."

Ruddik promptly showed great interest in his father's words.

"This plant grows in the sunny valleys beyond the confines of this town," the older man said. "I cannot tell you its exact location, nor am I allowed to point to the living plants. That is a secret of the medicine men alone. I will say only that when the plants are grown, they are picked, and the leaves are dried. Then they become indistinguishable from the broad dried leaves of the tobacco plant. Crumble these leaves together with the leaves of the tobacco plant in equal amounts, and give them to those who will fight. Let them fill their pipes with this mixture. When they have smoked a filled pipe of it, they will be eager and ready to take up combat for the Cherokee nation against any foe who would dare to oppose them.

"It is customary to provide a pipeful for each warrior when an impending war is to be announced. Then they may smoke a few pipefuls just prior to going into battle. When this happens they are mean

and ready for combat, no matter what the odds. If
you wish, I will give you some of it. The warriors of
the Cherokee may thus become imbued with the
proper fighting spirit in your effort to teach the white
settlers of Franklin a lesson."

"The story of this magic potion is too good to be
true," Ruddik said, his eyes shining.

His father shrugged. "Let me give you some of
this magic weed," Tebotha said, "and you may try it
when you please on any braves on whom you wish to
make the experiment." He rose and, going into the
adjoining room, returned with a large clay pot filled
with a crumbled weed that looked remarkably like
tobacco and a pot of tobacco.

His son sniffed it experimentally, but it had no
odor.

"This leaf," Tebotha said, "has no taste, and when
it burns, its odor is very much like that of tobacco.
Mix it so with tobacco," he went on, illustrating by
pouring a measure of the dried leaves into a pan with
an equal measure of tobacco, which he then mixed
together. "And then you will be unable to distin-
guish its odor."

Ruddik reached eagerly for the mixture.

His father held it from him, however. "Let me
issue one solemn word of warning to you, my son,"
he urged. "Be chary in your use of this strange plant,
and in its application to the warriors of our land.
Exercise caution in the quantities of the burning
leaves that you administer to any one man. A limited
amount makes him eager to fight and easy to handle.
Too much maddens him, much as our animals grow

mad when they chew too much of it in the fields.
Then he becomes unmanageable and no longer is
master of his own destiny."

"I hear you, my father, and I understand," Ruddik
said, although his tone indicated that he was not
concerned about the amount of the strange leaf that
any man inhaled. The one thing that mattered to him
was the result.

Tebotha gave his son a bowl of the strange plant
mixed with tobacco and smiled indulgently as Ruddik
hurriedly left to experiment on his fellow warriors.
His father was pleased at his enthusiasm. Perhaps
this gesture would help to solidify the bond between
them.

The old medicine man did not have long to wait.
From the interior of his house on the main square,
he could see a number of the younger warriors of the
nation gathering, apparently inspired by a call from
Ruddik. They entered the council chamber in ones
and twos, and Tebotha was interested to note that all
of them were placid and at ease. None were worked
up or showed any vigor for combat or for any warlike
endeavor. The last to appear was Ruddik, who carried the woven bowl filled with the contents his
father had given him. He stopped just outside the
entrance to the council chamber, looked across at his
father's house, and seeing Tebotha, he grinned and
waved cheerfully. He seemed certain that the gift he
had received would be the answer to his problem.

After a short time, Tebotha heard his son's voice
coming from the council chamber. The young war
chief spoke in a deep, resonant tone, his voice rising

to an impassioned pitch and then falling again. He
was an accomplished speaker, and his father smiled
at the thought that Ruddik had inherited his own
talents as an orator. Tebotha owed his position as
medicine man at least in part to his ability to speak
to the people of the nation.

The young warriors were smoking their pipes as
they listened to Ruddik's oratory. His father wondered anxiously what effect his words were having on
them. Suddenly the answer was self-evident. The
tension had been broken. The silence in the council
chamber gave way to a mighty roar, followed by loud
cheering and then the whoops of the tribal war cry.

Tebotha's grin grew broader. Combined with the
magical leaves, his son's views were having the desired effect, and the braves of the nation were being
worked into a patriotic lather, ready to fight on behalf of the Cherokee against any enemies.

The noise continued to mount as Ruddik's speech
went on. He was holding his audience in the palm of
his hand now, and they responded to every sen-
tence. He would say a few words and then would be
halted by a loud roar.

When at last the meeting ended, Tebotha hid in
the shadows as he watched the younger men filing
out into the night. Most of them looked wild-eyed,
unable to focus properly, one of the inevitable effects
of the strange drug. Several staggered slightly as
they went off down the street, and all were still in a
belligerent mood. Three or four argued violently
with each other, and several, conscious of their manhood, swaggered as they walked.

The last to appear was Ruddik, who hurried across the street. When he saw his father, he grasped him by the shoulders. Only a lifetime of strict training prevented him from hugging the older man. "Your magical tobacco has truly wonderful qualities!" he cried. "It has done all you said it would, and more. All I had to do was to make a short speech, and the men—all twenty of them, whom I gathered for experimental purposes—were ready to go out and start a war with Franklin immediately."

Tebotha was overjoyed that his son was so pleased. Now, perhaps, as a result of his intervention, they would be closer, as the old medicine man often had dreamed they would become.

"If you will give me an adequate supply of the tobacco, my father, I will be ready to begin my military campaign against Knoxville at any time. I am ready now for the supreme challenge. And if Loramas and Wegowa do not like it, they will have to be replaced."

Tebotha was startled. He had had no idea that his son was aiming so high—but having put the plan into operation, he did not see how he could possibly stop it.

Renno and Emily lovingly looked at each other across the campfire that he had made at the end of the day's march. While their supper was cooking, Emily smiled at him before she spoke. "It's odd, you know," she said. "We've had to devote so much time and energy to successfully concluding our adventure among the Seminole that we have given no time at all to our own plans for our future, after we are married."

Renno chuckled and shook his head. "I daresay," he replied, "that we will live happily ever after, as they say in your storybooks."

"I wish it were that easy," Emily said, "but life will be far more complicated. Things aren't as they were in our grandfathers' day, when many differences between white and Indian civilizations were only slight. Will you devote yourself to hunting and fishing, or will you perhaps cultivate some acreage? Will you have time for any of those pursuits when you inherit your post as head of the Seneca? You'll have many choices to make."

"I don't think we should try to make any decisions at all," Renno said, "sitting here in the wilderness removed both from your civilization and from mine. We'll need a far closer contact with the realities of the situation than we now enjoy."

He moved closer to Emily, and for the rest of the evening they dismissed thoughts of their place in the unforeseeable future.

Chapter X

Wegowa of the Cherokee and Casno of the Seneca conferred several times daily on many subjects concerning the governing of their two nations. Long before, they had abandoned any attempt at formality in their relationship.

Casno was weary now, as he entered the house of

the military commander of the Cherokee. Sighing heavily as he sat down, he leaned his back against the nearest wall and searched about him for his pipe and tobacco. "Our strategy," he said with a sigh, "is just not working. We thought that the belligerence that our people are showing toward the people of Franklin would disappear if we ignored it. But instead it grows worse."

"I must say that you are right." Wegowa prepared two gourds with water, into which he pressed crushed mint, and handed one of them to his guest. "I understand that last night young Ruddik had a party of warriors so worked up they were ready to march out then and there. Only the fact that Knoxville is far away deterred them."

"That is more or less what I gathered," his companion said. "We can be thankful that no white men were within sight. Either Ruddik is an unbelievably good speaker, which I am inclined to doubt, or the people of our nations are literally spoiling for a fight."

"Ordinarily," Wegowa said with a frown, "I know we could rely on Loramas to control our people. All he would need to do would be to talk sense to them and the warriors would listen, just as they have for a half century."

Wegowa began to pace up and down the room. "Unfortunately," he continued, "neither my father nor Ah-wen-ga can be relied on just now to make a sensible speech. They are both friends of the United States and of the people of Franklin, but you would never know it from their attitudes."

"Remember," Casno said, "they have both lived

the better part of their lives independent of the
white people and of their influence. They are both
members of the old school, and they are proud of
their heritage and their ability to stand up for themselves. So I do not think that either is much influenced by the feelings that are affecting the young
people."

"In any case, they are of no help to us," Wegowa
exclaimed angrily. "If we asked either of them to
make a speech to calm down the people, they would
make the situation much worse."

"Can't we reason with them?" Casno asked.

"I invited them to my house for supper last night,
and I tried—for all the good that it did. They would
not listen to reason. Loramas, who in the past has
spoken favorably of the white men, now thoroughly
distrusts them. As far as he is concerned, Rusog is
his grandson, and they have wronged him. Ah-wen-
ga's views are even more extreme. Obviously, Rusog
and Ena are favorites of the old couple, and they
have become distressed about the charge hanging
over Rusog's head in Knoxville. They are afraid that
the people of the United States are intending to
mock them, just as the British secretly mock them.
They have turned in their old age to all the old
hatred that is felt in just about every Indian tribe."

"All I can say," Casno replied, "is that they must
cooperate with the United States or both of our
tribes are doomed. It is easy enough to see the
handwriting on the wall now. With the war ended,
immigration has resumed again from Europe, particularly from the British Isles, and immigrants are

crossing the Atlantic Ocean in ever-increasing numbers. The cities of the seaboard are already filled, and that means the newcomers who seek land are going to come to Tennessee and Kentucky and the other communities west of the mountains. If we fail to reach a friendly accommodation with the United States that is fair to them and fair to us, we will be annihilated by the mighty tidal wave of newcomers."

"I tried to persuade my father and his bride to see those facts last night," Wegowa said, "but they refused to listen to me. They are as stubborn and as shortsighted in their own way as young people like Ruddik."

In a long silence that followed, Casno deliberately filled his pipe and lighted it with a coal from the fire. He took his time and appeared lost in thought. "So far," he said at last, "we are in agreement on the ailments that afflict our nations and on their causes. What we have yet to discuss is the possible cure."

Wegowa sighed. "I have been a military man all of my life," he said, "and I have spent many hours in combat with my nation's foes. I am guided by the son of the Corn Mother, and I have yet to fail. But this is a situation that requires a far different kind of expertise. I know nothing of the subtle ways of dealing with people, and I am at a loss. I have no thought of what to do or how we might go about doing it."

"I understand now how Ja-gonh, our sachem during the years of the war," Casno resumed, "must have felt when he was confronted by the desire of numerous warriors to break their treaty with the

English and side with the Americans. No matter how
he felt—and I must admit, I can sympathize with the
young people who feel that the Americans are violat-
ing their agreement with us—he could do nothing to
halt the dissension or stop the movement."

Wegowa continued to pace for a time, but suddenly he halted. "Only one possible solution occurs
to me," he said. "We must go once again to the
Franklin authorities and try to persuade them to
release their hold on Rusog. Whatever their laws
may be, they must exempt him from them and set
him free."

"You make good sense," Casno replied quickly, his
voice emphatic. "I see no other way, despite our
earlier discouragement. The choice of war or peace is
no longer up to us. The decision is the Americans'.
We must point out to them that unless they relax
their laws when it involves a man of Rusog's stature,
they will be forced to take the consequences. You
and I are mere men, after all, and we cannot hope to
assume the stature and the responsibilities of the
gods."

Preparing for their journey in great haste, Casno
and Wegowa selected as escorts senior warriors who
felt as they did on the issue of war or peace.

They set out at dawn the following morning and
managed to clip more than a half day off the usual
time for the journey. Arriving at Knoxville, they
approached the fortress by way of the river and once
more signaled their intentions by raising a white flag.
After only a brief delay, a large boat was sent across

the river, and the leaders of the Indian party were transported to the fort. As it happened, Lieutenant Thomas was the officer on duty in charge of the guard. The glare with which he greeted the two leaders revealed that their own subordinates were not the only people spoiling for a fight. Uncomfortably aware of the sharp antagonism of the young lieutenant, they were escorted to the office of Colonel Roy Johnson and were deposited there without ceremony.

Colonel Johnson tried to compensate for his officer's behavior by greeting them warmly, but he could sense their annoyance, and the meeting was off to a poor start.

Casno got down to business immediately. Mincing no words, he described the situation among the Cherokee, stressing the unhappiness of the younger men. Finally, he touched on the inability of Wegowa and himself to control over the hotheads.

Colonel Johnson listened with dismay to the account. He was reluctant to admit that the situation in Knoxville was no better than among the Indians and that bringing the two sides into close contact was highly inflammatory and dangerous.

When Casno finished his dismal tale, Wegowa was the first to speak. "We have told you all this, Colonel, because we need your help. We respect the treaty that we have signed with the people of Franklin, and we are convinced that Franklin also is interested in keeping its word with us and continuing to maintain the peace."

"Specifically, what is it you want?" Colonel Johnson asked sympathetically, despite his belief that all possible solutions had already been discussed.

"Forget the charges that have been lodged against Rusog! He is a fine young man, and those of us who know him are convinced he could not be guilty of having attacked and robbed you. I realize that you have no definite proof to that effect, but surely logic alone should persuade you that he is innocent!

"I am willing to admit the dictates of logic," Johnson said, "and I quite agree that it is highly unlikely that I was attacked by Rusog, as I have told you. Unfortunately, I do not possess the power to forget the charges, and neither does the judge who will hear the case. The only possible action can come from Governor Sevier. He can issue a decree in which the charges against Rusog are dismissed. I suggest you come with me now to his office and again plead your case in person. Perhaps then we can end this misunderstanding that is causing problems between our people."

The atmosphere appeared more optimistic. All three men had shared the same goal: elimination of tensions between Franklin and the two Indian tribes. They seemed to be united in the cause of peace as they made their way out of the colonel's office in the fort and walked to the new state house, where Governor Sevier's office was now located.

The presence of the two Indians with Roy Johnson created a considerable stir. Both Indians wore their conspicuous war paint, and their headbands were filled with the many feathers of their high rank. A number of citizens, particularly the elder men and the women, nodded pleasantly, but younger men scowled and their reaction created new tensions. Colonel Johnson wanted to explain that the younger men had no real hatred for the Indians but were excited by the emotions aroused by the entire affair revolving around Rusog. He decided, however, that it was best to let the matter ride for the present. The less said and the fewer explanations offered, he figured, the greater would be the likelihood that the incident could be resolved satisfactorily.

Governor Sevier was presiding over a meeting of military advisors, and since the matters under consideration were fairly complicated, he did not interrupt the meeting. Consequently, Casno and Wegowa were forced to wait in a reception room outside the governor's office where they sat wondering whether or not the governor was deliberately insulting them.

At last the visitors were comfortably settled in the governor's office. The Indians looked out of place in an office with the flag of the United States behind the governor on one side, and that of Franklin on the other. Wegowa began to outline his complaints and the reason for the visit. Speaking in true, formal Indian style—but employing the English words that he knew—he delivered a long speech that more and more came to resemble a harangue.

Colonel Johnson knew he should have warned him to speak succinctly and to present his case in the fewest words possible. But, having neglected to do so, he was forced to sit now and watch Governor Sevier squirming in his seat and listening with a lack of sympathy evident in his eyes. The thought of a war with the Cherokee and Seneca did not seem to dismay him. In fact, as Colonel Johnson looked at him, he suspected that the governor might secretly look forward to such a confrontation.

The truth was that the longer the visitors talked, the more convinced Sevier became that they were actually threatening him with armed conflict. His hackles rose, as they always did in contact with any Indians who seemed to dare to offer a threat. By the time that Wegowa and Casno were through presenting their case, Sevier was ready for full combat.

Crashing his fist on his oak desk, he glared at the Indians. "It strikes me," he said, keeping his temper only with difficulty, "that you are threatening to make war against my state unless we give in and set Rusog free without a trial. Common sense tells me that if your boy Rusog is so damn innocent, why are you afraid of a trial? If he is so free of blame, why do you refuse to let him go before a judge? If he is innocent, let the court act accordingly, and set him free. No mark would be made against him, and he will come and go as he pleases. But as I have told you and told you, Knoxville is in the State of Franklin, which is part of the United States of America, and in this country we have laws that apply to everyone. Sure, I know you have signed a treaty with us, but that doesn't give your people any special rights that don't apply to all people. In America, you must obey the laws of Americans. Therefore, I refuse to sign any paper that would set Rusog free, if that's what you have in mind. Let him come before the court, plead his case, and be judged as any other ordinary person would be. If he is innocent, he will be set free. If he is guilty, he will sure as hell pay."

There was a feeling of mutual hostility hanging heavy in the air.

The colonel was dismayed. He had seen Sevier lose his temper before in confrontations with Indians, but this would be a costly loss of control. His irate stand was certain to create problems with two powerful tribes that were his close allies.

Here were leaders, accustomed to supreme command, proud warriors who willingly faced any danger. Their pride was so great that now none of them could admit the possibility of an amicable way to solve their joint problem.

"I've made myself as clear as possible," the governor concluded firmly. "What more can you want? I assure you I can give you nothing more, and I am tired of these prolonged discussions. I intend to meet no more with you on this matter."

Casno drew in a deep breath. "I want nothing from Sevier," he said in the Cherokee tongue, with his meaning obvious to the governor and the colonel. "I willingly agreed to the treaty of peace because I trusted him. Obviously, that trust was misplaced. He gives me no choice now, and he forces me to take action that will cause the manitous to weep."

Reaching for the knife in his belt, he drew it and plunged it deep into the polished wood of Governor Sevier's desk. It quivered there, a barrier between the Seneca and the Cherokee on one hand, and the American people on the other. It was sharp, and its steel was hard.

Casno settled his multifeathered headdress firmly on his head, drew the robe of high office more tightly around his shoulders, and stalked out of the office. The die had been cast. There was no turning back.

Colonel Johnson accompanied the two Indians as they made their way to the canoe that would carry them across the river. Taking no chances, the colonel refused to allow anyone to approach them. He wanted no incident that might further disturb the peace or cause an outright incident.

He was sad as he walked in step with the two grimly silent Indians. They had fought side by side as brothers in memorable campaigns. Together they had defeated every major tribe within hundreds of miles, and together they had achieved a peace that had promised to allow the settlers on the Tennessee frontier and the Indians to live together in friendship and prosperity. Now all that was spoiled. An ugly war threatened, a war that had no cause except mutual misunderstandings and misplaced pride.

Frowning, unfriendly young militiamen opened the gate of heavy logs, and the three men walked down to the shore, where the boat awaited them. Wegowa was so upset that he climbed into the craft without saying a word of farewell, and there awaited his companion.

Casno hesitated, and after a moment, he extended his right hand in civilized style to the colonel, who offered his own hand, and they shook firmly, without hesitation.

"It appears," Casno said, "that we shall next meet on opposite sides of the battle line."

"That is the place," the colonel replied, "where I least wished or expected to be, now or ever. If conflict does come, then may the Almighty watch over you and preserve you and keep you from all harm. May you emerge whole and in good health from any ordeal that is to come. Meantime, I shall continue to do my utmost to prevent its coming about."

"May the manitous watch over you, now and always," Casno said sincerely. "May they protect you from harm, as they have protected you in past battles. May both of us meet again as friends when peace has returned to the land."

Ruddik smoked two pipefuls of the special tobacco that Tebotha had given him, and afterward, he was filled with an urgent desire to bring matters to a head.

He wandered into the woods behind the Cherokee town, and after pacing aimlessly for an hour or more, he decided that the time had come to act. He would lead the warriors of the nation to Knoxville, and they would make a public stand against the residents of Franklin. Still under the influence of the drug, he returned to the town and gave a series of impassioned speeches to the younger warriors, who responded to a man and announced they were ready to follow him anywhere.

The decisions that had been pending suddenly assumed a critical stance. Wegowa conferred at length with Casno, and they went together to Loramas and his Seneca bride. There it was decided that a large delegation would go at once to Franklin and, with a show of strength, would present the case for Rusog in a way sure to impress the authorities.

The result was that a scant thirty-six hours later a large party set out on the march eastward through the wilderness to Knoxville. It consisted of more than two hundred Cherokee and Seneca warriors, together with the titular leaders of the two tribes. In a few cases, it was deemed suitable for squaws to become part of the delegation, in order to help provide meals and meet other needs if a prolonged encampment proved to be necessary.

"I see no way of predicting the outcome of this journey," Loramas said in private to Ah-wen-ga. "The situation is too volatile, and dangers are present on every side. I am in hopes that when the Americans see our many warriors prepared to do battle they will reconsider their stand and will reach a reasonable accommodation with us."

"The Americans," Ah-wen-ga replied with a frown, "do not seem to be people who give in easily to threats or to promises of danger. They may react as our own Seneca react and put their backs against the wall, ready to fight at once. If that should happen . . ."

"I know," Loramas agreed. "That is my fear also. We shall have to await developments and pray to the gods that the entire affair will end satisfactorily. If only in some way we could control the young hotheads like Ruddik, we might have a chance to maintain the peace. Under the circumstances, however, we shall have to make progress slowly and hope for the best while making our own position unmistakable."

* * *

Renno was increasingly anxious to make the best possible time, so he urged that they travel more rapidly. He was particularly proud of Emily's ability to maintain the pace. Never complaining, she managed to keep up with him on the long daily treks, cheerfully walking for hours on end without respite, and eating what food her companions could shoot.

"Emily deserves to be married to a Seneca," Rusog said at the end of a particularly long, harsh day. "She is completely at home in the wilderness, and her energy is boundless."

Renno merely smiled. He considered that the woman he intended to marry was incomparable, and he needed no praise to remind him of her qualities.

As they came at last to the land near Knoxville, they found numerous farms. Renno thought, not for the first time, that the system of security established near such wilderness homes was inadequate. Instead of having the area patrolled by scouts, as Indian tribes did, it was left unguarded, except at night. Farmers carried their weapons when they went out to work in the fields. Only the main communities were guarded, and a zealous watch was maintained at the forts.

The Knoxville fort was well guarded, and when the three Indian figures were sighted, it caused a great deal of excitement. A longboat was launched across the river. Colonel Johnson was first ashore and he gathered his daughter into his arms and kissed her soundly. He shook hands warmly with Renno but was surprised to see Rusog in the same party.

He said nothing about the controversy about Rusog's fate, and the little party went off in triumph to the Johnson home. Nora Johnson and her daughter had a joyful reunion.

"I don't know how we can ever thank you for saving Emily," Mrs. Johnson told Renno. "You have more than earned the right to spend the rest of your days as her husband."

That evening, a large throng gathered at the Johnson home and listened to Emily's story, beginning with the attack on her and Rusog by Ben Whipple and his gang of freebooters. As she told the story, all the facts came out, including the important information that Rusog had been used as a dupe by Whipple, who had planted money and Colonel Johnson's personal belongings on him in order to shift suspicion for the robbery. The two gold coins were handed to Rusog, who solemnly gave them back to Colonel Johnson. Everyone applauded, and even Governor Sevier smiled.

"This account pretty definitely clears your name of any suspicion, Rusog," the colonel said. "I'm glad to say that this should end the crisis between us and our good Indian friends."

The newcomers looked blank, and Colonel Johnson proceeded to fill them in on the dangerous mounting tensions that threatened to destroy the peace.

"It seems to me," the colonel went on, "that this will immediately reduce the charges against you to a formality. I'm not the judge, of course, but I daresay that Judge Hill will find you completely innocent of any wrongdoing and will dismiss the case against you. You will be free again before you know it."

"Free again?" Renno asked in some bewilderment.

"Of course," Governor Sevier said, breaking in. "The charges against Rusog have been formally filed, and the only way to clear the docket is to present the evidence in open court and let the court set him free. That's in keeping with our system of government."

"If you will pardon my expression of an opinion," Emily said thoughtfully, "relations apparently are strained badly enough. Is it not possible to call off the case against Rusog here and now, and end the farce before relations become even worse?"

"That makes very good sense," Renno told her.

"I wish that it were that simple, but that is not the proper way to handle this matter. You don't understand, either of you," the governor objected.

"I am sure we don't," Emily responded angrily. "Rusog is innocent of any wrongdoing, so why even pretend to consider prosecuting him for crimes he did not commit? You are wasting time and making a mockery of justice."

"On the contrary," Sevier replied. "We are establishing a precedent for legal justice for the entire state for years to come. Look at the situation this way. Charges were brought against Rusog based on circumstantial evidence. Those charges apparently are mistaken. Let the case be lawfully expunged from the record by the judge because the evidence presented was faulty. In that way we have a legal precedent that will stand up under all normal scrutiny. I have no choice in the matter."

Rusog, the subject of the discussion, looked bewildered as the talk went on.

"It has all gone too far, Jack," Colonel Johnson advised. "He is no more guilty of wrongdoing than I am, and as Emily said, we're verging on a mockery of justice. Why not remand him into my custody, and he will stay here as my guest until this affair is settled amicably?"

"That sounds fair enough," the governor replied with a smile. "The only condition I will make is that Rusog stay with you until we get the case off the docket. I will speak to Judge Hill tonight, in the hope that we can get it wrapped up by some time tomorrow."

Everyone concerned was satisfied with this solution, and the party went on, no one dreaming of the danger that would arise the following morning.

The alarm drum sounded at the fort, followed by the blaring of bugles signifying that a large party of Indians had been sighted. A short time later word spread that a party of Cherokee and Seneca warriors had gathered on the far bank of the river. Renno was delighted; he had not expected to see family or friends that soon. He immediately arranged to have a boat take him and Emily to the Indian encampment.

There a series of surprises hit him. His mother and grandmother were glad to see him, but some members of the Indian party, including his sister, Ena, and his younger brother, El-i-chi, were reserved in their greeting and barely spoke to Emily.

He needed only a short time to ferret the truth from Toshabe, his mother, who explained their hostility over the treatment of Rusog.

Their anger increased when Renno revealed that
Rusog was in the town but was not free to join his
wife or see his father or grandfather until he was
released by the court. He took care to explain, however, that the presiding judge was making a special
effort to have the case resolved by the end of the
day, and that without doubt he would set Rusog free
and would dismiss all charges.

To his surprise, his statement had little or no
effect. Only Toshabe listened with any sign of sympathetic interest.

"Ruddik is right," El-i-chi said. "The settlers of
Franklin are going out of their way to insult Rusog
and all Cherokee."

Ena agreed heartily.

Renno and Emily were thoroughly bewildered by
their reaction.

Ena insisted on going into town with Renno and
Emily, and when she reached the Johnson house,
she met with her husband alone. After a short visit,
she demanded that Rusog be set free immediately.

Emily reported Ena's demands to her father, who
was sympathetic, but when he in turn went to Sevier,
the governor bristled. "I'll be damned," he said, "if
any Indians are going to teach me how to run the
state. When Judge Hill is ready to take up Rusog's
case, he will do so. But until the judge has acted, I
am going to do nothing."

Consequently Ena returned alone to the Indian
headquarters across the river. Ruddik, having obtained a supply of drugs from Tebotha, distributed
them to the warriors, and after they had smoked

their pipes, he made an impassioned, warlike speech, which was greeted with loud whoops and applause.

Hearing the commotion, Lieutenant Thomas became increasingly apprehensive and annoyed, and when he went off duty in midafternoon he proceeded to his brother's tavern. Over several glasses of heavy ale, he expressed his opinion of the Indians. "No damn Seneca or Cherokee is going to tell us what to do!" he shouted to a group of militiamen.

Appalled by the swift rise of harsh feeling on both sides, Renno invited Wegowa and Casno to a meeting in the Johnson house, where the problem could be discussed calmly.

There they learned of an unfortunate, last-minute complication. Another case that Judge Hill had been hearing was encountering difficulties and was not yet completed. Therefore, he had been forced to postpone any action planned in Rusog's case. The following day was Sunday, when no court would be held, so it would be at least noon on Monday before Rusog would be set free.

Ironically, Rusog himself, good-natured and complacent as always, was the only one reasonably satisfied with the current state of affairs. He knew he would be found innocent and had no doubt that the court would set him free, as Governor Sevier had stated. Because he had not been on hand while tensions were increasing, he was better able to avoid feeling any anger or bitterness.

Listening to the colonel, Renno realized that a dangerous crisis hung over them, a situation that threatened to fly out of control and to create new and different problems to all Americans, especially to the Seneca.

After the meeting ended, Renno and Emily went into the garden behind the house, and there he unburdened himself.

"This situation," he said, "in which your people and mine are pitted against each other, is like a nightmare that has suddenly come true. After all that we experienced on our long journey, it is indeed like a terrible dream to find our people snarling at each other, ready for a war."

"What can we do to stop it?" Emily asked.

Renno was silent for a time and then shrugged. "I do not see where it is possible for any one person to do anything," he said. "The situation appears to be out of control."

"But you must do something!" Emily insisted. "After all, you are Renno of the Seneca, and if any man can do anything for your people, you are that man. You have won the confidence of the gods. You alone have the power with your people and have the confidence of the manitous to do what you will to reconcile the Seneca and the colonists."

"I have never faced a problem like this," he announced. "I need more time to think."

"Then think well and with all your might," she urged. "Our future and the future of our unborn children are at stake. So are the relations of your people and mine in this land of great promise. Somehow, you alone must find the solution that will ease the needless enmity that has sprung up between them." She put her hands on his shoulders, reached up, and kissing him, hurried away.

He watched her as she disappeared from view. Then he began to pace. It was up to him to find the one solution that would reunite the Indians and the settlers of the State of Franklin.

As he weighed the issues he knew Emily was right: he should have known what she had been the first to understand. His position in the world, particularly in the Americas, was unique. He was not only the offspring but the namesake of the first Renno, who had acted as an intermediary between the Indians and the white settlers. He was in a position to speak for both sides in a dispute, to reach a common meeting ground between them, and to end the hatred that would destroy both the Indians' and the settlers' cultures.

A bold step was required to solve the problem without bloodshed and without causing further enmities. He had to make a move that would be dramatic yet simple, and would be virtually guaranteed of success. Such a formula was almost impossible to envision.

Staring up occasionally at the darkening sky, Renno finally felt an idea take root in his mind and grow into a full-fledged scheme.

Renno could not judge whether the notion was good or bad. He knew only that it was audacious, and that it might well accomplish the impossible.

He wrestled with the problem into the night. Unable to think clearly enough, he threw himself on the ground and slept on the bare earth, covering himself with his cloak, which was always with him though he rarely wore it. Then, when the first rays of daylight awakened him, he sat up, instantly wide awake and alert. He went over the scheme in detail and could find nothing wrong with it.

Before he launched such a venture, he wished that he might have the approval of the gods so that he would know whether or not it might succeed. In order to carry out the plan, he would need to absent himself for many days. He was uncertain whether he would be better advised to stay and try to hold the hotheads in check, or to leave and carry out his scheme.

Lifting his eyes to the cloudless skies of blue rimmed with the red of sunrise, Renno prayed to the manitous for a sign. Only they would know and be able to give him guidance.

He prayed earnestly, and then, still staring up at the sky, he began to contemplate his plan, coldly trying to separate the facts from his wish that such a scheme might be effective.

As he watched, several wisps of cloud began to drift into view and partly blocked the rising sun. He watched with interest as three of them blew from different directions and seemed to gather in front of him.

Suddenly he was electrified. He had asked for a sign from the manitous, and they were giving him the most visible of all possible signs! He saw the body and paws of a large bear form, and then another cloud blew in and settled on the top and became the head and ears of a bear. He could just make out the bear's snout.

This was the sign for which he had prayed. Renno knew now that his scheme was good and that he should follow it, regardless of any obstacles.

As he continued to look on in awe and fascination, the clouds began to dissipate, some drifting off slowly, others vanishing more rapidly. Within seconds, the image was gone; only the memory of it remained sharply etched in Renno's mind.

Now he knew beyond any doubt there was no time to be lost. Jumping to his feet, he realized it was too early to awaken anyone in the Johnson household, so he sprinted down the street to the waterfront. Finding one of the boats that were used by the militia to cross to the far bank, he rowed himself to the shore where the Indians were encamped. Not pausing for breath, he ran to his mother's tent and found Toshabe preparing her breakfast beside a small fire.

"I wish for your help, my mother," he said without preamble. "I need two containers. Let one be filled with the dried meat of venison and buffalo, and let the other be filled with the sun-dried fish from the waters."

"I will obtain them for you at once, my son," Toshabe said, rising and starting toward the rest of the community. "You are going on a trip." She made the statement flatly, not as a question, but as an expression of fact.

"I am going on a trip, my mother," Renno confirmed. "I shall be gone from this place for many days. When I return, I hope that the problem between us and the colonists will be solved for all time and we will be friends, as our gods and theirs decreed from the beginning."

Toshabe nodded and hurried away rapidly as she sought the traveler's sustenance that her son required. As Renno had known, she asked no questions and issued no warnings to him. She had sufficiently sublime faith in him and knew that he intended to carry out a mission that was for the good of all the Seneca. She had no need to question him or to caution him about pitfalls.

Within minutes she returned, handing him the two leather bags filled with the food he had requested.

"It is too early in the day for me to see Wegowa or Casno," he said, "and I cannot see my grandmother or her husband at this hour, either. Tell them, if you will, what I wish you also would tell my future wife—that I will return with all speed, and to join me in praying that my mission may succeed."

Toshabe silently placed a hand on her son's forehead, wishing him well on his journey.

He turned and left the encampment, soon reaching the speed known as the Seneca trot, which would enable him to maintain the pace for countless hours without tiring. He disappeared quickly into the forest.

Chapter XI

When she came downstairs, Emily was distressed to find Renno gone. But before she could ask her father if he knew anything about it, Toshabe crossed the river and came to see her.

They walked together into the garden, where they could speak privately. Toshabe told her future daughter-in-law about Renno's plans.

"Where did he go, my mother? And why was he in such a rush to leave that he could not even wait to tell me what he had in mind?" It was difficult for Emily to emulate the Indians and to hide her concern.

Toshabe smiled gently. "Renno did not answer these questions, nor did I ask him any of them," she said. "He was in a great hurry to depart, and I merely did what he asked. Then he went."

Emily recalled their final conversation the previous night. "I think perhaps I know why he took it on himself to go," she said thoughtfully. "He feels responsible for the problem that separates your people and ours, and he wants to do all he can to heal the breach."

"If that is his goal, let the manitous watch over him and guide him," his mother said fervently. "May he have the strength and the wisdom to carry out their wishes!"

"I don't for a moment doubt Renno's intent, nor do I question his ability to carry through any plan that he conceives," Emily said. "All the same, I do wish that he had allowed a few minutes to tell me what he had in mind, so that I could at least help him as best I am able from here."

Toshabe shook her head. "She who would become the squaw of a warrior destined to become a great leader," she said, "must learn and cultivate two qualities above all others: great patience and faith in her man's ability to overcome whatever obstacles may lie in his path. I know it is difficult for you, having lived in a different world, to accustom yourself fully to the ways of an Indian who stands alone and makes his own decisions. All I can ask is that you remember that Renno followed you for great distances, saved you from a very unpleasant fate, and brought you back here. He relied on the manitous for strength and courage, and they supported him, just as they are supporting him now. Have faith in him, as I have, and all will be well."

Emily had learned enough of Indian ways to realize that only one response was possible. She folded her arms across her breasts, lowered her head, and murmured in the language of the Seneca, "So be it."

Toshabe was pleased by her response. "I have only one additional request to ask of you," she said. "Renno made no mention that he wants his mission to gain general knowledge. Therefore, I ask you to treat his absence with great confidence and discuss with no one why you think he is gone."

"I will talk about the reason for his absence only with you," Emily assured her, "and will join you in your prayers to the manitous that he may succeed in his most difficult of missions."

Troublemakers on both sides continued to agitate during Renno's absence, and affairs remained at a dangerous fever pitch. On Monday afternoon, Rusog finally appeared in Judge Hill's court, and with both Roy Johnson and Emily testifying in his favor, he was soon released from custody. The judge offered Rusog the apologies of the state. The judge's action was unpopular, as expected, among some of the men present, including the Thomas brothers, and the little courtroom seemed on the verge of a disturbance.

But judging the temper of several of the men present, including the Thomas brothers, Colonel Johnson had ordered a full company of militia to stand by outside the courthouse.

When the hearing was concluded, the colonel immediately ordered members of the militia to surround Rusog and Ena and escort them into the street and lead them to the river's edge, from where they would be rowed across to the Indian settlement.

Ted Thomas, emboldened by whiskey, took a stance a few feet from Rusog, blocking the Cherokee's passage.

"You ain't going nowhere, buddy," he shouted. "String him up, boys. Even if the judge set him free, he won't get away from us!"

Colonel Johnson intervened swiftly. "If we have any hanging hereabouts, I'll take charge of it," he announced. "And if any man among you touches this Cherokee warrior and his wife, I promise you, it's you who will end up on the scaffold."

Rusog, as was his nature, accepted the incident with good-natured, philosophical calm. But Ena, indignant, complained loudly.

On the far shore, she found plenty of younger men to sympathize with her complaints, and no one was more vocal in support of her complaints than Ruddik. "This insult cannot be allowed to pass unnoticed!" he cried. "Let those responsible be punished for their sins against our people and our gods!" He passed out tobacco mixed with his drug, and as the men smoked, he kept them stirred with passionate oratory.

No one seemed to know precisely how the tragedy

came about. A party of fifty, including Rusog and Ena, sat together. Many of them were smoking the strange mixture and listening to inflammatory speeches by Ruddik and some of his followers. But everyone present admitted later that heated words passed between Ruddik and Tordel, a young warrior who was a friend of Rusog.

The argument became more and more impassioned, and before anyone even realized what was happening, the drug-crazed Ruddik drove his tomahawk into Tordel's skull, killing him instantly.

No crime was more serious than killing a fellow warrior. Rusog, who had not been smoking, immediately put Ruddik under arrest.

The entire encampment buzzed with the news of the horrifying event. The prisoner was turned over to Wegowa, and Loramas took personal charge of the case. In the morning, he called a council meeting of the Cherokee elders, and Ruddik was summoned before the group.

Loramas's questioning of Ruddik was brief. "What was the nature of your argument with Tordel?" he demanded.

Ruddik sat with his head in his hands. "I do not know," he said dully.

"What do you mean, you do not know?" Loramas demanded. "You were sufficiently incensed that you killed the man with a single blow of your tomahawk. How is it possible that you 'do not know'?"

"All of us were smoking the special mixture that Tebotha, my father, uses to inflame the minds of men," Ruddik replied ruefully after a brief silence.

"I do not know the cause of the argument. All I know
is that my anger was so great that I had to kill in
order to relieve it. I regret that my comrade Tordel
was on the receiving end of my tomahawk."

The issues were clear, Loramas told the board of
elders, and the punishment was automatic. A sacred
rule of the Cherokee required that any warrior who
killed a fellow warrior without cause be expelled for
all time from among his people. By a unanimous
ruling, Ruddik was exiled.

His war paint was taken from him, and he was
conducted to the edge of the encampment. There he
was told to go wherever he pleased but never again
to call himself a Cherokee. Then the elders marched
back into the camp, followed by the sobered young
people.

The unfortunate incident had the effect of cooling
the sentiment against the colonists. With Ruddik no
longer there to fuel the hatred and ignite emotions,
the warriors calmed down. Although a residue of
hatred remained, no further action took place. For
the time being, the precarious peace maintained by
the Seneca and Cherokee with the residents of Knoxville was safe.

Just as the expulsion of Ruddik provided relief
from the rising tensions, so the confrontation between Colonel Johnson and Ted Thomas give the
town a chance to think more seriously.

Mature residents were inclined to agree with the
colonel, who declared that they had no argument
with the Indians, their loyal friends over many years.

He made it clear that he could not agree with Governor Sevier, who continued to grumble that "the Indians should be taught a lesson." The fire was not out, by any means, but it burned much lower.

Emily and Toshabe, in particular, hoped that the cooling of tempers would provide a breathing period for Renno to find whatever solution he was seeking.

The crisis could heat up again and possibly explode as long as the Seneca and the Cherokee maintained their camp across the river from Knoxville. The Indians gave no sign that they intended to leave. They were waiting for something—though they did not know what.

If the Indians were anticipating a further apology, they were doomed to wait a long time. As Governor Sevier put it when Colonel Johnson mentioned the possibility, "I have never in my life apologized to a damned Indian for anything, and I'm too old to begin now!"

If Renno had been on hand, his marriage to Emily could have provided a fitting end to the hostility, but in his absence both sides could only continue to wait, and time dragged. The lessons learned when Ruddik was expelled and when Ted Thomas and Colonel Johnson clashed seemed forgotten. Tensions began to build again. The peace was once again seriously threatened.

The guard at Knoxville established a double sentry at night and the troops became increasingly belligerent. At about the same time, the Indians doubled their night guard and prepared to shoot on sight any outsider straying within the lines they had arbitrarily established.

The fighting men on each side yearned for active combat and would be satisfied with nothing less. They maintained their uneasy status quo, while each sought reasons to open hostilities.

War had not been avoided, as Toshabe and Emily had hoped. It had merely been postponed while the two sides regrouped.

Renno jogged eastward through the mountains of the Appalachians, going as quickly as he could through the forest. For hour after hour he pounded forward in the Seneca trot, seldom pausing to rest, paying no attention to whether it was daylight or dark night. When he came to shallow streams, he cupped his hands and gulped water as he passed through. When he came to rivers where he had to swim, he swam clenching his bag of gunpowder in his mouth and holding his rifle and his white cloak high over his head with one hand.

He ignored the presence of animals, even though he often passed within range of deer and other game that would have been easy for him to bring down with his bow. He had no time for such sport. It was urgent that he reach his destination as rapidly as possible, and his entire life's training was devoted to that single goal.

Occasionally, he grew faint, which served to remind him that he must eat. Then he usually dug into one of his provision carriers and chewed on a strip of leatherlike dried venison. At other times, he ate a chunk of dried fish instead but then kept going until he came to another stream where he could slake his thirst with quick handfuls of water.

At one point, he decided his pace was too slow and increased his speed slightly, moving even faster. Despite his superb physical conditioning, however, the speed was too great. His heart pounded in his ears, his legs felt like lead, and he began to gasp for breath. Afraid that he might fall and lose consciousness, thus costing many hours that he had labored so hard to save, he reluctantly reduced his speed to the customary pace of the trot.

The incident emphasized to him what he already knew. For generations, the Seneca had experimented with the trot and had arrived at a maximum speed that a healthy man could tolerate. To go faster would be to tax one's body too much, an invitation to catastrophe. He was obliged to exercise his patience, and to recognize that no human being could travel more rapidly under his own power.

Days and nights succeeded each other rapidly, and Renno soon lost all sense of the passage of time. Once in every twenty-four hours the weakness in his limbs and the exhaustion that overtook his entire body became so great that he knew he had to rest. He stumbled to a halt on high, relatively safe ground and immediately dropped off to sleep, but even his sleep was not so deep that he was unaware of his surroundings or of the potential of danger that might threaten him. Even when sleeping, he was conscious of any sound, be it animal or human, that might warn of attack. No incident disturbed him, and after sleeping for two or three hours—long enough to get rid of the worst effects of his exhaustion—he was wide awake again. Stuffing a strip of dried venison into his mouth, he started forward again.

Always in his mind was the knowledge that he alone was capable of saving the Seneca and the Cherokee from destroying themselves through war with the settlers of the State of Franklin. Regardless of which side was right and which was wrong, a war between them would be mutually catastrophic; neither side would gain. In fact, with both weakened severely, the entire region would be open again to the British, who could move into the vacuum to reoccupy the rich lands they had coveted. Only by carrying his own plan to fruition could he defuse the crisis.

As Renno covered mile after mile in the mountains that lay far northeast of Knoxville, he knew that the end of his ordeal was within sight. He had covered the greater part of the distance, and before long he would be reaching lowland plains of tobacco. That tidewater area would speed him toward his goal.

With the end in sight, he pressed even harder, and after jogging for twenty-four consecutive hours, he dropped to the ground, wearing his white cloak as a cover. He fell asleep almost immediately, so tired that his reflexes were not fully effective, and consequently he slept harder and deeper than he usually did.

He was nevertheless jarred awake by the sounds of a vicious fight. The high-pitched, penetrating sounds of a catlike snarl were compounded by the deeper roars of an angered bear. The battle was a short distance off to his right. Snatching up his bow, arrows, and rifle, he ran in that direction.

Suddenly, he slid to a halt. Directly ahead, and standing at the top of a high rock that commanded the immediate countryside, was a tawny mountain lion. Its great bulk seemed to be all muscle, ready to launch into the destruction of its prey. Renno saw at a glance that the lion was prepared to spring through the air and attack.

Below the lion was a brown bear that outweighed it three times over but was hardly a match for it in speed, strength, or cunning. Her cub, which had become a pawn in the battle, was lying at the base of the high rock. It had already been mauled by the lion. Its head was bloodied.

The bear was trying simultaneously to protect her cub and to kill the lion. But the need to keep the cub from further harm was paramount in her mind and distracted her from first killing the lion and then worrying about her young.

Standing on her hind legs, she pawed the air ineffectually as she roared, striking out with wide swipes but coming nowhere near her target.

The lion, snarling and ready to strike, was paying no attention to the cub but was devoting full attention to the mother bear. If it could destroy her, it could then turn on the cub.

Realizing she was at a distinct disadvantage, the bear tried to compensate by sidling closer to the cub while waving her front paws furiously and bellowing belligerently.

But her gyrations could not deflect the lion. Crouching at the top of the big rock, it was ready to spring and maul the more vulnerable animal in a series of swift blows.

Renno instinctively sided with the bear. As a member of the Bear Clan of the Seneca nation, he and his family had been personally associated with bears ever since the day his ancestor, the original Renno, had befriended an animal he named Ja-gonh. Since that day, the manitous had used bears to express their support of the successive heads of the family by stressing the friendship between man and animal.

Renno decided that he would use his bow instead of his rifle because he instinctively knew he should employ the traditional weapon of his people.

Dropping his rifle, he swiftly reached over his shoulder into his quiver and drew out an arrow, which he instantly nocked into the bow that he had carried over the other shoulder. He knew he not only needed to strike the lion fatally but to miss the bear and cub. He only had a split second to take aim.

As the lion crouched and sprang, Renno released the arrow. When the beast was in full flight, the arrow struck it in the forehead, penetrating the skull. The lion collapsed at the feet of the bear.

Brushing aside the dead lion with an air of disdainful anger, the bear took a stance above her cub, growling and ready to attack anything that dared come near.

Renno was not fazed. "Here, now," he called, "let us see the damage and find out what we can do about it." Paying no attention to the menace in the huge animal's stance, he bent down and picked up the cub. A trickle of blood was flowing from a cut in the scalp. Inspecting the wound, Renno knew that a cut inflicted by a cat's claw was almost certain to carry infection.

He looked around, saw a small creek flowing gently nearby, and promptly went to it. After lifting some moss from the bank he dipped it in the water. Returning to the cub, he began to rub the moss over the wound to cleanse it with a touch that was feather-light.

The bear did not attack or make any move in his direction while watching him closely. A single swipe of one of her paws could have broken every bone in Renno's arm, and a single bite of her powerful jaws could have inflicted lethal damage. Anyone familiar with the behavior of animals as ferocious as the bear would not have believed what they saw.

As for Renno, he took the bear's passivity for granted. He felt instinctively that even the protection of his cloak was unnecessary, for under no circumstances would the mother bear attack or harm him in any way.

After he had cleaned the cub's scalp to his satisfaction, he looked around the forest floor until he found a certain plant that he was seeking. In time to come, this plant, which would be known as sassafras, would win recognition for the qualities Renno saw in it. Breaking off several leaves, he rubbed them gently into the wound on the cub's head, cleansing it further and providing medication that could help it to

mend without infection. He spent an hour holding
the cub and rubbing the sassafras juice into the wound.

At last Renno finished his ministrations and placed
the cub on the ground. "There," he said, "you will
soon be as good as new."

The cub seemed to understand that the man had
completed the healing treatment and licked his hand
in gratitude.

Renno grinned and looked toward the mother bear.
The bear's black eyes and the man's blue eyes riv-
eted on each other.

Strangers might have sworn that the animal and
the man were communicating in some strange manner that only the two of them understood. The bear
was expressing her gratitude to him for having saved
her life and that of her offspring, and also, in some
unbelievable manner, was wishing him well and promising to intercede on his behalf with the manitous.
Only another Indian reared in the Seneca tradition
as Renno had been could have understood the significance of their encounter.

Guiding the cub with a gentle cuff on its backside,
the mother started her offspring into the forest and
waddled after it, close behind, a living shadow determined to protect it from harm.

Abandoning the temptation to skin the mountain
lion, Renno resumed his journey. He had lost valuable time, but the manitous had their own way of
compensating him for the delay.

Later that afternoon he came to a trail that crossed
the one he had been following. Uncertain which to
take, he halted and pondered. In the bright sunlight,

his shadow fell on the newer trail, and he decided instinctively to follow it. He soon discovered that he had done the right thing. It turned out to be a shortcut through the last stretch of mountains that led him to the fertile, rolling tobacco lands of Virginia. The route saved at least a day and a night of travel.

The manitous had chosen this way of thanking him for his kindness to the bear and her offspring in their time of trouble.

High on a hill overlooking a river, the white mansion seemed enormous, almost too big for a private dwelling. In addition, a large number of auxiliary outbuildings nearly surrounded it—kitchen, workshops, stables, carpentry and blacksmith establishments. Behind them, row after row of small buildings formed the slave quarters. As far as the eye could see, tobacco, its leaves rich and greenish-brown and wheat, barley, oats, and vegetables. Poultry, well fed and plump, walked between the feet of horses. There were sleek mounts for gentlemen and sturdier animals to pull carriages and wagons. This was Mount Vernon, home of the young nation's most honored and revered citizen. George Washington was now living in semiretirement after leading his colonial troops to victory in the long struggle for independence.

People were bustling in the kitchen, the stables, and other outbuildings. Renno paused to take in the scene. His journey had come to an end. His shoulders drooped; never had he felt so tired, but after more than a week on the trail, he felt the satisfaction of knowing that his efforts had been successful.

His feeling of pleasure was interrupted when two uniformed and armed horsemen rode up. Both were wearing blue jackets and white trousers that resembled the dress uniforms of patriot soldiers in the American Revolution. One of the pair, a sunburned, broad-shouldered man, looked down at the Indian and glowered. "What do you want here, Indian?" he demanded brusquely. "And who the hell gave you the right to come barging onto this property?"

Renno resented the tone but nevertheless replied civilly. "I have come to see the general," he said. "Tell him that Renno of the Seneca is here."

"I don't give a hang who you are," the guard replied. "Nobody gets to see him without an appointment, and you had better show me a letter from him inviting you here or you have no chance of being admitted into his presence!"

Energy suddenly flowed through Renno's body, and he was revitalized. Reaching up, he caught the guard's wrist, twisted it, and in a single, sharp, jerking movement, pulled him to the ground. As the man fell, Renno landed on top of him. Kneeling on his upper arms in order to immobilize him, he drew his knife from his belt and held it at the man's throat.

The other guard drew a pistol and pointed it at the Seneca.

"Drop that pistol! Fast!" Renno commanded. "Or this knife goes into the throat of your friend here."

The pistol dropped to the ground, and the guard beneath Renno looked up at him with wide, terror-stricken eyes, his officiousness having been replaced by fear.

"I have come all the way from the frontier lands of Tennessee," Renno said. "I want to see the general—and see him as soon as possible. Anyone who stands in my way or tries to stop me is going to end his days right now with a knife in his heart and his scalp on my belt!"

A white-haired woman hurried up and stopped directly behind the trio. "What is going on here?" she demanded in a soft, cultured voice.

The guard pinned on the ground tried to speak but could not. His companion also seemed incapable of speech. Renno looked up and, still holding the knife at the guard's throat, said politely, "Good afternoon, ma'am. I have come a long way to see the general, and these damn fools—if you will pardon the expression, ma'am—tried to stop me."

She peered at him and then blinked in surprise. "Why, Renno!" she said. "You look so disreputable I scarcely would have known you."

"I have been on the road, ma'am," he replied. "I am in such a terrible hurry to see General Washington that I did not bother to get cleaned up."

"Well, we will attend to that immediately," she said calmly. "Let Gilbert stand up, please, and he will take you to freshen up before you see the general."

With reluctance, Renno released his hold on the guard, who scrambled to his feet.

"Take him to a washroom where he can make himself presentable," Martha Washington instructed the guard, "and then conduct him to the solarium, where the general will be having his noon meal soon. But be sure you treat this gentleman with great care. He served with his father on the personal staff during the war, and the general was always very fond of him."

"Yes, ma'am!" the guard replied, and although he favored Renno with a murderous look, he led him to a washroom, where he provided a fresh basin of warm water and a towel, together with a dish of yellow soap.

Renno quickly cleaned himself and then proudly added a fresh coat of yellow and green war paint, the colors that his ancestors had made famous. The guard silently walked him across the compound in front of the house and, taking him indoors, led him to the doorway of a large room where George Washington sat alone at a long, mahogany-topped table.

His dark hair was gray as well as black, giving it a salt and pepper effect, and his strong, regular features were serene. His skin was permanently tanned by having lived most of his life in the open. He looked in good trim and he held himself erect. His clothes were well tailored, as befitted a man of means.

As Renno appeared hesitantly in the doorway, he was lifting a wine-filled silver goblet. He stared for a moment, put down his wine, and jumped to his feet. "Renno!" he cried out. "You are the last person I expected to see here just now. Come in, boy! Come in! Don't stand around cooling your heels." He took Renno's hand in both of his and pumped it vigorously.

The guard departed, obviously cursing the day that he had gotten on the wrong side of an Indian who turned out to be a close friend of the master of the establishment.

"What are you doing here?" The general did Renno the honor of pulling another chair up to the table and waving him to it. "The last I heard of you, you were off on the Tennessee frontier trying to fill your father's shoes. You don't know how much I regret that he met an unfortunate accident. He was a grand gentleman and a first-rate scout."

"He will rest in peace now," Renno informed him grimly. "I followed his enemy to the Floridas and got rid of him."

"How glad I am that you and I are on the same side!" the general exclaimed jovially. "What brings you here?"

"I have come to see you on a matter of state that requires your attention," Renno said, getting down to business. "It concerns a problem that only you can solve."

"Apparently you starved yourself while you were coming here," Washington interrupted shrewdly. "You will join me for lunch, of course."

Renno started to protest but was cut short. "This is not a subject for discussion," his host said. "It is an order. The meal's all prepared, for I am fortunate enough to have a cook who never asks whether the company has come, but whether the hour has come. Therefore, I am meticulous about punctuality at the table!"

"Yes, sir," Renno replied meekly, and made no objection when the general rang a bell. A liveried

servant came to the room and was instructed to set
another place at the table.

The first course was oysters cooked in the shell
with a sauce of various herbs to make it even more
palatable. Renno, who had subsisted on dried food
for a full week, found the food so delicious that he
assented willingly when his plate was refilled.

He then settled down to the main course, large
pieces of chicken cooked with potatoes and a variety
of vegetables in a rich sauce that had a faint taste of
wine in it. After he had eaten two servings, he
became self-conscious and declined more.

"That is wise, I think," the general said genially.
"Save some room for the apple crumb cake." He
watched in approval as his guest ate the dessert and
finished the meal with a brimming mug of ale.

"Now, then," he said at last, "perhaps you can tell
me about the crisis that brought you here."

Speaking succinctly, Renno told him of the attack
on Colonel Johnson and the charges against Rusog.
He explained, as best he understood it, the rise in
tension on both sides that was approaching a state of
war by the time he had decided to bring the problem
to the general, seeking his aid. He ended with a
heartfelt appeal for the general's personal intervention in ending the dilemma.

As Washington listened, he occasionally interjected
a brief question. But in the main, he allowed Renno
to do the talking, and when he finally had grasped
the entire situation, he shook his head.

"Jack Sevier," he said, "is a first-class fighting man

and able enough as a leader, but his suspicion of Indians can get in his way and interfere with his judgment. I'm not saying that he is completely at fault, because I am sure that at times your people may be equally blameworthy. A man of Ghonkaba's stature, as a friend of Sevier, was needed to calm them and make them see the right way to behave, but the situation Sevier has created is far more serious than he knows. Already, opposition to existence of the State of Franklin exists in the state's next-door neighbor to the east, North Carolina. If Sevier becomes involved in a war with the Cherokee and the Seneca, North Carolina, acting under its rights in the Articles of Confederation that bind the United States together, will be sure to veto the admission of Franklin to the union. They are looking for an excuse now, and Sevier would be handing them the perfect reason. From Canada, the British are watching the situation closely. They are convinced that squabbling between the states is going to mean the breakup of the new country. All they want is an excuse to send divisions of redcoats south to occupy territory they have lost and reclaim it in the name of the Crown."

Renno was shaken by the information. He had not realized that the frontier situation in the Tennessee country might endanger the existence of the entire nation.

"You were wise to come to me." General Washington drummed on the table for a few minutes, and suddenly he smiled. "Do I judge correctly—based on your condition when you arrived—that you ran all the way from Knoxville?"

"Yes, sir," Renno replied, and smiled as though apologizing for his extraordinary feat.

"I am glad that you came. I am not sure what I can accomplish, but I agree with you that I must try. The growth of the United States depends in part on the amicable solution of this problem. I have spent too long here at home supervising the growing of crops and eating far more than is good for my health. I need a touch of exercise, and I'm sure my wife won't mind in the least getting rid of me for a time. At least she could paint the place, which I have forbidden when I am in residence. But if you think that I'm going to indulge in a Seneca trot all the way to the Tennessee wilderness, you are very much mistaken. We will travel my way. You haven't forgotten how to ride a horse, I trust?"

In spite of the severity of the general's tone, Renno could not help grinning. "No, sir," he said. "I remember it very well."

"We will take a company of state militiamen with us. A full company of cavalry should be enough to satisfy my protectors. They won't let me travel these days, you know, unless I am surrounded by rifles. How soon can you start?"

"I am ready to leave right now, sir," Renno replied eagerly.

"It may take us a few hours to organize for travel, so I suggest that in the meantime you go to bed and get some sleep. We will leave sometime this afternoon."

Renno was conducted to a private chamber, where a huge four-poster bed awaited. He tumbled into it and soon was sound asleep. His training allowed him to relax completely, putting aside all fears, and when he was awakened late in the afternoon he felt refreshed, ready to begin his new adventure.

One of the servants brought him a large tub and filled it with hot water, a luxury he had not enjoyed in many months, and after bathing he shaved on either side of his scalp lock and applied fresh war paint. Picking up his weapons, he was ready to depart. In the courtyard below, he found a full company of Virginia militia. Assembled and ready for duty, these men were serving on a voluntary basis, and all were veterans of the great conflict with Britain.

Renno had been with some of them in the war, and the men, particularly some noncommissioned officers, greeted him heartily. While he was shaking hands with them, the company commander, a Captain Trumbull, appeared and smiled broadly. "You're like a Rhode Island penny, Renno," he said. "It's impossible to get rid of you.

"All the same," the captain went on, "we're grateful to you. We were not looking forward to a full month here with little to do. Thanks to you, we're going to see a little action. I don't know how you talked the old man into it, but he's eager to be on his way."

For the next hour Renno studied maps of the area to the west and went over them with Captain Trumbull, selecting the best route for the party to take on the ride to Knoxville.

A sergeant soon appeared from the stables with a

lively young bay horse for Renno's use. He also was given a kit containing a blanket, cooking utensils, and a supply of food. He accepted it all without comment but had no need for any of it. If necessary, he could return to his own people in the way that he had left; he needed nothing but his own sacks of emergency rations, and he required only his own legs to get him there.

Eventually, General Washington appeared on the back of a huge white horse. He was wearing his wartime uniform with a tricorn hat and his rank of major general visible on the epaulets on his shoulders. Because the weather was cool, he wore a long cloak of blue and white. His appearance was so familiar that Renno, who seldom gave in to emotions of the moment, felt his eyes becoming misty.

The members of the militia surrounded the general, forming a loose square about him, and when Captain Trumbull gave the signal, they moved out and took a road that headed toward the west. They rode with the expert ease of men who spent their lives in the saddle, and they made good time as they traveled down the well-used roads of the Virginia farming country. Renno had been given no assigned place in the line of march but took up a position directly behind Captain Trumbull. He assumed he would be used as a scout when they left the farm country and came to the wilderness.

They rode hard about two hours after sundown, when they halted for the night in a copse of trees that adjoined a large farm. Captain Trumbull took the precaution of visiting the farmer in his dwelling and obtaining his permission to spend the night in the little wooded area.

The men reacted with singular efficiency. They unsaddled their horses, turning them loose to drink from the small stream and to graze in the rich grass of the area. A tent was erected for the general, but most of the men elected to sleep in the open. Two personal servants of the general began to prepare dinner, while the men made smaller fires for their own meals. Ultimately, when the time came to eat, Captain Trumbull and Renno were summoned to Washington's table.

Renno could not help marveling. The table was covered by a cloth of double-damask, and the plates, knives, forks, and water goblets were among the finest made. The cutlery was fashioned of heavy, solid silver, and no expense had been spared on any details of the general's mess.

Dinner consisted of a fine vegetable soup, which had come from the kitchen of the Washington estate; steak and potatoes that had been cooked over the open fire; and a generous portion of salad greens, also provided by the general's domestic cooking staff.

Nothing of substance was discussed during the meal, but after it was finished, Washington leaned back in his chair and began to discuss the crisis in Franklin. Occasionally, he called on Renno to explain various aspects of the situation, but he had already grasped the essence and knew exactly where things stood.

Captain Trumbull looked thoughtfully beyond the fringe of trees toward the farm's neatly planted cotton fields. "I have never met Colonel Sevier," he said, "but I understand he's a stubborn old cuss who has his own opinions of everything. Now that he's governor of Franklin, we may be hard put to control him. What if he refuses to listen to reason, General? Then what do we do? Or what happens if the Cherokee and the Seneca won't respect your authority and decide to take independent action? Then what happens?"

Washington smiled and his voice was soft, but in his pale eyes a hint was reminiscent of the steel in his sword.

"I find it is a waste of time to speculate needlessly," he said. "We will see what develops, and we will act accordingly. We know your company is faithful and will obey orders."

The general turned to Renno. "Could we count on a number of your braves to throw in their lot with us if the situation demands it?"

"I have no doubt that the entire company of scouts that served in the war will do what you order, General," Renno said proudly. "As for the rest, I am reasonably confident that I can count on the personal loyalty of as many as one hundred of the younger braves."

Washington nodded. "That should be sufficient for our purposes," he said. "I don't see anyone raising his musket to combat the will of the Virginia militia and the Seneca."

A short time later, after drinking coffee imported

from the Caribbean, the general announced that it was time for him to turn in.

Renno spent the night wrapped in his white buffalo cape. He had to smile as he thought of the differences between this and his previous journey. He consoled himself with the fact that General Washington was moving as rapidly as any elderly colonist could under the circumstances.

Chapter XII

Loramas and Ah-wen-ga sat beneath a chestnut tree near the river that fronted Knoxville. They were holding court. Seated nearby were the members of Ah-wen-ga's Seneca family, and on either side were arranged both Seneca and Cherokee warriors, all heavily armed.

Wegowa, the son of Loramas, and chief military man of the Cherokee, rose to his full height. With his arms folded across his chest, he spoke slowly and impressively.

"I have called this meeting," he announced, "to inquire when we are going to put this visit behind us and return to our own home. We sit here for day after day, waiting for some development—I know not what it may be—but nothing happens. We live in a dangerous place and in an unsettled time. The longer we live next to the settlers of Franklin, the greater the chances are for an explosion that both sides will regret. I urge the leaders of these tribes to take their leave of this place at once and to lead us on a return to our own homes."

Ena was on her feet instantly, her black eyes shining with indignation. "We are in this place," she said, "because we have been waiting in vain for an apology due to be made to my husband by the settlers who call themselves citizens of the State of Franklin. They made a grievous error when they arrested Rusog and charged him with a crime he did not commit! In so doing, they insulted the family that rules the Cherokee. And at the same time, they cast aspersions on my family, which has led the Seneca for generations. If they are truly our friends, as they claim, they will offer us an apology for their mistakes and will swear that they will do nothing further that would stand in the way of resuming our mutual friendship."

The men nodded in agreement. She was voicing a common thought.

Rusog sat quietly during her diatribe and merely nodded silently from time to time. He appeared to be in complete agreement.

"Each day," Ena continued, "we awaken with the hope that this will be the day the colonists apologize to Rusog for doubting his manhood and his honesty. Each day we tell ourselves that before the sun falls from the sky they will make amends for the mistakes they have made. But, when the day ends, nothing has been done—no steps taken, no friendship renewed."

She brandished a fist above her head. "We will not leave and return to our own town until the wrong has been righted. If no apology is issued, we will know that the treaty of friendship that the colonists signed with us is nothing but a mockery. And we shall know how to deal accordingly with it! This is a time for friendship to be genuine—or be revealed as the sham that I fear it has become!"

Everyone roared in approval, and Loramas looked pleased, as did Ah-wen-ga. The honor of the Indians was truly being upheld.

Wegowa looked across the intervening space until his eyes met and held those of Casno, the regent and chief medicine man of the Seneca. They were of one mind, but they could do nothing to avert the terrible tragedy that threatened their people. They alone recognized the peril of a confrontation with the citizens of Franklin.

While the Indians waited in vain for their sacred honor to be satisfied, affairs in Knoxville were rapidly approaching a climax. The militia officers were becoming increasingly apprehensive about the Indians' presence, and they were demanding that some action be taken to end the threat to their well-being. Colonel Johnson called a meeting of senior officers and urged his subordinates to exercise patience. The Cherokee and Seneca, he explained, were still smarting over the inadvertent insults to Rusog. If the colonists kept their tempers now, the incident could be passed over peacefully, he said, but by insisting on a showdown, they would lose their only Indian allies. Soon, they might find themselves alone, facing the entire Indian population of the frontier. His argument, good-tempered and balanced, would have been effective. Unfortunately, however, Governor Sevier, formerly the colonel in command of the militia, was standing at the rear of the room, listening incredulously and with growing ire.

When the speech was finished and the officers began to indicate their approval, the governor jumped to his feet, flung a hand into the air, and shouted, "Hold on a minute!

"Before you lads break your necks approving what you have just heard, let me say a thing or two," he declared. The assembled officers rapidly became quiet.

"In my opinion, the Indians are remaining in the neighborhood in order to trick us. They are waiting until we lower our guard, and then they aim to attack us. I don't see any question about their motive."

The attitude of the officers began to shift. These words were being spoken by their former commander.

Roy Johnson did what he could to salvage the

situation in favor of peace. "I beg to disagree with you, Governor," he called. "The warriors assembled across the river aren't alone, you know. Three women are with them, including Ah-wen-ga, who is virtually a goddess to the Seneca. Surely they wouldn't be present if the warriors were planning to attack us!"

Sevier shook his head. "You are a good fighting man, Roy," he said, "but damned if you're not too trusting sometimes. The women are present for one reason only: to keep us off guard and make us lax in our watch. When the fighting begins they'll vanish and put a lot of miles between them and the hostilities. You can bet your boots on it."

Johnson had no intention of becoming involved in a bet. He knew far better than anyone that his own situation was vulnerable. His daughter was engaged to be married to Renno, the future leader of the Seneca. Anything he might say that could be interpreted as pro-Indian would be suspect. Certainly he had no wish to be regarded by anyone as an apologist for the Indians, especially since men of the caliber of the Thomas brothers were just waiting for him to show too much sympathy for the Indians. He thought it best, therefore, to speak softly now. "Time will prove one of us right and one wrong, Governor," he said. "But until then it's senseless for us to argue."

"I'm not arguing, Roy. I simply want to protect Knoxville from attack. The younger boys are all screaming for scalps, and I can't say I would blame them if the Indians provoke trouble."

A few of the most belligerent of the younger officers began to applaud.

The governor raised a hand. "I'm not suggesting that we do anything for the sake of glory," he said. "These Indians supposedly have been our friends. Now they are acting otherwise, and I think we must teach them a lesson. They need to learn that a treaty of friendship can't be dealt with lightly and that an agreement to maintain the peace means exactly what it says. If we deal firmly with our friends, that ought to make the other tribes of the area take notice. If we are firm now, we will run into a whale of a lot fewer troubles than if we don't take a strong stand."

An even larger number of officers applauded.

Roy Johnson knew better than to fight. He was losing to Jack Sevier, and in the end bloodshed between his people and the Indians undoubtedly would occur. He had no idea what this would do to the forthcoming marriage of his daughter. He could not imagine her enjoying a happy life with Renno if their people went to war.

He had no idea where Renno had gone—or why— but he was grateful that at least he was not on hand during this ugly period of distrust and recrimination. He and Emily might be spared some of the worst of the bad feelings.

Under the best of circumstances, Emily would have a difficult time adapting to the Seneca's ways. Now, it began to seem virtually impossible for her and her husband to find a common meeting ground.

As much as Roy Johnson's heart ached for the young couple—particularly after all they had undergone that kept them separated—he knew he could not only consider them.

The issue of war or peace loomed over everyone, and his responsibilities to all the people of Franklin had to come first. He did not see how it was possible for the settlers to avoid bloodshed, just as he found it impossible to believe his daughter and Renno would escape unscathed.

Farms became scarcer, and the unclaimed forests grew thicker as the company under Captain Trumbull's command proceeded across the Allegheny Mountains. Renno took over as the scout. The matter wasn't discussed, it was just assumed by Trumbull and the other officers that he would revert to the role he had played with such success during the war.

Leaving his horse with the main body, he ranged ahead on foot, covering twice as much territory as the riders. Nothing escaped his attention, and he examined every sign that might warn of the presence of other people as he scoured the countryside.

His routines were the same as they had been during the war. Up early, he left the camp before the men woke up. He ranged far ahead through the day and returned to the company when night had fallen. Usually the men had eaten their supper by the time he got back, and he therefore was invited to eat by the general, who was customarily served after all his men had finished their meal.

The conversation was always the same. "Any luck today, Renno?" General Washington asked.

"No, sir. I spotted a few deer. I passed a pond where some ducks were resting, and I could have snagged some rabbits in the forest if you had needed them. But I did not get as much as a sign of any humans in the area."

"No sign of Indians?"

"No, sir, not a one. Whoever was about was smart enough to stay out of reach."

"No settlers?"

"No, sir, not in this wilderness."

One night Renno's reply was somewhat different. "Now that you mention it, General," he said. "I ran into a couple of scouts today."

Washington was instantly alert. "Scouts? What kind of scouts?"

"As near I can make out," Renno said, "it is a band of no-goods. I followed their trail back to their main hideout, and it looked to me like a gang of mountain renegades, men thrown out of various communities— the kind who survive by robbing innocent folk heading south or westward over these trails to establish homes on the frontier."

"You have reported all this to Captain Trumbull, I assume?"

"Naturally, sir."

The following morning, while Renno was eating his solitary meal before going out on patrol, Captain Trumbull came to him. "Renno," he said, "I have been thinking about that report of yours. I don't like to take unnecessary risks with the general's well-being. At the same time, I prefer to avoid bloodshed. Maybe we can work out something beneficial all around."

"I had more or less the same notion myself," Renno said.

Together, they worked out a scheme, then called in a sergeant and three of his men to put it into effect.

Renno got a late start that morning but without much trouble located the renegade scouts and allowed them to see him. They were intrigued and promptly followed him.

He stayed within their sight for the better part of the day, but giving no indication that he knew he was being followed.

By midafternoon, he decided that the time had come to end the charade, so he slowly headed back to the camp, where a halt had been called for the evening. The general's tent had been erected, and he was sitting outside it, enjoying a glass of herbal wine.

Still concealed in the woods, Renno could see Captain Trumbull and several of his men hiding in the undergrowth and nodded at them to indicate that the scheme was working perfectly.

The two scouts from the renegade band were behind him and paused to inspect the general through the screen of trees.

They had no idea that they were being watched, and that had either reached for a weapon, he would have been killed instantly by a sharpshooter. Aware of the risk, the sergeant and the squad had the pair covered with rifles and were ready to shoot instantly if they saw the slightest sign of a hostile movement, which never materialized.

The renegade scouts, both tall, burly men dressed in homespun linsey-woolsey, had stopped short and were staring at the general, looking at him as though they had just seen a ghost.

"My God!" one muttered.

The other was somewhat more articulate. "I can't believe I'm seeing right!" he said. "It's General Washington!"

For a moment or two longer, the two renegade scouts continued to stare at George Washington. Suddenly they turned and bolted, going back the way they had come as they hurriedly beat a hasty retreat through the forest.

When Renno and Captain Trumbull were sure that the pair had gone, they emerged from the woods, both chuckling.

The general looked up from his glass of wine, a question in his eyes.

Captain Trumbull explained to him what had just happened.

Washington was even more perplexed.

"It is a simple matter, General," Renno said. "We planned it carefully. By allowing the scouts for the renegades' party to identify you, it was sure to guarantee that they will put as much distance as possible between themselves and you. You can bet your last dollar that they are leaving the area and will not come anywhere near the company."

"Why not?" Washington was still unconvinced.

"In the first place, they prefer to avoid a confrontation with my troop of cavalry," Captain Trumbull said. "That goes almost without saying. But, even worse than that, suppose they had attacked you. They would have been the objects of the greatest manhunt in American history. They wouldn't have been safe anywhere. Every man who served under you in the war—regardless of whether he was enrolled in the Continentals or was a member of a state militia—would have been gunning for the whole gang. Not a member of that band could have lived for a single day anywhere in the United States, believe me," he went on. "They would have been hounded and persecuted and, if captured, undoubtedly shot without the formality of a trial."

"We decided it would be wiser," Renno added, "to reveal your identity rather than to take them on in a pitched battle. Even the criminals in this country know enough to respect you and to keep out of your way."

"I suspect," the general said, "that you're inclined to exaggerate, gentlemen."

Quite the opposite was true, as Renno well knew. Washington was universally regarded as the officer who had won the long war with Great Britain and was responsible for the independence of the United States. He enjoyed unparalleled popularity with people of every class. In fact, that was what had led Renno to think of appealing to him to mediate in the dispute between the Seneca and Cherokee of the Tennessee country and the people of Franklin. Only Washington could perform the miracle of convincing them to reconcile their differences without bloodshed.

Every day, the Cherokee and Seneca warriors behaved more and more like an invading army. Paying no attention to pleas of Wegowa and Casno, they sent out scouts into the surrounding countryside to learn if any reinforcements were on their way to relieve the citadel of Knoxville.

Surprised to encounter such warlike conditions when he came in advance of Captain Trumbull's escort company, Renno was relieved that at least he was in time to prevent a major tragedy.

Hoping for success with tactics he had used successfully before, he sought out the Seneca scouts who were prowling in the wilderness and gave each a simple message. "You may transmit word," he said, "that Renno has returned."

His authority was such that no one questioned his word, and the Seneca warriors did exactly as instructed.

Excitement spread through the Indian camp as the drums throbbed out the message. The younger warriors, belligerent and eager for combat, reasoned that their leader's return was a signal to begin the attack. Even Ah-wen-ga, his grandmother, thought much the same.

As the party drew still nearer to the Indian camp, Renno mounted his horse for the first time in days and led the procession.

When his colleagues saw that he was riding at the head of the company of blue-uniformed white men armed with modern rifles, they felt betrayed. It was inconceivable to them that Renno would be a traitor to their cause, but here he was. As they watched in growing astonishment, General Washington appeared, resplendent in his gold-trimmed uniform.

The first to recognize him were members of

Ghonkaba's loyal battalion of scouts, who had served faithfully under Washington from the early days of the war in Massachusetts to the terrible winter at Valley Forge. They gaped in astonishment. The first to react was Casno, who exuberantly fired his musket high into the air.

Others soon followed his example as they raced forward, and the sound of gunfire rattled through the otherwise silent wilderness.

Someone unleashed a Seneca war cry, and soon the sound of shouting filled the air.

General Washington enjoyed the display enormously, calling out greetings to his former comrades. His memory was surprisingly accurate, and he greeted most of them by name.

The Cherokee, who had not played an active role in the main theaters of war, were reluctant to come forward, although they recognized Washington by name and by description.

Renno, who had fallen back in the procession and now rode on the left-hand side of the general, remedied the situation by presenting the leaders of the Cherokee to the wartime commander in chief, taking special pride as he introduced Loramas, Wegowa, and Rusog. General Washington took pains to congratulate Wegowa on his steadfast patriotic stance and his insistence that the word of the Cherokee be kept in their dealings with the settlers. Then he looked at Rusog and said, "So you are the one who is responsible for all this?"

Startled, Rusog did not know how to respond. Only when Renno laughed did he realize that he was being teased, and he grinned appreciatively, though he could not understand all of the general's words.

The ranks of the warriors parted, and standing beyond them, alone, was Ah-wen-ga. Straight-backed and white-haired, her face was set in masklike, impenetrable lines as she folded her arms across her breasts and looked directly at General Washington.

Renno did not need to present his grandmother to the general. Washington intuitively understood the situation, and it was evident that he already recognized her as she gazed at him with an inscrutable expression. He approached her and bowed. "I bring greetings to the first lady of the Seneca," he said. "Your husband was a great warrior, your son was a great warrior, and your grandson gives evidence that he, too, will be great. I salute you on behalf of the American people and myself."

Without showing her age, Ah-wen-ga easily sank to the ground, dropping from a standing position with grace as well as dignity. Then, her arms still folded, she bent forward and touched her forehead to the ground in a sign of fealty.

No living person had ever seen her bow her head to another human being. Toshabe, her daughter-in-law, gasped aloud, and all three of her grandchildren stared at her in astonishment. Her subservience to George Washington spoke volumes for her sense of independence and for principles she held dear.

She did not speak, but rising again, she smiled slightly and extended her right hand. The general took it and found her grip firm. They, like Loramas, were years older than most others present. Their memories of the long roads traveled by both the settlers and the Indians transcended the hopes and fears of those who had come after them. They had achieved an understanding based on deeds, not only on words, and were satisfied with what they had found.

The bursts of musket fire in the forest opposite the fort caused a brief panic in the Knoxville bastion. Trumpets and drums were sounded at once, canceling all military leaves. A messenger was sent to Colonel Johnson to order him to the fort immediately.

At the fort, he was handed a telescope, which he immediately fixed on the scene across the river. He watched in silence for some time, then complained, "There is so damn much milling around over there that I can't quite see what is happening."

After a long pause, he exclaimed, "Good Lord! Renno is back! Somebody be good enough to notify my daughter immediately!"

He continued to scrutinize the scene until Emily showed up and demanded breathlessly, "Is it true, Papa? Has he really come back?"

"No question about it," the colonel replied. "He's there." He handed her the telescope, and she studied the scene for a moment.

"He looks well," she said, "and healthy, for which I'm grateful to God." She put down the glass and turned to the militiamen gathered behind her. "Who will row me across the river?"

A long moment's silence followed. "We're none

too sure it's safe on the far side for you, Miss Emily,"
one man offered.

Emily reacted furiously. "In case you don't know
it, sir," she replied, "I'm going to be married to
Renno. I'm as safe there as I am here. In fact, from
what I have seen of the blundering mess made by
men on this side, I'm inclined to think I'm much
safer over there!" She was prepared to continue her
diatribe, but her father cut her off by instructing a
sergeant to row her across as soon as he found it
convenient. The noncommissioned officer promptly
disappeared with Emily, and peace was momentarily
restored.

As he continued to watch the scene across the
river through the telescope, Colonel Johnson suddenly stiffened, and his voice took on a new urgency.
"Lieutenant Thomas! Be good enough to fetch Governor Sevier and ask him to get down here as fast as
he's able!"

"Yes, sir!" Thomas, thinking that the break with
the Indians had come at last and that the battle for
which he had longed was about to be fought, bolted.

When he returned, breathlessly followed by Sevier,
he found Colonel Johnson still wrapped up in what
he was watching on the far side of the river.

"Do we attack," the governor demanded, "or are
we going to stand off an assault first?" By way of a
reply, Colonel Johnson handed him the telescope.

Adjusting it, the governor muttered under his breath
and finally settled into studying the scene as his jaw
dropped.

"My God, Roy! Is he really standing there, big as life and natural as you please?"

"So it seems," Colonel Johnson replied quietly.

"How in hell did he get way out here on the frontier?" Sevier asked incredulously.

"I reckon my future son-in-law is pretty much responsible for it," the colonel replied. "He's back too. You may have noticed that he's standing near the general."

"Damned if he isn't!" Sevier finally found his voice and began to bellow for a full crew to row a large dinghy across the river.

Then, accompanied by Colonel Johnson, he hurried down to the waterfront.

Lieutenant Thomas followed, evidently very much concerned. "You're not going to run the risk of going over into Indian territory, are you, Governor?" he demanded.

Sevier halted, put his hands on his hips, and hooked his thumbs into his belt as he replied angrily, "Nothing is going to happen to me over there, you damn fool! General Washington himself is over there right this minute. Any place safe enough for him is sure as hell safe enough for any other American!"

Leaving the lieutenant speechless, he climbed into the boat, and motioning Colonel Johnson to follow, he gave the order to push off.

When Emily's boat put into the shore, Renno was standing at the water's edge, ready to greet her. He helped her from the boat, and paying no attention to the shocked Indians or the grinning members of the general's escort, he swept her into his arms, then embraced and kissed her.

Emily looked up reproachfully. "You could have told me where you were going," she said. "I've been dreadfully worried about you."

"I'm sorry," Renno said. "When I suddenly had the idea of appealing to General Washington, I thought I had to make the best possible time in reaching him."

"You mean you went all the way to Mount Vernon— and you're back in so short a time?" Emily asked in disbelief. She wondered if she could ever become accustomed to this extraordinary man whom she was marrying. He took his accomplishments so lightly. It would not be easy to be his wife, she knew, even if they had been members of the same race and nation.

Renno took her to the general and proudly presented her.

Washington removed his hat and favored her with a low bow, as though they were meeting at a grand public function.

"You are much to be admired, young lady," the general told her. "Not only do I respect your personal taste, but if every American followed your example, our troubles soon would be over. This country will become stronger and greater only as her people mix and become one."

The approach of another boat from the fort cut short the conversation as the general moved down to the waterfront. When the vessel manned by members of the militia pulled up onto the bank, Governor Sevier and Colonel Johnson emerged and saluted.

"This visit is quite a surprise," Sevier said. "Welcome, General."

"I am in the process of getting acquainted with some old allies," Washington said. "Why don't you join us, gentlemen?"

He escorted them to a circle before a low fire, where Loramas and Ah-wen-ga sat, surrounded by young people.

Even Wegowa and Casno, who had favored an amicable solution with the colonists, barely nodded their heads in greeting the officers, and in return received slight smiles of acknowledgment. No words were exchanged.

"Governor," Washington demanded, "do either you or Colonel Johnson represent the faction in favor of making war against the Cherokee and Seneca?"

"Not really, sir," the governor replied. "We do have some officers who are pretty much the leaders of that faction."

"Then by all means we must get them here," the general replied, and asked that a dinghy be sent back to the fort to pick up the officers in question.

"Is the warlike faction already well represented in this gathering?" Washington inquired. A number of the Indians, particularly the younger braves, nodded affirmatively, and several pointed to Rusog and then to Ena, who was translating.

Rusog promptly objected. "I have no interest in making war with anybody," he said. "All I want is a chance to live in peace, as we are bound to do under our treaty."

"I think our friends were talking about me, rather

than you," Ena said, her manner still belligerent. "In which case, I can only agree with them. It is true that I am against the people of Franklin and all they stand for, and I demand that my husband be compensated for the grievous injury that he has suffered!" She glared at Governor Sevier, who would have retaliated verbally had not Colonel Johnson put a hand on his arm and whispered that it would not be seemly to argue in the presence of George Washington.

Ena was a more articulate spokesman for the dissident group than Ruddik had been and she enjoyed one additional advantage; as the daughter of Ghonkaba and the sister of Renno, her prestige was almost as great as her brother's.

"If you are planning on holding a full-scale meeting, General," Governor Sevier said, "I recommend that we leave this site and cross the river to the fort, where we'll be far more comfortable."

Several Indians bridled at the suggestion.

Washington was quick to pick up their reaction. "We shall stay right here," he said. "Some of the Cherokee and Seneca object to going into the enclosed fort. They suspect they might be subjected to trickery there, and I can't blame them, so we will meet right where we are now."

Even the more radical of the young Indian dissidents were surprised by Washington's fairness. This was a man of whom they had often heard, but were now seeing in action for the first time. Everything that they had heard about him seemed to be true. He was going out of his way to be fair to both sides, and even though he was more closely related by blood to the settlers, he was refusing to favor them.

When the dinghy pulled up at the shore, it discharged passengers, who represented every phase of public opinion in Knoxville. They included the judge who had discharged the case against Rusog, the Thomas brothers, and a handful of other young firebrands.

Inevitably, their arrival caused a change in seating. The Indians sat in rows on the ground behind Loramas and Ah-wen-ga, while the settlers congregated near Governor Sevier and Colonel Johnson.

What most impressed Renno was the lack of friendly give-and-take between the young warriors of the Indian nations and the members of the militia. These men, who had fought side by side together to defeat the Creek, the Choctaw, and the Tuscarora, now looked at each other as strangers. They exchanged hard stares, rather than greeting each other as comrades. This more than anything else illustrated the hostility that was eating into the souls of the former allies.

Men spoiling for a fight were surly and uncommunicative. The women, notably Ah-wen-ga and Ena, were even more open in their emotions than were the men, patently ignoring the white men from the fort. Only Emily, who was utterly appalled by the confrontation, showed what she was feeling. Her face was white and drained of all blood, her fists were clenched, and she looked as though she might burst into tears.

George Washington was equal to the situation.

What many of his admirers failed to realize, but what Renno knew, was that he was more than a man of military accomplishments. He was a diplomat who had presided at countless sessions during the war and had somehow managed to iron out the vast differences between the various groups.

Superbly calm now, he seemed removed from the fray and from all emotional involvement as he looked first at one side and then the other. He drew his sword and stuck the point into the ground directly in front of him. The blade stood upright, waving slightly, and it became a symbol of the justice he intended to dispense. Before he could say anything, however, Renno interrupted.

"Many words have been spoken in anger in this ridiculous dispute," he said. "Now an attempt is going to be made to settle with words rather than with deeds the problems that divide us. I would like to offer my arms as a symbol of my own peaceful intention."

He threw his rifle, bow, and arrows out onto the ground and followed by adding his tomahawk and his skinning knife. "I am descended from the greatest warriors the Seneca nation has ever known. Soon I will be married to the daughter of a great American warrior. Let my own desire for peace spread to all who are gathered here, and let all follow my example."

A long, tense silence followed his words, and then Colonel Johnson dropped his rifle and brace of pistols at his feet. "I follow the example of my future son-in-law," he said. "I indicate my own peaceful intentions in the same way he has done."

With General Washington nodding encouragement, Wegowa and Casno were the next to discard their weapons.

Rusog, theoretically the cause and heart of this dispute, smiled broadly as he dropped his weapons. He released them with such force, in fact, that his bow bounced and skidded away, causing a burst of merriment on the part of some warriors, who were stunned by the unexpected turn that Renno had inaugurated.

In the next few moments, a brief pause was followed by the throwing down of arms by several younger warriors and militiamen. All seemed reluctant and were simply following the example set by their superior.

Washington looked hard at Loramas and smiled slightly. "Is the family of Loramas of the Cherokee less great than is that of Ghonka and Renno the elder of the Seneca?" he inquired.

His jibe was immediately effective. Loramas looked ashamed, and when Ah-wen-ga whispered to him, he threw down his bow, arrows, and tomahawk.

Washington turned to Jack Sevier, and a hint of mockery was in his voice as he asked, "Is the governor so fearful that he keeps his weapons at hand, even when those whom he regards as his enemies have relinquished theirs?"

Sevier responded forcefully. Flushing so that his face became as red as a sunset, he threw down his sword and followed with a brace of pistols.

Washington raised both hands. "I have come to Franklin," he said, "from my own home in Virginia in response to the earnest plea of Renno. He is interested first and foremost in maintaining peace between good friends, on whom depends the future of true republican government in this part of the world. I have intervened because a failure to do so well might result in a war. Such an occurrence would so weaken the cause of Americans that Great Britain or even Spain might intervene and claim this land for themselves. You exist here on tenuous ground, my friends. Don't think that because we have signed a treaty with Britain that we are through with the forces of the Crown for all time. They are still envious and want to regain what they have lost. These lands west of the mountains are rich and promising, and they will do anything they can to gain possession of them. So, too, will Spain, if we relax our vigilance and friendship there. Freedom must be earned, my friends. We must be strong and prepared to fight our common foes for the protection of rights that we hold sacred. Please keep these factors in mind."

Renno was at peace with himself. He felt reassured that he had been right to go to Mount Vernon and seek General Washington to come to mediate a dispute that seemed insoluble. Only Washington had the stature and the respect necessary to command the obedience of the men on both sides of the senseless though dangerous conflict.

"This dispute arose," Washington continued, "because Rusog of the Cherokee was falsely accused of having committed a crime. Am I right?"

Rusog hauled himself to his feet, and shaking off the restraining hand that Ena placed on his arm, he looked around the assemblage. "I was caught in a trap that was set by a clever man," he said, speaking in his own tongue, which Ena translated, as she had the general's remarks. "He probably had nothing against me, but it seems that I happened to appear at a convenient time. He chose me as the means of avoiding the guilt that otherwise could have been directed only at him. I have heard much about the justice of the white man in my trial. I must admit that his laws are truly just, as are the ways of administering them. During the brief period I was held in jail, I was given enough to eat and drink. I was never abused, nor did any man try to strike me or torture me. The cause of justice was always first in the minds of those who had arrested me. And when my innocence became clear to them, I was released at once. I have no bitterness for the wrongs that were mistakenly done to me. I have fought beside the soldiers of Franklin, and I am prepared, as of this moment, to fight beside them again if it should become necessary.

"I hold no hatred in my heart," he concluded, "for those who accused me. I urge my fellows to be forgiving also as they look back at the unfortunate experience."

As he sat down, Renno let loose with a noisy cry of approval, and several joined him in cheering Rusog's words, which had made it clear that any further attempt to maintain a feud with the colonists was a waste of time.

General Washington drilled the point home even harder.

"We have heard the words of Rusog," he said. "As

we ponder them, let us hear what the sachem of his family and the Cherokee nation think of the present dispute. Let Loramas tell us in his view what is wrong with the friendship that his people have had with the men of Franklin."

Loramas rose slowly and adjusted the cape that was a mark of his high office. "I object," he said, "because the white men dared to criticize the grandson of the sachem of his people and to brand him as a criminal. I agree that justice has been served, and the blot against the name of Rusog has been erased. But I have waited in vain for the white men to apologize for their error. Are these colonists so proud they cannot admit when they have made a mistake? Are they unable to see the light and to bow their heads before a justice that is greater than their own?"

Roy Johnson jumped to his feet and replied before anyone else could intervene. "When our court found Rusog innocent of the charges that were brought against him," he said, "that was the end of the matter in our minds. Under our system, the action of our court speaks for itself, and no other words are necessary. If Rusog wants an apology, or if those who are close to him demand an apology, I freely make it on the part of my colleagues and myself. I was the object of an attack, but let me say that at no time did I myself consider him guilty. Nor did I resent him for his supposed attack on me. I knew him as a warrior who fought side by side with us, and I admired him for his bravery and his courage in battle. Never have I had an unkind thought toward him, never have I denigrated him in my own mind." He sat down abruptly.

Loramas was highly pleased, as was Ah-wen-ga. Their Indian sense of justice now had been fulfilled, and they had no further need to feel they had been slighted in any way by the people of Franklin.

Only one element in the dispute remained to be satisfied, and the general turned to Jack Sevier. "What are your views on this matter, Governor?" he asked.

Sevier took his time, standing slowly, looking over the audience, and hitching up his trousers.

George Washington braced himself. He knew that Sevier, a native of the Virginia frontier, had spent all his adult life in North Carolina and in the Tennessee wilderness as an Indian fighter. His views on the subject of relations with Indians could be inflammatory.

On the other hand, he had a sound military background and had been one of the heroes of the Battle of King's Mountain, one of the turning points of the Revolutionary War in the South. He was a patriot who loved the United States and had made sacrifices in accordance with his beliefs. Washington, therefore, could not be harsh on him.

"Some folks may claim," Sevier said in a rasping voice, "that I don't think highly of Indians. I have been fighting them all my life, and I haven't seen much good in any one tribe. When I first came out to this country from North Carolina, it was empty. Not a soul was living within hundreds of miles in any direction. Well, sir, as soon as we got it settled and began to populate it, the Cherokee appeared and claimed that this whole region was part of their own hunting grounds. Maybe it was and maybe it wasn't. I'm damned if I know."

Loramas started to rise, intending to dispute his words, but Renno reached out and, taking hold of his arm, shook his head strongly. He saw no point in arguing with Sevier, whose prejudices were so powerful that it was impossible to enjoy a reasonable conversation with him.

"I'll grant you that we made a mistake when we arrested Rusog," Sevier went on, "but it was an honest mistake, based on what appeared to be convincing evidence. Our system is good—in fact I know of none better on earth—and we proved it by determining him to be innocent. What more does he want? For us to get down on our knees when we apologize? We don't do things that way. In fact, any Indian who has the view that we are going to crawl to him on our hands and knees is very much mistaken!"

The general forced a chuckle. "You and Rusog appear to be on the same side of the fence, Colonel Sevier," he said. "He stressed just what you said, that he expects no apology and wants none. It strikes me you are on the same side of the argument."

Sevier looked rather confused.

Renno was on his feet again in an instant. "Do we need a threat from a legion of Choctaw warriors to unite us?" he demanded. "Must we stand apart until several divisions of British troops sweep down on us from Canada and threaten to engulf us? Or are we sufficiently advanced to become friends for our own sake? The white men came into this land to which we Indians gave up all our claims in return for a promise that we can have lands of our own, with our own hunting grounds, where we rule ourselves in peace—and we ask nothing more. The United States is a young nation—young enough so that citizens from Europe and those who come from the native forests may band together and become great together. Let us join forces here and now, and march on together to meet our common destiny!"

No one moved or spoke. The entire assemblage seemed frozen.

Washington was uncertain as to whether he should be candid with Sevier. The governor's position was at best precarious. He was still considered a local resident by North Carolina, where he was resented for his attempt to form a separate state in Tennessee. North Carolinians were threatening to veto the admission of Franklin to the union. If that happened, where the people of Franklin might turn seemed questionable.

Casno looked at Wegowa, his lips moving silently.

Wegowa knew what his Seneca counterpart was doing. The medicine man was praying to his ancestors and to the manitous for a convincing sign that would impress on everyone present the need for unity and friendship.

Renno was doing the same thing. Clasping Emily's hand tightly, he prayed to his ancestors, asking for a dramatic sign that would convince those present that it was urgently essential they unite for the common good, so America could survive in these virgin lands west of the mountains.

Renno, the white Indian, had never failed his people, nor had the great Ghonka. According to family tradition, they heard the pleas of Renno and Casno, and from their homes on the far bank of the Great River, they responded. Perhaps, however, it was merely a coincidental phenomenon of nature that occurred and had no connection whatever with their ancestors.

The sky directly overhead grew quickly darker as heavy clouds blew in from the mountains and covered the entire area. The wind blew stronger, and it appeared that a storm was brewing up.

Ena was concerned, but a look at her grandmother calmed her. Ah-wen-ga sat erect with her hands folded, her expression tranquil, her brow untroubled.

Loramas took his cue from his wife, and he, too, appeared serene. Renno seemed to be relaxed, but Emily, who was learning to interpret him, realized that he was experiencing unusual tenseness. His face and body showed nothing, but she sensed his inner tension and knew that his prayers to his ancestors were about to be answered in a most dramatic manner.

The sky continued to darken, the winds rose, and whitecaps appeared on the river. It was soon impossible to see more than a few feet, and the howling of the wind increased, becoming so loud that conversation was impossible.

In spite of her education and her refusal to accept superstitious beliefs, Emily became frightened and gripped Renno's hand all the harder. He said nothing but in his own way reassured her. His grip became tighter, letting her know that she could rely on him, no matter what might happen.

Suddenly, the entire area was filled with light, as though by magic. A bolt of lightning appeared overhead in the sky and creased downward, threatening to hurl itself into the fort or, perhaps, into the river. Instead, the bolt sought the near bank, and a crash was followed by a loud, persistent sizzling as the lightning struck an oak tree.

The area was now as light as day as the tree caught fire and burned with a bright, phosphorescent light that spread quickly and dispelled all shadows. The entire tree was consumed by the flames, and only a long, ugly scar remained on the ground where it had stood.

Daylight returned as the clouds evaporated. The wind dissipated, too, and the river became glassy and calm. The storm was over, and tranquility reigned.

George Washington remained skeptical of what he had seen. He was much under the influence of a young neighbor and friend, Thomas Jefferson, author of the Declaration of Independence, a philosopher and naturalist who claimed that superstition had no place in modern thinking. Many natural explanations existed for what he had just seen, Washington knew, and he only had to decide which were applicable.

Everyone, white settlers as well as Indians, was deeply impressed. Almost without exception they were ready to agree with Renno, that his prayer to his ancestors had been answered, and they had given a sign.

Even Governor Sevier felt as Renno did. He had
dealt with Indians for many years and had come to
understand enough of their beliefs to put aside logic
and depend on the evidence of his senses, rather
than of his mind.

Renno knew what had to be done now. Not saying
a word to anyone, he jumped to his feet, walked
across to where Governor Sevier sat, and held out
his hand.

John Sevier was on his feet instantly. He shook
Renno's hand, and they smiled at each other.

Pandemonium broke out, and cheers echoed across
the river. Men watching the scene from the fort fired
a battery of cannon, one after another, in salute. The
manifold problems created by Rusog's imprisonment
were at an end.

Chapter XIII

The peaceful termination of the dispute that had simmered for so long resulted in a sudden outpouring of joy on both sides. The women of Knoxville prepared a banquet for their Indian guests. Their menfolk responded by providing fish from the river and venison from the forest for the feast. The Seneca and

Cherokee, not to be outdone, traveled far from the fort and found a small herd of buffalo. They brought down two to add to the celebration.

Although only three women were in the camp of the Indians, they refused to be outdone and prepared a number of their favorite dishes, including a chowder that had been popular among the Seneca for generations. Its principal ingredients were corn, chunks of potato, and wild onions, into which a variety of herbs were added.

The men roasted whole sides of buffalo over pits dug in the ground, and the colonists, following their example, did the same with sides of venison.

Rusog led a small party of hunters into the wilderness, and they were fortunate to encounter a flight of large, plump geese. They brought down several of the birds, and they, too, were added to the menu.

Some residents of Knoxville contributed precious flour for making johnnycakes, and Toshabe borrowed enough to make a cake in the Erie style, which consisted of many layers separated by crystallized syrup.

The throng attending the banquet was so large that no building in Knoxville could hold it, so tables were set up in a park opposite the town hall.

General Washington, who was spending the night at the Johnson house, was the guest of honor. The leaders of both the Indians and the residents of Franklin shared his table.

The general was completely at ease with each person to whom he spoke. He was one of the native-born American aristocrats, a man of considerable wealth, but having grown up among Indians, and knowing the frontier well from his early days as a surveyor, he understood the ways of the Indians and the settlers. He was so down to earth that all who talked with him found it difficult to realize that this man had been responsible for the defeat of the armies of the most powerful nation in the world and for the colonies' independence. He showed familiarity with the hunting grounds of the area in his talks with the men, and to the pleased surprise of the women, he cordially accepted several choice recipes for his cook at Mount Vernon. He put on no airs, and everyone, delighted to be treated like an equal by the hero, was able to forget his own self-consciousness.

Despite his geniality, the general had some strong candid words for a few among the throng. At one point, he drew Lieutenant Al Thomas aside.

"Some reports I've been hearing from Colonel Johnson are disturbing to me," he said in a low tone, while coldly scrutinizing the lieutenant's uneasy expression. "As an officer in the militia and as a good citizen of this community and state, you have a responsibility that apparently you have not been fulfilling. You should demand more of yourself, and your fellow citizens should expect more, than to act as a rabble-rouser playing on prejudices. Your performance, as it is described to me, leaves much to be desired. It is not at all in keeping with the expectations of our fellow countrymen for the behavior of all Americans. I strongly urge that you, as an officer and a gentleman, give much thought to mending your ways."

The young officer responded with a prompt "Yes, sir!" and a sharp salute, but his eyes were downcast as he withdrew from the general's company.

Only one other man stood somewhat apart. John Sevier, who had won a large measure of fame, felt overshadowed by the presence of Washington and retreated, silent and withdrawn, rather than taking charge in his customary ebullient manner.

During the dessert, Washington turned to Renno and Emily. "When are you two young people to be married?" he asked with a twinkle in his eye.

Emily smiled shyly and looked at Renno to reply.

"We have been so busy handling the crises of our people," he said, "that we have had no opportunity to make our personal plans. So far, we have not yet set a date."

"From all I have heard," Washington remarked genially, "it seems to me you should have been married months ago." He looked at Colonel and Mrs. Johnson for corroboration, and in return Johnson grinned and his wife nodded affirmatively.

It was Renno's turn to become shy, and he withdrew into silence.

Emily sat close to him and slipped her arm through his. Their hands met, and they clung together, neither sure of what was proper to say or do.

"It strikes me as fitting," the general said, "if we conclude this chapter in the relations between settlers and Indians with a wedding that will unite the two people."

Ah-wen-ga, who had been silent for some time, exchanged a meaningful glance with Toshabe and then spoke vigorously. "The Great Sachem of America," she said, "is a wise man. I know of nothing that could better cement the relation of the Seneca and the Cherokee with the people of Franklin than the marriage of Emily and Renno."

"Their marriage is especially important," Colonel Johnson said, "because of all they have contributed to the welfare of our people. If it had not been for them, we might well be at war now. Our debt to Renno, particularly, is too great to be paid. I would like to have a wedding we all will remember for the rest of our days."

Everyone nearby began to cheer.

"I know of no time like the present," General Washington said. "If you can arrange to be married while I am here, I would like it very much."

Emily smiled, then looked at Renno, and finally at her mother, who nodded agreement. "I am ready any time," she said, taking a deep breath. Her grip on Renno's hand tightened.

He responded by holding her hand more firmly. Events were moving rapidly now in a direction that he could not personally control. In fighting or in making most major decisions, he knew exactly what had to be done. In this situation, however, he was ill at ease, uncertain as to how to proceed.

Casno leaped into the breach. "I will be glad to perform one of my functions as a medicine man and marry these two people at the earliest time they choose," he announced, and another cheer arose.

"I think it would be appropriate," Judge Hill said, "if we had a double wedding, so to speak—one in which the couple marries in an Indian ceremony and also according to our traditions. I would be honored to be allowed to officiate at the latter."

Demonstrating the change of heart that General Washington had advised, Al Thomas now decided the time had come to compensate for his contribution to bad relations. "Hold on a second, Judge," he said. "This is the week when the Reverend Mr. Wilson can be expected to be preaching somewhere in the vicinity of Knoxville."

His brother Ted quickly picked up the idea. "He's right! I'll volunteer to go on a search for him tomorrow morning!"

"So will I!" A half-dozen voices were raised in enthusiastic shouts.

The party ended on a cheerful and busy note as Emily's mother with several friends returned home to finish the wedding dress.

Citizens of Knoxville and Indians alike went to work to finish building a small house that had been partially constructed in a quiet part of town. Declaring that it must be a proper honeymoon cottage, friends donated suitable furnishings.

Virtually everyone played some part in making ready for the event. So much had already been provided for the banquet that only a large wedding cake was needed now, and several women promised to make and decorate it.

Early the following morning, Al Thomas led a group out to search for the traveling clergyman. They found him shortly before noon in a small village twelve miles away and escorted him back to the town in triumph. The wedding that evening was assured. General Washington's presence added to the sense of festivity.

Emily was so busy with fittings for her wedding dress that she had no opportunity to see Renno until he came to the Johnson house in the middle of the afternoon.

She slipped away from her mother and the ladies who were helping her and joined Renno in the parlor. Kissing him chastely, she led him into the garden, where they would not be overheard. She sat on a bench and looked up at him anxiously. "I'm so glad you are here," she said. "We had no chance to talk last night, and I was afraid I would not see you until time for the ceremony. I have to talk with you."

He was aware of the gravity of her tone and asked quickly, "What is wrong?"

"Everything—and nothing. I think that we are on the verge of making a mistake."

"You mean that getting married tonight is a mistake?" he asked.

Biting her lower lip, she shook her head. "As you said last night," she told him, "we have been racing from one crisis to another. We have had no time to think of ourselves. Just ask yourself how long it has been since we have behaved like two people who are betrothed and preparing to be married. No romance is left in our lives, and I fear there will be none."

To Emily's astonishment, Renno chuckled aloud. She stared at him.

"I hope," he said, "that you have no worries greater than those you have just expressed. I know you love me because I can see it in your eyes every time you look at me. You feel uncertain of me because I am an Indian and I have been raised in the tradition of the Seneca. I do not show my feelings. I love and admire you as much as any man has ever loved any woman."

"You left here on a dangerous journey," she said. "You ran all the way to General Washington's house without even saying good-bye to me."

"I had no opportunity to bid you farewell," he replied. "A crisis loomed, and every minute of every hour was important. I had to get there fast. I couldn't wait to explain."

"I knew you felt that way," Emily said, "but I had to hear you say it in your own words. I realized it right after you left. It wasn't until you came back that I began to have some doubts."

Renno took her in his arms and kissed her, ending the discussion. "I will see you next when we come together to be married," he said, and hurried off down the street to return to the Indian camp, where he was expected to bathe in cold water before dressing for the wedding.

General Washington led the Knoxville settlers to the scene of the ceremony, only to find Renno stretched out on the ground before Casno, motionless.

Emily, resplendent in a white gown, was holding her father's arm. Although she had known what to expect, she nevertheless looked concerned when she saw the prostrate figure of Renno.

Suddenly he leaped to his feet and raised his arm in a formal greeting to Emily and her father. A very

slight increase in a drum's tempo, almost inaudible
to an inexperienced ear, had told him that his bride
was at hand.

Casno began to sing an incantation to the gods, in
which Renno joined, and occasionally all the Seneca
also sang. This was an almost tuneless, singsong refrain that seemed endless in its repetitions, invoking
every member of the pantheon of gods, whose aid
was asked for the coming marriage. No deity wor-
shiped by the Seneca was omitted.

Then it was Emily's turn to respond. She had been
well coached by Toshabe. Toshabe now sat on the
ground half facing her, and she moved her lips in the
words that Emily was to sing. With Toshabe's help,
the bride managed to go through the entire ritual
without an error. Ena had been worried because
even the slightest mistake would bring bad luck to
the bride and groom.

Renno, too, was overjoyed and could not help but
smile proudly at the young woman who was in the
process of becoming his wife.

At last it was time for the bride and groom to
begin to dance. This they did while a drum throbbed
in accompaniment and all the Indians, the Cherokee
as well as the Seneca, joined in singing another
repetitious refrain. The couple faced each other. At
no time did they touch. It was customary for the
bride to invent a complex step and for Renno to
repeat it after her. This Emily did again and again,
increasing the tempo and making the steps more
intricate.

The challenge became so great that she kicked off

her slippers and began to dance in her bare feet on the grass. Renno entered the spirit of the occasion, and they grinned at each other as they moved in perfect harmony, whirling and dipping, almost flying from one end of the field to the other.

Ah-wen-ga expressed what every Seneca present felt. "Emily has the true spirit to become my successor," she said happily. "In her spirit lives the successor to Betsy, wife of Renno the elder, and I can tell by the way she moves, by the way she acts, that everything I have meant to the Seneca, she also will come to mean."

The ceremony ended on a brief but impressive note. Casno took a slice of raw venison that had been soaked in brine and cut it in half. He handed one piece to the bride and the other to the groom. Without hesitation, they ate the meat and then offered their thanks to the manitous for the sustenance they would receive in all the years they were married.

The ceremony was over, and in the eyes of the Seneca, Renno and Emily were now man and wife.

With scarcely a pause, the Reverend Mr. Wilson stepped forward. The bride and groom stood in front of him, and facing the assemblage, he spoke the words familiar to the settlers, the ceremony from the Book of Common Prayer.

As the ceremony continued, Renno gave his responses in a loud, firm voice, audible to everyone present. Emily spoke more softly, but her voice was equally steady. Both affirmed they knew exactly what they were doing and had no doubts as to the outcome of this wedding between representatives of two very different civilizations.

When the time came to produce a ring, Renno reached into a pocket of his cape and took out a band of solid gold that had a long and honorable history. Bought by Renno the elder for Betsy, it had been worn then by Ah-wen-ga and Toshabe. Toshabe had presented the ring to Renno the previous evening, and he had accepted it eagerly as a symbol of the continuity and good that would come of his union with Emily.

The ceremony ended with the customary kiss of the white man, and as the young couple embraced, even the Indians, whose sense of modesty ordinarily was offended by the public display of affection, cheered.

The marriage was a fitting symbol of the reconciliation of the Indians and the settlers.

The wedding supper went off without a hitch. General Washington offered a toast to the bride and groom, and everyone present participated.

The Thomas brothers and some of their followers were interested in playing some of the usual frontier wedding tricks on Renno and Emily, but wiser heads prevailed. Renno, it was explained, had undergone so many hardships prior to his marriage that his sense of humor was unlikely to tolerate any crude displays of humor. Recalling Renno's quick reactions and expertise with every weapon, the would-be hazers decided to leave well enough alone.

In midevening, after responding to all who had

wished them well, the bridal couple made their way through deserted streets to the house designated as their honeymoon cottage. When they reached the front door, Renno raised the bolt and then unexpectedly took Emily into his arms, sweeping her off her feet and kissing her soundly as they entered the house.

Her arms curled around his neck, Emily laughed breathlessly as she looked at him. "You surprise me," she said. "I didn't know you would be aware of this particular custom."

"I know many of your customs," Renno admitted. "If I choose to ignore them for Indian ways, it is because I often find the customs of the Seneca are superior."

They had waited too long, and their relationship was too free of subterfuge to permit them to delay now in their lovemaking. Renno went straight to the bedroom, and when he lowered Emily to the four-poster bed, she reached up, caught hold of his shoulders, and as he kissed her, pulled him down beside her.

They made love honestly and directly, giving free rein to their emotions and holding back nothing in reserve. They knew each other so well that neither felt embarrassment or a false shyness. They gave freely, and the secret was in the giving. Each was interested almost exclusively in the joy of giving pleasure and not knowing or caring what was received in return. The result was explosive and prolonged. Starved for love, they made love repeatedly until they were so tired they fell asleep for a few hours. When they awakened they were again swept into each other's arms.

After a breakfast of fish, fruit, and cups of steaming chocolate, they wandered into town, holding hands with no sense of self-consciousness. Not until they approached the fort did they realize something out of the ordinary was occurring. Leaders of the settlement and prominent Indians were hurrying there, all intent on reaching it as soon as possible. Renno halted a Cherokee who was preparing to enter the fort. "What is happening?" he asked.

"A messenger has just arrived, and General Washington has agreed to see him. That is all I know," the brave answered.

Soon thereafter, Colonel Johnson arrived, and with him Renno and Emily went inside. There they encountered a very tall and thin stranger, about six inches over six feet in height. His skin was pale, but with a heavy coating of freckles across the bridge of his nose and on his forehead. His hair and beard were a carrot-colored red. His footgear was made of buffalo hides held in place by thongs around his legs. His shirt and trousers were sewn of animal skins. He carried a long rifle.

Captain Trumbull called the assemblage to attention, and everyone stood respectfully as General Washington came in and shook hands cordially with the stranger. "I was scheduled to leave this morning," he explained, "but when I heard that an old acquaintance, Cal Hopple, had arrived for the specific purpose of seeing me, I not only delayed my departure but I agreed to meet him in the presence of as many of you as could be gathered here on short notice."

"General," the visitor said, speaking in a slow drawl, "I've been chasing after you for quite a spell now. You and that there Indian guide of yours travel like greased lightning."

General Washington's eye found Renno's and he nodded in private amusement.

"I come from a place that some folks here probably never even heard of—a new settlement on the banks of the Cumberland River, called Nashborough. The captain of the militia sent me all the way to where the Congress of this country is meeting, and they told me I would have to find General Washington, wherever he might be, and beg his help." He paused, shifted a wad of chewing tobacco in his mouth, and unleashed spittle, which landed neatly in a spittoon.

"What is it you want from me?" Washington asked.

"That is a right interesting question," Cal Hopple replied. "I didn't realize until now how many prominent Cherokee Indians are here. I don't know what's going on, but the fact that they have all come east to Knoxville shows one reason why we are having troubles. Half a dozen tribes out west are kicking up their heels and causing all kinds of trouble that never would have come up if the Cherokee were home keeping the peace."

"What tribes are causing trouble?" Loramas demanded in a loud voice.

"Well, sir," the visitor replied after the request was translated for him, "the Taposa, of course, and the Chakchiuma. The Tunica have wandered north, and the Shawnee, who are a big, nasty nation who live north of us, have wandered south. Then the Quapaw have crossed the Mississippi, and they are all looking for spoils. I reckon they figure that with the Cherokee otherwise occupied, they want to move into the territory, and while they are about it, they will kick out any white folks they happen to see. We have only about sixty men we can muster at Nashborough.

"Anyway, I am sure that the militia leader would want me to ask General Washington, now that I have found you, to take charge and boot out the interlopers. What do you say, General?"

Washington looked deeply regretful. "I am sorry to have to tell you that I am not in any position to take charge of a military campaign," he said. "I have other obligations, and my place is at home in Virginia. I came here to Knoxville under special circumstances, to repay a debt to the Seneca, to whom I owe so much. But I cannot give the help that you need to drive out the Indian intruders from your district."

Looking at Loramas, Wegowa, and Casno in turn, Washington said, "The Cherokee and their Seneca allies have concluded their business here and are about to return to their own homes. I suggest they cooperate to the fullest extent possible with those in Nashborough who are eager to expel the Indians from their land that is actually under the jurisdiction of the Cherokee. I will also go one step further. One member of your company has long been familiar with my ways and knows how I deal with military situations. Therefore, I designate Renno of the Seneca as my personal deputy and authorize him to act in my name in any way he may see fit. Is this satisfactory with you, Renno?"

Startled by the unexpected responsibility, Renno had no choice and replied out of habit, "Yes, sir."

"I must also appeal to Renno's bride," Washington said with a smile, "and I apologize to you for interrupting your honeymoon. Do you agree with this designation?"

Emily sat erect in her chair and her voice rang out. "I am willing to do anything necessary, General, to further the advance of the Seneca, my husband's people and now my people."

The Seneca responded with whoops of delight, and in that moment their acceptance of Emily as a true Seneca was complete.

Renno rose and looked in turn at each of the other rulers of the Seneca and Cherokee. Pulling his white cloak about his shoulders, he spoke quietly but decisively. "I suggest we prepare for our march home at once. Then I will proceed to Nashborough to see what can be done about the situation that this gentleman describes."

On the far side of the Great River, where dwelt only those persons whose spirits had departed from the earth, Ena, wife of the great Ghonka, and Betsy, her daughter-in-law as the wife of their adopted son, Renno, sat close together, staring down into the cool waters of a deep pool.

Both were utterly absorbed by what they saw, and

with good reason. Mirrored in the depths of the lake were activities in the world of the living. By staring into the waters, they could see the world they had left behind them and the events taking place there.

As they watched, they were recalling the recent dissension between the Seneca and Cherokee and the white settlers at Knoxville.

"The young warriors of our nation are fools," Ena said bitterly. "If all that had happened in Ghonka's time, he would have severely punished these disturbers of the peace. They have no right to behave so and risk all that the Seneca in Tennessee stand to gain."

"Not in all the years that Renno was chief sachem of the nation and of the Iroquois League, would he have tolerated such conduct," Betsy added indignantly. "I don't know what has come over the younger generation. They seem to have no respect for the values that all of us held dear."

They continued to stare in fascination at the scenes unfolding in distant Knoxville.

They were still absorbed when Ja-gonh, the son of Betsy and Renno, appeared nearby. Like them, he was cured of the ailments that had taken his life and was completely hardy as he approached along the trail, a deer carcass slung across his shoulders.

Pausing to pay his respects to his mother and grandmother, he became aware that they were uncharacteristically distressed.

He listened in silence for some moments before he spoke. "Man learns in one of two ways," he said. "Either he is corrected by his own mistakes, or he learns from the mistakes of others. Today's youth, having known the taste of rebellion, will be forced to swallow their own errors in order to learn. Now I must hurry to meet with my father and my grandfather. Forgive me for not lingering, but I am late."

He hurried on and came at last to a modest building made of thatched straw. Cross-legged on the floor in front of a small fire was the dark-haired Ghonka, a large man with an impressive physique. Seated opposite him was his fair-haired adopted son, Renno. Between them, they had won great battles for the people of the Seneca nation, and they appeared celebrated in scores of songs and legends, but they were modest and unassuming. Each was lost in his own thoughts but was prepared to listen, as well as to instruct and give orders. Ghonka smoked a long pipe, which he passed to Renno occasionally, each drawing on it thoughtfully and tamping its contents rather absently. Long before Ja-gonh came into their presence, Renno, still endowed with almost superhuman hearing, looked up and then smiled as his son arrived. "Ah," he said, "you had success on your morning's hunt, I see."

Ja-gonh nodded companionably. "I was fortunate," he said. "I shot the buck no more than a couple of miles from camp."

"We can rejoice that, here, the spirit of life will be restored to the buck," Renno said, "though we shall partake of a feast."

Warriors on this side of the Great River still continued to hunt, but the game they shot was granted new being.

"I thought we should exchange views," Ghonka told them, "about what we might do further on behalf of young Renno. Are we ready to make up our minds how—if at all—we are to intervene in his interests?"

"It seems to me," the elder Renno said, "that we have already done everything in our power to help my namesake fulfill his sacred mission at this stage of his life. He has shown great prowess, and after a start that dismayed us for a time, he shows great devotion to the ideals of our people. And he is embarking on a marriage that suggests that much happiness is in store for him."

His father nodded understandingly, waiting for other opinions.

Ja-gonh spoke up. "The gods have provided him with a magic cloak that gives him great power over his foes," he said. "As you suggest, we have done our best to assure that they will guide and lead him. We have asked them to protect him from harm. In response, they have sent bears and hawks to guide him. We have been the servants of the gods in leading him in the paths that it is advisable for him to take."

Both his father and grandfather looked at him in agreement, but it was Renno who now resumed.

"Every means of assistance that is suitable for us on these shores of the Great River to undertake for young Renno has been done," he concurred. "He has been protected and guided. He has been led and advised and helped. He is, after all, descended from ancestors of whom many legends have been made. If he is a true descendant, as we believe, he will make his own way from this point, and he will triumph regardless of the odds, regardless of whether or not we request the gods to help him."

Ja-gonh interrupted. "As you know, my son, Ghonkaba, so recently arrived among us by virtue of his own son's dedication and courage, is enjoying the pleasures of our wonderful forests today. But I am certain, after talking at length with him, that he agrees with the ideas you express, my father."

"So I urge," Renno continued, nodding in recognition of Ja-gonh's information, "that from this time forward, we let Renno stand on his own. Let him live up to his name, let him fulfill his destiny in his own way, without further intervention from us. Let him carve his own future with a knife that he has honed himself. And as for us, let us be confident that he will carry out our highest expectations in fulfillment of the great Seneca tradition!"

The three old warriors clasped hands in silence as the rosy hue of the skies above them brightened with a new light.

Author's Note

If George Washington had been requested, as suggested in this book, to intervene personally in the dispute between the citizens of eastern Tennessee and the Seneca and Cherokee, he might well have complied in the manner described here. He and the aged Benjamin Franklin were, by all means, the most popular living Americans, and it is not coincidental that when the new Constitution of the United States was written and submitted to the states for ratification, some four years after the period at which this book ends, Washington was elected President almost by acclamation.

Certainly he handled numerous other disputes as he did this argument. His activities since the beginning of the American Revolution had led him to live such an active life that he was already becoming ill at ease with the small challenges of life at his Mount Vernon estate. We are justified in a belief that he would have welcomed an appeal such as that made to him by Renno.

D.C.P.

Coming in 1992
A special-edition volume in the best-selling
WHITE INDIAN Series . . . Book #22:

SENECA
PATRIOTS

For an exciting preview, turn the page . . . .

The American brig *Dora E.*, laden with naval stores, had all sails set before a fair breeze for Naples. Taking the air on the *Dora E.*'s deck was a man dressed in a drab suit just a bit too tight for his soft, slightly overweight body. His name was William Eaton. He was a Connecticut man who had made his permanent residence in Brimfield, Massachusetts, with a contentious woman almost old enough to be his mother.

Slightly before midday the wind became less favorable, and the brig wallowed in the troughs as she held to her course. Eaton was not the best of sailors, and the uncomfortable motion sent him to his cabin. He threw himself into his bunk after loosening his collar and waistcoat and prayed earnestly to be allowed to live long enough to feel solid land under his feet. He dozed and did not hear the commotion on deck that was caused by the sighting of a sail. The bellowed orders of the *Dora E.*'s captain did not wake him as the brig was slowly overtaken by a swift, low, black ship of war. It was the change in the ship's movement that revived him and sent him on deck to see that the *Dora E.* was lying dead in the water with a sinister-looking vessel closing on her.

"I'd advise you to go below, sir," a seaman said as he hurried past.

Eaton stood stiffly as the dark ship flying the flag of the pasha of Tripoli grappled the *Dora E.* Swarms of swarthy, bearded Arab seamen dressed in dingy, one-piece robes and sweat-soaked head windings scrambled aboard the brig and began to scream orders that were incomprehensible to everyone but William Eaton. Two of the pirates leaped toward him, their scimitars at the ready. One of them said in the patois—a mixture of Italian, Turkish, and Egyptian Arabic—that was the lingua franca of the North African pirate nations, "Your clothes. Take them off."

Eaton replied in the same language: "You fly the flag of Yusef Karamanli, Pasha of Tripoli. Before you act further, consider what he will say upon learning that you have insulted the United States consul to the Barbary nations."

"Your clothing, infidel," the pirate said, jerking at Eaton's coat.

Eaton made the same decision that had been made by the captain of the *Dora E.* The captain had known that for his unarmed ship to fight the Tripolitan man-of-war would mean death for his crew and him. Surrender meant slavery for the ordinary seamen, but at least there was hope of repatriation as long as the men were alive. Eaton could see murder in the eyes of the two pirates who demanded his clothing. To resist meant death. The captain of the Arab ship would have to account to the pasha for the captured ship and its cargo. The personal possessions of the crew and passengers were loot for the pirates. Clothing—shirts, vests, trousers, smallclothes—all were valuable commodities in the scruffy cities of the North African coast.

To be shamed, to be stripped naked before the crew of the *Dora E.* and the scabrous Arabs, was to remain alive to do the job to which he had been assigned by Thomas Jefferson. Eaton had no doubt that if he resisted, he would be killed in spite of his diplomatic credentials. After all, his captors were savages by ancient Greek definition. The Barbary Coast: coast of the barbarians, home to merciless pirates for centuries. And of the four Barbary states—Algiers, Morocco, Tunis, and Tripoli—the last was the most barbaric. Tripoli's ruler, Yusef Karamanli Pasha, had declared a unilateral war not only on American shipping but on the United States as a whole.

As he removed his clothing, being prodded more than once by the sharp tip of a Moorish scimitar, he vowed that he would not leave North Africa alive with his purpose unfulfilled. Within moments he stood naked on the deck. Gone along with his clothing were his watch, his purse, and a pair of gold-rimmed eyeglasses that he used for reading.

His cabin was thoroughly ransacked while the crew of the *Dora E.* was herded roughly onto the pirate vessel, to be imprisoned belowdecks. Arabs in their filthy, flapping robes leaped to the orders of an especially evil-looking brigand to set the captured ship sailing before the wind toward the African coast.

To the surprise of Eaton and the *Dora E.*'s officers, they were put ashore not in Tripoli but in Tunis. The officers were put under light guard in a vermin-infested mud building. Two days later Eaton was able to obtain an audience with the bey Ahmed Pasha, as much a pirate as his ally in Tripoli, but, perhaps, a bit more aware of the affairs of the world outside North Africa.

Eaton's anger did not move Ahmed, nor did a formal written protest receive an answer. "I have been appointed by President Thomas Jefferson as special consul to the Barbary nations," Eaton told the impassive pasha. "Moreover, I am attached to the United States Navy as a special adviser. You are going to find, sir, that the time when the Barbary nations can prey on unarmed American ships with impunity is past."

Ahmed Pasha made no reply. He could respect the power of the Royal Navy and the navy of the French, although even those great nations chose to buy peace with the pirate states rather than assure it by force of naval arms. Once, that obscure little nation across the Atlantic, the United States, had been under the wing of the Royal Navy. Now, however, with war looming between the two giants of Europe—Great Britain and France—the impotent United States was left to her cwn devices in the Mediterranean. Ahmed smiled benignly at the brash infidel. It was quite amusing to listen to his empty threats.

"It can be arranged that your ships will have safe passage through Tunisian waters for modest sums," Ahmed said. "One hundred fifty thousand dollars—"

Eaton snorted.

"—and certain quantities of ship's stores," the bey continued.

"And what of the waters of Tripoli, Morocco, and Algiers?" Eaton asked.

"I fear that you will have to discuss that question with my brothers in those countries," Ahmed said with a smile.

Ahmed, as had other men before him, underestimated William Eaton. On the surface the American looked weak, pudgy. In Ahmed's estimation he would not have been a match for the smallest man in the pasha's bodyguard. The ruler of Tunis did not think it worthwhile to inquire into William Eaton's background. The bey was not even curious as to why the president of the United States had sent such an unprepossessing man as Eaton to negotiate with the Barbary nations. He assumed that if President Thomas Jefferson had sent such a plump little dumpling to do his work, then Jefferson, too, was weak. The bey would have been surprised if he could have read the contents of William Eaton's letters to Jefferson, far away in Washington.

"I would use American arms to force these brigands to respect our flag. Only gunshot and powder will compel the deys and the beys of Barbary to treat us in a civilized manner, to honor the lives and property of American citizens. Their attitude is insulting not only to every American but to every man who considers himself to be more than a savage barbarian. Pray consider my urgent request that a fleet of American warships be sent to the Mediterranean along with five thousand trained, armed, and well-equipped American infantrymen and cavalrymen. With these troops at my disposal I can guarantee that the rulers of the Barbary Coast will sing a new song more to our liking.

Oddly enough, Eaton had long taken an interest in Islam. Before joining the American Legion and fighting with Anthony Wayne in the Ohio Valley Indian War, Eaton was reading the *Koran* and other volumes about the Mohammedan countries. In his journal he wrote at that time, "I wish to learn Arabic and to find out all I can about the Ottomans. Someday I shall visit that far-off part of the world, and if the Almighty wishes it for me, may even live there for a while."

Later, Eaton would call it kismet, the Arabic word for a predetermined fate willed by God, for there had been no evident reason for him to become interested in North Africa or the Middle East. There was to be no mention of Algiers, Tunis, Morocco, or Tripoli in American newspapers until sometime in 1797.

By the time William Eaton joined the consular staff in the Barbary states, the United States had paid over one million dollars in blackmail to the dey of Algiers. When Eaton walked the streets, Arabs spat at him and cursed him, not knowing that he understood their language. He restrained himself on those occasions, as he did when he was presented to the dey of Algiers, Hussein, whom Eaton described as "a great, shaggy beast, sitting on a low bench with his hind legs gathered up like a tailor or a bear."

He was compelled to kiss the dey's hand.

"The animal at that time seemed to be in a harmless mood," he confided to his diary. "He grinned but made little noise."

Eaton astounded the dey and other diplomats by speaking in flawless Arabic. Later he wrote in his journal, "I believe it is my kismet to treat these thieves with the contempt they deserve."

He had only to bide his time and to convince Thomas Jefferson to send him men, ships, and guns.

For an event of such great magnitude, it happened quickly. The French-language treaty to transfer the Louisiana Territory to the United States—thus doubling the size of that young country—was signed with Napoleon, and the Senate quickly ratified the document. The House passed the necessary acts of appropriation so the land could be purchased. A date for the formal ceremony of transfer, to be held in New Orleans, was set. Jefferson himself wanted to attend, but he knew that his place was in the drafty executive mansion. He named men to represent him. He penned a personal letter to a man to whom he had written once before, because he remembered the advice given to him by George Washington: Maintain communications and friendship with those Indians who were allied with and were friendly to the United States. It was to Renno, sachem of the southern Seneca, that the president addressed his personal request to represent the Indian nations at the ceremony of transfer of the Louisiana Territory in New Orleans on 20 December 1803.

Thomas Jefferson's letter reached Knoxville and was subsequently carried to the Seneca village in the

Cherokee Nation by Renno's ex-father-by-marriage, Roy Johnson. Renno's youngest offspring, Ta-na, and his cousin Gao, son of the shaman El-i-chi, greeted their "Grandfather Roy" with enough enthusiasm to make Roy stagger and almost go to the ground under the combined attack.

"By gum," Roy said, ruffling the thick, Indian black hair of the two boys, "if you two aren't big enough to cut up and fry for breakfast."

"The hunting has been good, Grandfather," twelve-year-old Ta-na said. "But we can't get our fathers to take us."

"Well, we'll see about that," Roy said, "if you two rapscallions will turn me loose long enough to see if Toshabe's cookpot is full or empty."

"Horsemeat stew," Gao said, licking his lips with satisfaction at the memory of the meal.

"Horsemeat?"

"A panther got one of Beth's colts," Ta-na said, referring to his stepmother.

"Well, waste not want not," Roy said.

Toshabe, mother of Renno, El-i-chi, and Ena, having heard the rumpus, came out of her longhouse and smiled to see Roy approaching, with two wild young warriors leaping and cavorting on either side.

"Welcome," Toshabe said. Her almost six decades of age rested lightly on her. She was not as slim as a maiden, but the fullness of her breasts and hips became her. Her French blood both lightened her skin and emphasized her Erie characteristics— high cheekbones, dark eyes, and thick, straight hair snow-sprinkled with gray.

"I thank thee that thou art well," Roy said in perfect Seneca.

"Will you take food?"

"With the greatest of pleasure," Roy said, grinning widely. He turned to the boys. "You two find Renno and tell him I've got a letter for him."

"Shall I take it to my father?" Ta-na asked.

"Nope." He winked at Toshabe. "We old ones get nosy, you see. I want him to open it here so Toshabe and I can hear what it says."

The boys went whooping off, and Toshabe ushered Roy into the longhouse that she had shared with two husbands, both of them victims of murder, the great Ghonkaba, grandson of the original white Indian, and the Seneca senior warrior Ha-ace, the Panther. Within minutes Roy was seated cross-legged on a mat and eating horsemeat stew from a delicate bone-china plate that had been a gift to Toshabe from her daughter-in-law Beth.

"One of Beth's good colts?" Roy asked around a mouthful of savory, tender meat.

"She was very upset. She herself demanded to be allowed to shoot the panther."

"And did she?"

Toshabe shrugged. "She is the chosen wife of Renno."

"Meaning she did?"

Toshabe nodded.

Roy laughed. "Might as well face it, Toshabe—she's quite a gal, that Beth."

"But she is not Seneca," Toshabe said.

Roy finished his plate and accepted seconds, soaking up thick potliker with cornbread. After a comfortable silence he said, "I'm not exactly Seneca, either, Toshabe."

"That is true," she said, looking at him questioningly.

"That's why I've been reluctant to speak what's been on my mind," Roy said.

"The grandfather of my grandchildren should feel free to speak."

"Well, that's it," Roy said. "We have a lot in common, you and I. We both love our grandchildren, Little Hawk and Renna, and those other scamps out there. You know that I still look on Renno as a son and . . ."

Toshabe was silent. She looked straight ahead, her face giving no hint of her thoughts.

"And well, Toshabe, I'm sick and tired of living alone in Knoxville. I'm tired of playing part-time soldier in the Tennessee Militia with Andy Jackson, 'cause most often when they talk about fighting, they want to fight the wrong people. I don't get a kick out of it anymore. I don't find anyone in Knoxville I want to talk to or be with. I keep thinking about how Renno and I covered a lot of ground up north with Anthony Wayne, or I remember being off and away over a ridge with El-i-chi or with Little Hawk, the way we used to hunt before he went off to become an officer and a gentleman at West Point."

He paused. Toshabe looked straight ahead impassively.

"You're not making it any easier," he said accusingly.

"I have always known that you were like my sons and my grandsons in many ways," she said.

"Well, there are other things I'm tired of, too, Toshabe. I'm tired of not having anyone to help me warm my bed." He flushed.

There was a long silence.

"There are widows," she suggested. "Young widows."

"I don't want a damned young widow," Roy said. "I want you."

She turned to face him and her expression softened. "I am old, and much of the warmth has gone from me."

"Fiddlesticks," Roy said. "You're more striking than most women half your age." He reached out and took her hand. "How about it, Toshabe? Think you could put up with an old codger like me?"

Toshabe spoke in English. "You will become a squaw man?"

"Now you hush that mess," Roy said. "If you'll have me, I want to live here in the village."

"And leave me at a whim to go off on a hunt or a ramble?"

He grinned. "Well, not for a while, Toshabe. Not for a while." He felt the need for her. He had been long without a woman. He pulled her into his arms and kissed her neck, her cheek.

"Old man," she said, "the boys will be back soon."

"Yep, and that's too bad," he said, for she was responding to him, pressing her body to his. "Do I take this unmaidenly behavior of yours to be agreement?"

"If you can put up with me, I think I just might be able to put up with you," she said.

"Good girl," Roy said, then muttered in frustration when he heard the noisy approach of Gao and Ta-na.

Renno entered the longhouse immediately after the two boys burst in. He exchanged greetings with Roy, shared the warrior's handclasp, then sat down cross-legged before he accepted the letter. He gave an un-Indian-like frown when he saw that it was from the president. The last letter he had received from Jefferson had taken him south to New Orleans and to encounters with evil of a force he had not experienced since his battles with the shaman Hodano, so long ago.

Now he was content and didn't want to go anywhere. He led his tribe with relaxed but steady discipline. He lived with a wife whom he loved deeply. Although Renna was far away in France and Little Hawk was in New York State, he had the pleasure of raising Ta-na, his full-blooded Seneca son. There had been no pressures against the Cherokee Nation, of which his Seneca had become a part.

"Well, are you going to open it or not?" Roy demanded.

Renno smiled and extended the letter toward Roy. "Here, you do it."

"Well, don't think I won't," Roy said, jerking the letter from Renno's hand.

"Might as well," Renno said. "Save me the time and trouble of telling you what it says."

"It's from President Thomas Jefferson," Roy said.

"That much I know," Renno said.

Roy wrinkled his brow with the effort of reading Jefferson's handwriting. "You hankering for a trip, Renno?"

"Do me the favor of throwing the letter into the fire," Renno said.

"No, wait. This one might be fun," Roy said. "Mr. Jefferson wants us all to go down to New Orleans to represent Indian interests at a fancy shindig."

"All?" Renno asked. "He mentions names other than mine?"

"Well, not exactly," Roy admitted. "But he says that you should take other representative members of the tribes."

"And of what tribe are you a member?" Renno teased.

"Well, if you want to be technical about it," Roy said, "Little Hawk made me a blood brother of the Seneca years ago." He chuckled. "Almost cut my finger off trying to draw blood."

"Well," Renno said, "since the president wants us all to go to New Orleans, you can go in my stead."

"Now, Renno," Roy said, "it's you he really wants, but he says to take along any other representatives who would do credit to the Indian. I reckon I meet that definition if I brush my hair and shave. It'll be fun, Renno. We can take El-i-chi—"

"And me," Gao and Ta-na said as one.

"And Beth. I'll bet she gets cabin fever, even if she does live in a house big enough to hold three barns and a goat farm."

"So," Renno said, reaching for the letter to read the words for himself. He left the longhouse, followed by Gao and Ta-na.

"You forgot rather quickly," Toshabe said to Roy.

"Nope, I didn't forget. I thought you'd enjoy a trip down to New Orleans."

"I am too old and tired for such nonsense."

"Fiddlesticks. I'll buy you a French gown, and we'll show those youngsters how to dance."

"I have no need of a French gown," she said. "And I was never good at the white man's dancing." She put her hand atop his. "I have said yes to you, Roy Johnson, but that is no reason why you can't go with Renno. I will be here when you return, the manitous willing. We have lived almost sixty years without being man and wife. Another few months won't matter."

"Well," Roy said.

A Proud People in a Harsh Land

THE SPANISH BIT
SAGA

Set on the Great Plains of America in the early 16th century, Don Coldsmith's acclaimed series recreates a time, a place and a people that have been nearly lost to history. With the advent of the Spaniards, the horse culture came to the people of the Plains. Here is history in the making through the eyes of the proud Native Americans who lived it.

❏ 26397-8	**TRAIL OF THE SPANISH BIT**	$3.50
❏ 26412-5	**THE ELK-DOG HERITAGE**	$3.50
❏ 26806-6	**FOLLOW THE WIND**	$3.50
❏ 26938-0	**BUFFALO MEDICINE**	$3.50
❏ 27067-2	**MAN OF THE SHADOWS**	$3.50
❏ 27209-8	**DAUGHTER OF THE EAGLE**	$3.50
❏ 27344-2	**MOON OF THUNDER**	$3.50
❏ 27460-0	**SACRED HILLS**	$3.50
❏ 27604-2	**PALE STAR**	$3.50
❏ 27708-1	**RIVER OF SWANS**	$3.50
❏ 28163-1	**RETURN TO THE RIVER**	$3.50
❏ 28318-9	**THE MEDICINE KNIFE**	$3.50
❏ 28538-6	**THE FLOWER IN THE MOUNTAINS**	$3.50
❏ 28760-5	**TRAIL FROM TAOS**	$3.50
❏ 29123-8	**SONG OF THE ROCK**	$3.50
❏ 29419-9	**FORT DE CHASTAIGNE**	$3.99
❏ 28334-0	**THE CHANGING WIND**	$3.95
❏ 28868-7	**THE TRAVELER**	$4.50

■■■■■■■■■■■■■■■■■■■■■■■■■■■■■
Available at your local bookstore or use this page to order.

Bantam Books, Dept. LE 10   414 East Golf Road, Des Plaines, IL 60016
Please send me the items I have checked above. I am enclosing $_____
(please add $2.50 to cover postage and handling). Prices are $1.00 higher per book in Canada. Send check or money order, no cash or C.O.D.'s, please.

Mr/Ms._____

Address_____

City/State_____Zip_____
Please allow four to six weeks for delivery.
Prices and availability subject to change without notice.   LE 10 12/91

THE EXCITING NEW FRONTIER SERIES
BY THE CREATORS OF
WAGONS WEST

STAGECOACH
by Hank Mitchum

"The STAGECOACH series is great frontier
entertainment. Hank Mitchum really makes the
West come alive in each story."
—*Dana Fuller Ross, author of Wagons West*

☐ STATION 50: BUCKSKIN PASS   (28799-0 $3.50)

☐ STATION 51: WILD WEST   (28826-1 $3.50)

☐ STATION 52: THE LAST FRONTIER (28879-2 $3.50)

Buy them at your local bookstore or use this handy page for ordering:

Bantam Books, Dept. LE6, 414 East Golf Road, Des Plaines, IL 60016

Please send me the items I have checked above. I am enclosing $_____
(please add $2.50 to cover postage and handling). Send check or money
order, no cash or C.O.D.s please.

Mr/Ms _____

Address _____

City/State _____ Zip _____

LE6-7/91

Please allow four to six weeks for delivery.
Prices and availability subject to change without notice.